I0744177
GEORGE
HELLFLOWER
SMITH

HEATHEN EDITIONS
THEIR BOOKS. OUR WAY.

Published in the good ole United States of America
by Heathen Editions, an imprint of
Heathen Creative
P.O. Box 588
Point Pleasant, WV 25550-0588

Heathen Editions are available at quantity discounts.
For information and more tomfoolery, check us out online:

heatheneditions.com

@heatheneditions
#heathenedition

First published 1952
Heathen Edition published March 11, 2023

Heathen logo, colophon, design, Heathenry, and footnotes
Copyright © Heathen Creative, LLC 2023

Book and cover design by Sheridan Cleland
Set in 10.5pt Century Schoolbook
Chapters in Eurostile

ISBN: 978-1-948316-43-9

FIRST HEATHEN EDITION

"When he keeps the horseplay within bounds and really bends to his task, Smith can produce a highly readable book. He has done just this in **Hellflower**, perhaps the swiftest-moving story of interstellar conspiracy ever written. It is well-plotted and packed with surprises . . . In short, despite a few shortcomings, it's a lot of fun to read."
—Fantastic Universe

"George O. Smith's big beautiful space novel."
—Startling Stories

"**Hellflower**, by George O. Smith, is a piece of pure 'space opera' — and what an end!"
—Richard Preston, *The Sydney Morning Herald*

"A thrill-packed story of unscrupulous men—and women—at war in an age when inter-planetary travel has become commonplace."		*—Nebula Science Fiction*

"This new book by the author of *Venus Equilateral* will fascinate the fans. George Smith started writing in the early days of the war. Scientist as well as writer, the science part of his fiction is unimpeachable." —O. Gartrell, *Tulsa World*

"**Hellflower**, by George O. Smith, is a fast, exciting story that manages to miss all the opportunities the plot gives for space opera — and increases in value accordingly."
—Authentic Science Fiction

"Swash-buckling, fast-moving, a melodramatic novel that keeps going all the way through. Here is a yarn for those who want something different."
—R.G., *The Montgomery Advertiser*

"Along with romance of faraway planets, George O. Smith chooses an exotic theme in **Hellflower**, which succeeds *Venus Equilateral*, his first science fiction novel . . . Scientific-slant literature devourers, here are the sky trails. More space travel awaits you. Contact!"
—The Cedar Rapids Gazette

"I'M YOUR MAN NO MATTER
HOW YOU WANT IT PLAYED."

For Doña

HEATHENRY:
THOUGHTS ON THE TEXT

George O. Smith's *Hellflower* was originally published in the pulp sci-fi magazine *Startling Stories*, May 1952,[1] then republished as a standalone hardcover by Abelard Press in 1953. Pyramid Books then took the reins, republishing it twice in paperback: a first printing arrived November 1957, with a second printing in February 1969.

What we Heathens love most about this story is that it's most certainly a product of its time: the main character Charles Farradyne, even when things look dire, never misses an opportunity to kick back, smoke a cigarette, and sip a Scotch highball while trying to sort out the who's who of an intergalactic drug smuggling cadre. And that highball is nonalcoholic, by the way. He'll also smack a woman around when he deems it necessary, then kiss her and call her "baby."

Hellflower is like film noir meets *Mad Men* in space.

What's not to love?

It's just a good old-fashioned sci-fi romp.

Now, as for the text, surprisingly, (or not,) considering its age, we've kept our usual Heathening to the bare minimum.

---

[1] Smith, G. O. (1952, May). The Hellflower. *Startling Stories*, 26(1), pp. 12-92.

Our only changes being a few instances of adding Oxford commas (which we do with most of our books), and removing some hyphens.

The majority of our attention, therefore, was focused on the annotations, and we've furnished the text with over 70 footnotes, mostly to clarify certain terms, phrases, and quoted sources utilized by Smith.

Additionally, as a preface of sorts, we have included a short biographical introduction that Smith penned for the March 1955 edition of *Imagination: Stories of Science and Fantasy*[2] — because who better to tell you about the author than the author himself?

Finally, we'll leave you with this *Hellflower* introduction as printed by *Startling Stories*:

Bad space opera has been the plague of science fiction—good space opera may be its savior. In a very real sense, space opera is science fiction at its best, utilizing fully the terrific concepts of space and time and immensity which is science fiction's greatest asset. It affords the greatest scope for imagination, the most color and movement. And within its framework, any kind of additional sub-plot may fit. It can embody that other controversial child of science fiction—the purely cerebral story, the story of complex ideas. Or it may offer relief from it.

From any standpoint, a good space opera is a thing of beauty and a joy forever. And *Hellflower* is a good one. No blonde priestesses, no BEMs,[3] no intelligent insects sending short waves from their antennae—but plenty doing, and some characters you'll wish you had met before.

—*The Editor*

---

[2] Introducing the Author: George O. Smith. (1955, March). *Imagination: Stories of Science and Fantasy*, 6(3), pp. 1,88-89.
[3] Acronym for Bug-Eyed Monsters.

INTRODUCING THE AUTHOR:
GEORGE O. SMITH

When William Hamling[1] proposed that I turn out this thumbnail sketch of myself, my first thought was that any guy who has been cluttering up the science fiction magazines for twelve long years hardly needs any introduction. But William hastily pointed out that while a million or more words speaks for itself, not a word of them tell much about the man who did the deed. At this I indulged in some higher mathematics and came up with a grand average of about a hundred thousand words per year since 1942, which is no great shakes for any writer. So maybe a word of explanation is in order.

I shall now enter the competition for the Grand Prize by completing the statement, "I write Science Fiction because——" in twenty-five words or more. But first, a Word from your Correspondent!

By the time you read this, I shall be shoving the age of Forty-Four hard and close. This puts me a solid twenty years in the electronics engineering field, with some years

[1] William Lawrence Hamling (1921–2017) was an American writer and publisher of both science fiction digests and adult magazines and books, active from the late 1930s until 1975.

before that of amateur interest. I was among those kids who wound doorbell wire around an Oatmeal Box back in the mid-Twenties; and who listened to the famous Dempsey-Tunney "Long Count" heavyweight battle[2] on a radio set of my own build. Atoms were still indivisible when I first became intrigued with the notion of science, and the proposal of the "Expanding Universe"was still a new idea. The 100 Inch Telescope on Mount Wilson had just provided some evidence that certain spiral, misty clouds were actually distant galaxies made up of billions of stars collected into "Island Universes"similar in size and shape to our own galaxy. Early hints were coming in that a new outermost planet had been discovered; Pluto was confirmed and named just in time to cinch my interest in science. I majored in physics and mathematics, and took some minor courses in astronomy and celestial mechanics.

This background puts me in an exclusive but diminishing club of science fiction writers who can fall back upon their training for their science. Of course, the day when science fiction had to be liberally peppered with snibbets and bits of science — both honest fact and bafflegab[3] — is diminishing too. And while this makes for a more interesting story line, let's face one fact: You can't eliminate science from science fiction and still have science fiction. And so the possession of a technical background helps any writer stay away from gross errors, as well as provide an air of verisimilitude[4]

---

[2] The Long Count Fight, or the Battle of the Long Count, was a professional boxing 10-round rematch that took place on September 22, 1927, at Soldier Field in Chicago between world heavyweight champion Gene Tunney (1897–1978) and former champion Jack Dempsey (1895–1983), which Tunney won in a unanimous decision. "Long Count" is applied to the fight because when Tunney was knocked down in the seventh round the count was delayed due to Dempsey's failure to go to and remain in a neutral corner. Whether this "long count" actually affected the outcome remains a subject of debate.

[3] Unclear, incomprehensible, or wordy jargon; gobbledygook.

[4] Having the appearance of reality or truth.

even to those spots still remaining where fact must give way to their imagination.

As an author, however, I lack the standard colorful background. I've never hunted walrus, slung hash in the Andes, mined gold (or uranium), nor piloted a bulldozer. I don't wear a beard and I don't fancy red checkered shirts. I have yet to spend a night in jail, although I did once collect a traffic ticket for jaywalking in Cincinnati, where crossing the street is apparently illegal.

This mundane and conventional life of mine may be the cause of my only turning out about a hundred thousand words per year. I'm sure I could do better if my life were more complicated. So now with this explained, we'll get back to the original question:

I Write Science Fiction Because——

1. I fell heir to a typewriter in 1942 and I'm the kind of guy who can't stand to see machinery grow rusty from disuse.
2. Rumor holds that magazines pay money for printable material. This rumor is true, although it is also true that some rumors are louder than others.
3. There aren't enough of the kind of story I prefer; I have helped to fill this crying need by writing yarns that I like to read.

And so a review of the past twelve years indicates that there are just enough people who agree with Item 3 to make Item 2 provide me with three subsequent replacements to Item 1.

Hoping you are the same——

——George O. Smith

1

The book had been thrown at Charles Farradyne. Then they had added the composing room, the printing press, and the final grand black smear of printer's ink. So when Howard Clevis located Farradyne working in the fungus fields of Venus four years later, he found a beaten man who no longer burned with resentment because he was all burned out. Farradyne looked up dully when Clevis came into the squalid rooming house.

"I am Howard Clevis," said the visitor.

"Fine," mumbled Farradyne. "So?" He looked at one of the few white shirts in a thousand miles and grunted disapprovingly.

"I've a job for you, Farradyne."

"Who do you want killed?"

"Take it easy. You're the Charles Farradyne who——"

"Who dumped the Semiramide into The Bog, and you're Santa Claus, here to undo it?"

"This is on the level, Farradyne."

Farradyne laughed shortly, but the sound was all scorn and no humor. While his raw bark was still echoing in the room, Farradyne added, "Drop it, Clevis. With a thousand licensed spacemen handy everywhere, willing to latch onto an honest buck, any man that comes halfway across Venus to offer Farradyne a job can't be on the level."

Clevis eyed Farradyne calculatingly. "I should think you might enjoy the chance."

"I'm a bum, but I'm no murderer."

"I told you——"

"You've said a lot of nothing. So you came here to offer me a legit?"

"Yes."

"It doesn't look good."

Clevis smiled calmly. He had the air of a man who knew what he was doing. He was medium tall, a sprinkle of gray in his hair and determined lines near the eyes and across the forehead. There was character in his face, but nothing to show whether this character was high or low. Just strong and no doubt about it. "I'm here, Farradyne, just because of the way it looks. The fact is that I need you. I know you're bitter, but——"

"Bitter!" roared Farradyne, getting to his feet and stalking across the wretched little room toward Clevis. "Bitter? My God! They haul me home on a shutter so they can give me a fair trial before they kick me out. You don't think I like it in this rathole, do you?"

"No, I don't. But listen, will you?"

"Nobody listened to me, why should I listen to you?"

"Because I have something to say," said Clevis pointedly. "Do you want to hear it?"

"Go ahead."

"I'm Howard Clevis of the Solar Anti-Narcotics Department."

"Well, I haven't any. I don't use any. And I don't have much truck[1] with them that do."

"No one is on trial here and nothing that you say can be used in any way. That's why I came alone. You're on the

---

[1] In this context: to have dealings with.

wrong trolley. But I'll tell you this, Farradyne, if I were in your shoes I'd do anything at all to get out of this muck field."

"Some things even a bum won't do. And I don't owe you anything."

"Wrong. When you dumped the Semiramide into The Bog four years ago, you killed one of our best operatives. We need you, Farradyne, and you owe us one. Now?"

"When I dumped the Semiramide no one would listen to me. Do you want to listen to me now?"

"No, I don't."

"I got a raw deal."

"So did the man you killed."

"I didn't kill anybody!" yelled Farradyne.

Clevis eyed him calmly even though Farradyne was large enough to take the smaller, older man's hide off. "I am not here to argue that point," he said. "And I don't intend to. Regardless of how you feel, I'm offering you a chance to get out of this mess. It's a space job."

"What makes you think I'll play stool pigeon?"

"It's no informer's job. It's space piloting."

"I'll bet."

"You bet and I'll cover it a thousand to one."

Farradyne sat down on the dingy bed. "Go ahead and talk, Clevis. I'll listen."

Clevis dug into his briefcase and brought out a flower. "Do you know what this is?" he asked, handing the blossom to Farradyne.

Farradyne looked at it briefly. "It might be a gardenia, but it isn't."

"How can you tell?" asked Clevis eagerly.

"Only because you wouldn't be coming halfway across Venus to bring me a gardenia. So that is a love lotus."

Clevis looked a bit disappointed. "I thought that maybe you might have someway——"

"What makes you think I'd know more than a botanist?"

Clevis smiled. "Spacemen tend to come up with some oddly interesting specks of knowledge now and then. No, I didn't really hope that you'd know more than a botanist. But——"

"So far as I know, there's only one way of telling. That's to try it out. Thanks, I'll not have my fun that way. That's one thing you can't pin on me."

"I wouldn't try. But listen, Farradyne. In the past twelve years we have carefully besmirched the names and reputations of six men hoping that they could get on the inside. For our pains we have lost all six of them one way and another. The enemy seems to have a good espionage system. Our men roam up and down the system making like big-time operators and get nowhere. The love lotus operators seem to be able to tell a phony louse when they see one."

"And I am a real louse?"

"You've a convincing record."

Farradyne shook his head angrily. "Not that kind," he snapped. "Your pals sloughed off my license and tossed me out on my duff to scratch, but no one ever pinned the crooked label on me and made it stick."

"Then why did they take away your license?"

"Because someone needed a goat."

"And you are innocent?"

Farradyne growled hopelessly. "All right," he said, returning to his former lethargy. "So just remember that all the evidence was still my unsupported word against their assumptions. I was acquitted, remember? Lack of evidence stands on the books. But they took my license and tossed me out of space and that's as bad as a full conviction. So where am I? So I'll stop beating my gums about it, Clevis."

Clevis smiled quietly. "You were a good pilot, Farradyne. Maybe a bit too good. Your trouble was being too sure of yourself. You collected a few too many pink tickets for cutting didoes[2] and collecting women to show off in front of. They'd have marked it off as an accident if it hadn't been Farradyne. Your record accused you of being the hot-pants pilot, the fly-fly boy. Maybe that last job of yours was another dido that caught you. But let's leave the ghost alone. Maybe you've learned your lesson and are willing to make a stab at it again. We need you."

Farradyne grunted and his lips twisted a bit. He got up from the unmade bed and went to the scarred dresser to pour a stiff jolt from an open bottle into a dirty glass. He took a sip and then walked to the window and stood there, staring out into the dusk and talking, half to himself. Clevis listened.

"I've had my prayer," said Farradyne. "A prayer in a night-mare. A man fighting against a rigged job, like the girl in that old story who turned up in her mother's hotel room to find that every trace of her mother's existence had been erased. Bellhops, and cab driver, steamship captain and the hotel register, all rigged. Even the police deny her. Remember? Well, that's Farradyne, too, Clevis. Do you know what happened? My first error was telling them that someone came into the control room during landing. They said that no one would do that because everybody knew the danger of diverting the pilot's attention during a landing. No one, they said, would take the chance of killing himself, and the other passengers would stop anyone who tried to go up the stairs at that time because they knew the danger to themselves.

"Then they practically scoffed me into jail when I told them that there were three people in the room. A pilot might just as well be blindfolded and manacled to his chair during landing. He hasn't time to play games around tables and chairs. So I heard three people behind me and couldn't look. All I could do was to snarl for them to get the hell out. So

---

[2] A dido is a caper, trick, or prank.

ch. ends p. 9

then we rapped the cliff and dumped into The Bog, and I got tossed out through the busted observation dome. They salvaged the Semiramide a few months later and found only one skeleton in the room. That made me a liar. Besides the skeleton was of a woman, and they all nodded sagely and said, 'Woman? Well, we know Farradyne!' and I got the works. So," said Farradyne, bitter-sounding once more, "they suspended me and took away my license. No jobs for a man trained for space and nothing else. They wouldn't even let me near a spacer—maybe they thought I might steal one, forgetting that there is no place to hide. Maybe they thought I'd steal Mars, too. So if I want a drink they ask me if it's true that jungle juice gives a man hallucinations. If I light a cigarette I'm asked if it is real laughing grass. If I ask for a job they want to know how hard I'll work for my liquor, and so I end up in this godforsaken marsh, playing nursemaid to a bunch of stinking toadstools." Farradyne's voice rose to an angry pitch. "The mold grows on your hide and under your nails and in your hair, and you forget what it's like to be clean and you lose hope and ambition because you're kicked off the bottom of the ladder, but you still dream of someday being able to show the whole damned solar system that you are not the louse they made you. Then, instead of getting a chance, a man comes to you and offers you a job because he needs a professional bastard with a bad record. It's damned small consolation, Clevis."

Farradyne sniffed at the glass and then threw it out the window with a derisive gesture. "I'll ask for a lot of things," he said quietly, now. "And the first thing is for enough money to buy White Star Trail instead of this rotgut."

"That can be done, but can you take it?"

"It'll be hard," admitted Farradyne. "I've been on this diet of soap and vitriol too long. But I'll do it. Give me a month."

"I can't offer you much," said Clevis. "But maybe this can be hope for you. Help us clean up the hellblossom gang and you'll do a lot toward erasing that black mark on your record."

"Just what is the pitch?"

Clevis took a small leather folder from his briefcase and handed it over. Farradyne recognized it as a space pilot's license before he opened it. He read it with a cynical smile before he asked, "Where did you get it?"

"It's probably the only official forgery in existence. The Solar Anti-Narcotics Department—SAND—has a lot of angles to play. First, that ticket is made of the right paper and printed with the right type and the right ink because," and Clevis smiled, "it came from the right office. The big rubber stamp, 'Reinstated,' is the right stamp and the initials are put on properly, but not by the right man. The license will get you into and out of spaceports and all the rest of the privileges. But it has no listing on the master log at the Bureau of Space Personnel. It's an excellent forgery, it will not be questioned so long as you stay out of trouble. The only people who will check on the validity will be the ones we hope to catch. When they discover that your ticket is invalid, you may get an offer to join 'em."

"And in the meantime?"

"In the meantime you'll be running a spacer in the usual way. We've a couple of sub-contracts you can handle to stay in business. You'll pick up other business, no doubt. But there are two things to remember, always."

"Two?"

"Two. The first is that you've got to play it flat, no nonsense. Just remember who and what you are. And just to make sure of it, I'll remind you again that you are a crumb with a bad reputation. You'll be running a spacer worth a hell of a lot of dough and there will be a lot of people asking a lot of other people how you managed the deal. Probably none of them will ever get around to asking you, but your attitude is the same as the known gangster whose only visible means of support for his million-dollar estate and his yacht and his high living is the small string of hot-dog stands or the dry-goods store. That he owns all these things is only an indication of thrift and good management."

"I get it," grinned Farradyne.

Clevis snapped, "This is no laughing matter. What goes along with this is important. You'll play this game as we outline it to you and in no other way. The first time we find you playing hanky-panky, we'll have you by the ears in the morning. And if you cut a dido and get pinned for it, there you'll be with a forged license and a spacer that will have some very odd-looking registration papers so far as the Master Log runs. And no one is going to admit that he knows you. Certainly the SAND office won't. And furthermore, if you do claim any connection at any time for any reason whatsoever, we'll haul you in for attempting to impersonate one of us. You're a decoy, a sitting duck with both feet in the mud, Farradyne, and no damned good to anybody until you get mired deeper in the same stinking mud. There'll be more later. Now for the second item."

"Second? Weren't there ten or twelve in that last delivery?" grunted Farradyne.

"That was only the beginning. The second is this. Do not, under any circumstances, make any attempt to investigate that accident of yours."

"Now look," snapped Farradyne hotly, "I've spent four years——"

"In the first place, nothing that you could possibly do would convince anybody that you were the innocent bystander. So——"

"But I'm telling you——"

"The game you are going to play will not permit you to make any attempt to clear up that mess. As a character of questionable background, your attitude must be that of a man caught in a bad show and forced to undergo visible suffering long enough for the public to forget, before you can resume your role of professional louse. Got this straight?"

Farradyne looked at Clevis, gaunt has-been looking at success. The window was dark now, but there were no stars visible from the surface of Venus, only Terra[3] and Jupiter and Sirius[4] and Vega[5] and a couple of others that haloed through the haze. The call of the free blackness of space pulled at Farradyne. He turned back from the window and looked at the unmade bed, the insect-specked wall, the scarred dresser, the warped floor. His nose wrinkled tentatively and he cursed inwardly because he knew that the joint reeked of rancid sweat and mildewed cloth and unwashed human body, and his nose was so accustomed to this stink that he could not smell it.

Farradyne came to understand in those few moments while Clevis watched him quietly, waiting for his decision, that his oft-repeated statement that there were some things that even a bum wouldn't do was so much malarkey. Farradyne would have joined the hellblossom operators for an opportunity to get out of this Venusian mire. He turned to Clevis.

"Let's go," he said.

Clevis cast a pointed look at the dresser.

"There's nothing in the place but bad memories," said Farradyne. "I'll leave 'em here. Good, bad, or indifferent, Clevis, I'm your man no matter how you want it played. For the first time in years I seem to want a bath and a clean shirt."

As Clevis headed toward the door Farradyne aimed a solid kick at the dresser, putting one more scar on its marred flank. "I'm behind you," he said.

---

[3] Another name for Earth in classic science fiction.

[4] Known as the Dog Star and in the constellation Canis Major, it's the brightest star in the sky after the sun.

[5] The fifth brightest star in the sky, and the brightest in the constellation Lyra.

2

He was rustier than he had realized. For it was not only four years away from the levers of the control room and the split-second decision of high speed, it was four years of rotting in skid row. His muscles were stringy, his skin was slatey, his eyes were slow and he had lost tone. He was flab and ache and off his feed. He was slow and overcompensating in his motions. He missed his aim by yards and miscalculated his position and his speed and his direction so badly that Donaldson, who rode in the co-pilot's seat, sat there with his hands poised over the levers and clutched convulsively or pressed against the floor with his feet, chewing his lips with concern as Farradyne flopped the sky cruiser roughly here and there. They practiced on Mercury where the traffic was very light, in a Lancaster Eighty-One which was a fine piece of space-cruiser by any man's opinion, and Farradyne punished the ship like a recruit.

It took him a month to get the hang of it again. A solid month of severe discipline, living in the ship and taking exercise and routine practice to refine his control. He found that making the change from the rotgut jungle juice to White Star Trail was not too hard because his mind was busy all the time and he did not need the high-powered stuff to anesthetize. White Star Trail was a godsend to the man who liked the flavor of fine Scotch whiskey but could not afford to befog his coordination by so much as a single ounce of the pure quill. It was a synthetic drink that tasted like Scotch but lacked the alcoholic kick, and Farradyne learned soon enough that he could forego the jolt of high-test liquor in favor of the pleasant flavor because he had discovered ambition again.

Eventually they "soloed" him. Donaldson sat in the easy chair in the salon below talking to Clevis and he could hear them discussing problems unrelated to him. Their voices came over the squawk-box clear enough to understand. It gave Farradyne confidence. He took the Lancaster Eighty-One into the sky and circled Mercury for a landing, and for a moment relived that black day in his past, vividly.

He had called the spaceport, "Semiramide calling North Venus Tower."

"Aye-firm, Semiramide, from North Venus Tower."

"Semiramide requesting landing instructions, give with the dope, Tower."

"Tower to Semiramide. Beacon Nine at one hundred thousand feet, Landing Area Twelve. Traffic is One Middleton Seven-Six Two at thirty thousand taking off from Beacon Two and one Lincoln Four-Four landing at Beacon Seven. Keep an eye peeled for a Burbank Eight-Experimental that's been scooting around at seventy-thousand. That's all."

"Aye-firm, Tower."

Then had come the voice of a woman behind him. Just a murmur, perhaps a sigh of wonder from a woman who had just been shown for the first time in her life the intricacies of rack and panel, of meter and gauge and lever and shining device that surround the space pilot to demand every iota of his attention during take-off or landing. In Farradyne's recollection, there were two kinds of people; one kind stood in the center of such an array and held their hands together for fear of upsetting something, and the other kind couldn't keep their hands off a button or a lever if it meant their own electrocution.

There were thirty-three people aboard, thirteen of them women and Farradyne wondered which of them it was. He didn't care. "Get the hell below," he snarled over his shoulder. The man who had brought her up made some sound. Farradyne was even shorter with the man. A woman might wander up, interested, but a man should know that this was a deadly curiosity. "Take her below, you imbecile," he snapped.

An older man chimed in with something that sounded like an agreement with Farradyne's order. There was a brief three-way argument that lasted until one of them had fallen for the lure of a dark pilot lamp and an inviting pushbutton. The Semiramide bucked like a wasp-stung colt and the silver-dull sky over Venus Spaceport whirled . . .

●

Farradyne was shocked out of this vivid daydream by the matter-of-fact voice of the Mercury Port's dispatcher, "Lancaster from Tower, you are half a degree off landing course. Correct."

Farradyne responded, "Instructions received, Tower. Will correct. Will correlate instruments after landing."

"Aye-firm, Lancaster Eighty-One."

Farradyne's remembrances ended and his solo landing was firm and easy; almost as good as he used to do in the days before . . .

He put it out of his mind and went below to Clevis and Donaldson. The latter asked him what had been the matter with the course.

"I hit a daydream of the Semiramide," admitted Farradyne.

"Better forget it," suggested Clevis, dryly.

"I came out of it," said Farradyne shortly.

"Okay?" Clevis looked at Donaldson. The pilot nodded. "Okay, Farradyne, you're ready. This is your ship; you're cleared to Ganymede[1] on speculation. You'll play it from there. There's enough money in the strong-locker to keep you going for a long time on no pickups at all; you'll get regular payment for the Pluto run. Play it flat, and help us out. Just remember, no shenanigans."

"No games," promised Farradyne.

Clevis stood up. "I hope you mean that," he said earnestly. "If nothing else remember that your—er—misfortune on Venus four years ago may have put you in a position to be a benefactor to the mankind you hate at the moment. I hope you'll find that they are as quick to applaud a hero as to condemn a louse. Don't force me to admit that my hope of running down the hellblossom outfit was based on a bum hunch. Don't let me down, Farradyne."

Clevis left then, before Farradyne could find words. Donaldson left with him, but stopped at the spacelock to hurl one sentence. "Pilots are a proud lot, Farradyne. Luck, fella."

An hour later Farradyne was a-space between Mercury and Ganymede. On his own in space for the first time in four long, aching years. Not quite a free man, but at least no prisoner. He took a deep breath once he was out of control-range and could put the Lancaster on the autopilot. Gone were the smells and the rotting filth of the fungus fields and here were the bright, clear stars in the velvety sky. Here was freedom—freedom of the body, at least. Maybe even freedom of the soul. But not freedom of the intellect, yet. He had a tough row to hoe and the tougher row of his innocence to turn up into the light of day. But for the first time since he was thrown flat on his face he felt he had a chance.

---

[1] The brightest and largest of the four moons of Jupiter. Discovered by Galileo in 1610, it is the largest satellite in our solar system.

ch. ends p. 21

Eventually he hit the sack . . .

Ganymede was in nightfall and Jupiter was a half-rim over the horizon when he landed. He checked in at the Operations Office and listed his Lancaster as available for a pickup job. The clerk that took his license to make the listing raised a mild eyebrow at the big rubber stamp reading "Reinstated" across the face of the card, but made no comment. Farradyne's was not the only one so stamped and Farradyne knew it. Pilots had been suspended for making a bounce-landing with an official aboard or coming in too slantwise instead of following a beacon down vertically.

He folded the leather case and slipped it back in his pocket. He looked at the pickup list which was not too long. Farradyne knew that he had a fair chance of picking up a job here, and if he did it would add to whatever backlog Clevis had left him. The space business was an odd one and Farradyne found himself able to figure his chances as though he had not spent his time digging mushrooms on Venus. His chances were excellent; the pilot that owned his own ship outright was a rare one. The rest were mortgaged to the scuppers and it was a touch and clip job to make the monthly payments. Some pilots never did get their ships paid off but managed to scratch out a living anyway. A pilot with a clear ship could eventually start a string of his own. This was the ultimate goal which so many aimed at but so few achieved. With no mortgage to contend with, Farradyne could loaf all over space and still make out rather well, picking up a job here, a job there.

He waved a hand at the registry clerk and went out into the dark of the spaceport.

Rimming the edge of the field were three distant globs of neon, all indicating bars. One was as good as the next, so Farradyne headed toward the nearest. He entered it with the air of a man who had every right to land his ship anywhere he pleased and head for the nearest bar. He waggled a finger at the barkeep, called for White Star Trail, and dropped a ten-spot on the bar with a gesture indicating that he might be there long enough for a second.

Then he turned and hooked one heel in the brass rail, leaned back on the mahogany with his elbows and surveyed the joint like a man with time and money to spare, looking for what could be found.

Appropriately, it was called The Spaceman's Bar even though the name indicated a lack of imagination, for there were about sixteen hundred Spaceman's Bars rimming spaceports from Pluto to Mercury. The customers were about the same, too. There were four spacemen playing blackjack for dimes near the back of the room. Two women were nursing beers, hoping for someone to come and offer them something more substantial. Two young fellows were agreeing vigorously with one another about the political situation which neither of them liked. One character should have gone home eighteen drinks earlier and was earning a ride home on a shutter with a broken nose by needling a man who showed diminishing patience. A woman sat in a booth along the wall, dressed in a copy of some exclusive model. The copy had neither the material nor the workmanship to stand up for much more than the initial wearing, and it looked now as though she had worn it often. The woman herself had the same tired, overworked look as her dress. She was too young to have that look, but she had it and Farradyne wondered how she had earned it. He looked away, disinterested. He favored the vivacious brunette who sat gayly across the table from a young spaceman and enticed him with her eyes.

Farradyne shrugged, the girl had eyes for no one else and she probably couldn't have been pried away from her young man by any means, fair or foul. It occurred to Farradyne from the way she was acting, that if some other guy slipped her a love lotus, the girl would take a deep breath, get bedroom-eyed, and then leave the guy to go looking for her spaceman. Farradyne grinned at the idea; the hapless spendthrift who bought the love lotus would probably go roaring back to the seller raising hob about being rooked on the deal because the lotus hadn't worked.

He finished his drink and then turned back to the bar for a refill. As he turned to face the road again he saw that a man had come in and was standing just inside the door, blinking at the light. He was eyeing the customers with a searching look.

Eventually he addressed the entire room, "Who owns the Lancaster Eighty-One that just came in?"

"I do," said Farradyne.

"Are you free?"

"Until the third of August."

"Terran, I see."

"Right. Anything wrong in being Terran?"

"Not at all. Just an observation. I'm Timothy Martin of the Martian Water Commission and I'd like to hire you for a trip to Uranus."

"My name is Charles Farradyne and maybe we can make a deal. What's the job, Mr. Martin?" Farradyne eyed the room furtively, wondering if the mention of his name would ring any cracked bells among the spacemen. It didn't seem to, and Farradyne did not know whether to be gratified at man's forgetfulness or depressed.

"Only three of us and some instruments," said Martin.

"That's hiking all the way to Uranus empty, you know."

"I know, but this is of the utmost importance. Government business."

"It's up to you; I'll haul you out there on a three passenger charter, since you probably haven't enough gear to make it a payload. Okay?"

"It's a bit high," objected Martin, "but this is necessity. Can you be ready for an early morning hop off?"

"You be there with your gear and we'll hike it at dawn." He turned to the barkeep and wagged for a refill, then indicated that Martin be served. The government man took real bourbon but Farradyne stuck to his White Star Trail. The two of them clinked glasses and drank. Farradyne was about to say something when he felt a touch against his elbow. Her glazed eyes were small and glittering, and her face was hardened and thin-lipped.

"You're Charles Farradyne?" she asked in a flat voice. Beneath the tone of dislike and distrust the voice had what could have been a pleasant throatiness if it had not been strained.

Farradyne nodded.

"Farradyne—of the Semiramide?"

"Yes." He felt a peculiar mixture of gratification and resentment. He had been recognized at last, but it should have come from a better source.

She shut him out by turning to Martin. "Do you know whom you've hired?" she asked in the same flatness of tone. Profile-wise, she was not much more than a girl. Maybe twenty-three at the most. Farradyne could not explain how a woman that young could possibly have crammed into the brief years all the experience that showed in her face.

Martin fumbled for words. "Why, er——" he started, lamely.

"This rum-lushing bum is Charles Farradyne, the hot-rock that dumped his spacer into The Bog."

"Is this true?" demanded Martin of Farradyne.

"I did have an accident there," said Farradyne. "But——"

The woman sneered. "Accident, you call it. Sorry, aren't you? Reeking with remorse. But not so grief stricken that you'll not take this man out and kill him the way you killed my brother."

Farradyne grunted. "I don't know you from Mother

ch. ends p. 21

Machree,"[2] he said. "I've had my trouble and I don't like it anymore than you do."

"You're alive, at least," she snarled at him. "Alive and ready to go around skylarking again. But my brother is dead and you——"

"Am I supposed to blow out my brains? Would that make up for this brother of yours?" demanded Farradyne angrily. Some of the anguish of the affair returned. He recalled all too vividly his own mental meanderings and the feeling that suicide would erase that memory. But he had burned himself out with those long periods of self-reproach.

"Blow your brains out," advised the girl, sharply. "Then the rest of us will be protected against you."

"I suppose I'm responsible for you, too?" he asked bitterly.

Timothy Martin gulped his drink down. "I think I'd better find another ship," he said hurriedly.

Farradyne nodded curtly at Martin's back. He looked down at the girl. He felt again the powerful impulse to plead his case, to explain. But he knew that this was the wrong thing to do. Martin had refused the job once Farradyne had been identified. This might be the start of the game that Clevis wanted. Farradyne could louse it up for fair by saying the wrong thing here and now. So instead of making some appeal to the woman, Farradyne eyed her coldly.

There was something incongruous about her. She looked like the standard tomato of the spacelanes; she dressed the part and she acted it. The rough-hewn language and the cynical bitterness were normal enough but her acceptable grammar and near-perfect diction were strange. He had cataloged her as a drunken witch but she was neither drunk nor a witch. Nor was she a thrill-seeking female out slumming for the fun of it. She belonged in the "Spaceman's Bar" but not among the lushes.

---

[2] "Mother Machree" is a 1910 American-Irish song with lyrics by American songwriter and playwright Rida Johnson Young (1875–1926).

He caught it then. He had been too far from it for too long. The glazed, bored eyes, the completely blasé attitude gave it away first; then the fact that she had become animated at the chance to start a scene. Dope is dope and all of it works the same way. The first sniff is far from dangerous, but the second must be larger, and the third larger still until the body craves a massive dose. In some dope it is physical, in others the effect is mental. With the love lotus it was emotional. The woman had been on an emotional toboggan; her capacity for emotion had been dulled to such an extent that only a scene of real violence could cut through the emotional scars to give her a reaction. Someone had slipped the girl a really topnotch dose of hellflower.

"Who are you?" he asked.

"Norma Hannon," she snapped. "And I don't suppose you remember Frank Hannon at all."

"Never met him."

"You killed him."

Farradyne felt a kind of hysteria, he wanted to laugh and he knew that once he started he could not stop easily. Then the feeling went away and he looked around the room.

Every eye in the place was on him, but as he looked at them and met their eyes, they looked down or aside. He knew the breed, they were spacemen, a very strange mixture of high intelligence and hard roughness; Farradyne knew that to a man they understood that the most damaging thing they could do to him was to deny him the physical satisfaction of a fight. He could rant and roar and in the end he would be forced to leave the joint. It would be a lame retreat, a defeat.

He looked back at the girl. She stood there in front of him with her hands on her hips, swaying back and forth and relishing the emotional stimulus of hatred. She wanted more, he could see. Farradyne wanted out of here; the girl had done her part for him and could do no more. To take her along as a possible link to the hellblossom operators was less than a half-baked idea. She would only make trouble because trouble was what she relished.

"I've got it now," she blurted. Her voice rose to a fever-pitch, her face cleared and took on the look of someone who is anticipating a real thrill. Norma Hannon was at that stage in addiction where bloody, murderous butchery would thrill her only to the same degree as a normal woman being kissed goodnight at her front door. "I've got it now," she said, and her voice rang out through the barroom. "The only kind of a rascal that could dump a spacer and kill thirty-three people and then turn up with another spacer is a big-time operator. You louse!" she screamed at him. Then she turned to the rest of the room.

"Fellows, meet Charles Farradyne, the big-time hellflower operator!"

Farradyne's nerves leaped. He knew his spacemen. A louse they could ignore but a dope-runner they hated viciously. Their faces changed from deliberate non-recognition of him to cold and calculated hatred, not of Farradyne, but of what he represented. Farradyne knew that he had better get out of here quickly or he would leave most of his skin on the floor.

Something touched him on the shoulder, hard. He snapped his head around. The bartender had rapped him with the muzzle of a double-barreled shotgun.

"Get the hell out of here, Farradyne," said the barkeep between narrowed lips. "And take your rotten money with you!"

He scooped up the change he had dropped beside Farradyne's glass and hurled the original ten-dollar bill at him. It went over the bar and landed in a spittoon between the brass rail and the bar.

"Pick it up," growled the barkeep coldly. He waved the shotgun and forced Farradyne to retrieve the soggy bill.

"Now get out—quick!" Then his voice rose above the growing murmur of angry men. "Sit down, God dammit! Every bloody one of you sit the hell down! We ain't going to have no trouble in here!" He covered the room with the shotgun.

Farradyne left. It was an ignominious retreat but it kept him a whole skin. He burned inwardly, he wanted to have it out, but this was the game Clevis wanted him to play and it was the price of his freedom from the fungus fields. So he left, burning mad. He took it on the run to his Lancaster, knowing that the barman would hold the room at bay only until a bare escape was made.

He took the ship up as soon as the landing ramp had been retracted and only then did his nerves calm down. He looked at the whole affair—he seemed to have started with a bang. If Clevis wanted a decoy, what better decoy than to make a noise like a small guy muscling in on a big racket? The word would travel from bar to bar, from port to port until it reached the necessary person.

Time was unimportant now. The word must get around. So instead of driving to some definite destination, Farradyne set the Lancaster in a long, lazy course and let the big ship loaf its way into space.

3

Big Jupiter and tiny Ganymede were dwindling below by the time Farradyne was finished at the control panel. He was hungry and he was tired, so he was going to eat and hit the sack. He turned and saw her.

Norma Hannon sat in the computer's chair behind the board. Her hands were folded calmly and her body was listless. She had been quietly waiting for him to get finished with the important part of his piloting before she started anything. Farradyne grunted uncertainly because he was completely ignorant of her attitude, except perhaps the feeling that she would enjoy violence.

"Well?" he said.

"I caught the landing ramp as it came running in."

"Why?"

"You owe me a couple," she told him. "You're a lotus runner, you can give me one. Simple as that."

"How do you figure?"

"You killed my brother," she said. There was more vigor in her tone as the anger flared again. "So you owe me more than a couple of blossoms for it, at least."

"What makes you think——"

"Another thing," she interrupted. "I wanted to come along with you."

"Now see here——"

"Don't bother pretending you give a damn for the lives of the people you sell those things to. Run your dope and get your dough and skip before you have to see the ruin you bring." The flare of anger was with her and she wriggled in her chair with an animal relish that was close to ecstasy.

"But I can't——"

"Keep it up," she said. "You'll satisfy me, one way or another." She eyed him critically. "You can't win, Farradyne. I've had my love lotus, and all that is left of my feeling is heavy scar-tissue. Pleasure and surprise are too weak to cut through; only a burning anger or a deep hatred are strong enough to make me feel the thrill of a rising pulse. I can get a lift out of hating you, but if you kissed me it would leave me cold." She paused speculatively. "No, would it? Farradyne, come here."

"But why?"

"Because I hate your guts. Of all the people in the solar system, I hate you the most. I can keep telling myself that you killed Frank, and that does it. And I add that you are a love lotus runner and in some way part and parcel of this addiction of mine and that builds it up. Now if you came over and kissed me, I'd let you and the very thought of being kissed and fondled by such a completely rotten reptile as Farradyne makes me seethe with pleasant anger."

Farradyne recoiled.

"Afraid?" she jeered, wriggling again. "You know, as a last thrill I might kill you. But only as a last thrill. Because then the chance to hate you actively would be over and finished and there could be no more. So between hating your guts and getting an occasional hellflower from the man I hate, I can feel almost alive again."

Farradyne shook his head. This sort of talk was above and beyond him. No matter what he said or did it was the wrong thing, which made it right for Norma Hannon.

He did not know much about the love lotus. All he knew

ch. ends p. 32

was from hearsay. But that did not include this sort of completely illogical talk. Like many another man, Farradyne had always scorned the use of any chemical means to lower the inhibitions of a woman. He wanted them to love him for himself, not because of a sniff of perfume that made them any man's woman.

Seeing this end result actually made Farradyne feel better about the lot he had been cast in. If Clevis was the kind of man who boiled inwardly from a sense of outraged civic responsibility, Farradyne was beginning to feel somewhat the same.

He looked at Norma Hannon more critically. She had been a good-looking woman not too long ago. She had probably laughed and danced and fended off wolves and planned on marriage and happy children in a pleasant home. Someone had cut her out of that future and Farradyne felt that he wanted to get the man's neck between his hands and squeeze. He shook himself and wondered whether this addiction to hatred were contagious.

He said softly, "Who did it, Norma?"

Her eyes changed. "I loved him," she breathed in a voice that was both soft and heavy with another kind of anger than the violence she had shown just a moment before. This was resentment against the past, while her previous flare had been against the physical present. "I loved him," she repeated. "I loved the flat-brained animal enough to lead him into the bedroom if that's what he wanted. But no, the imbecile thought that the only way I would unfreeze was with a hellflower. So he parted with half a hundred dollars for one. The idiot could have rented a hotel room for a ten-dollar bill," she added sourly. "Or bought a marriage license and had me for the rest of his life for five."

"Why didn't you refuse it?" he asked. "Or didn't you know that it wasn't a gardenia?"

Norma looked up with eyes that started to blaze, but

they died and she was listless again. "Maybe because people like to flirt with danger," she said. "Maybe because men and women don't understand each other."

"That's the understatement of the century."

There was no flicker of amusement in her face. "Look at it this way," she said. "I did say I loved him. So naturally he wouldn't be the kind of man who would bring me a love lotus. Or if he did I could wear it for the lift they bring without any danger, because any man worth loving would not take advantage of his sweetheart while she's unable to object. So I wore it and when I woke up after a real orgy instead of a mild emotional binge, I was on the road toward having no feelings left. I've been on the road ever since and I've come far."

She looked at him again. "See what you and your kind have done?" she demanded. Farradyne knew that she was whipping herself into a fury again. "I was a nice, healthy woman once, but now I'm a burned out battery. It takes a spot of violence to make me feel anything. Or maybe a sniff from a lotus. Maybe by now it would take more than one."

"But I haven't any."

She snarled at him. "You can afford to part with one stinking flower."

Norma leaped out of her chair and came across the room, her face distorted, her hands clutching at his face. Farradyne fought her away, and saw with dismay the look of animated pleasure on her face. It was an unfair fight; Farradyne was trying to keep her from hurting him without being forced to hurt her. She went at him with heel and fingernail and teeth.

He gave up. Taking a cold aim at the point of her jaw, Farradyne let her have it. Norma recoiled a bit and her face glowed even more. In his repugnance at hitting a woman he had not struck hard enough. She came after him again,

ch. ends p. 32

enjoying the physical violence, looking for more of the same. Farradyne gritted his teeth and let her have it, hard.

Norma collapsed with a suddenness that scared him. He caught her before she hit the metal floor and carried her to the salon below, where he laid her on the padded bench that ran along one wall. His knowledge of things medical was not high, but it was enough to let him know that she did not have a broken jaw. Of one thing there was no doubt: Norma was out colder than he had ever seen man or woman.

He carried her to one of the tiny staterooms, and stood there contemplating her and wondering what to do next. He would have been puzzled as to the next move if Norma had been a completely normal woman. As it was, Farradyne decided that no matter what he did it would be wrong. She would be as angry at one thing as at another. The cocktail dress would not stand much sleeping in before it came apart at the seams, but she would surely rave if he took it off to save it for tomorrow. If he left her in it, she would rave at him for letting her ruin the only thing she had to wear.

Farradyne gave up and slipped the hold-down strap across her waist and let it go at that.

He would take what happened when she woke up.

Then he went to his own stateroom and locked the door because he didn't want anymore ruckus and confusion. He slept fitfully even though the locked door separated him securely from both amour and murder—both of which added up to the same end with Norma.

It was a sixty-hour trip from Ganymede to Mars. Each hour was a bit more trying than the one before. Norma bedeviled him in every way she knew. She found fault with his cooking but refused to go near the galley herself. She objected to the brand of cigarettes he smoked. She made scathing remarks whenever he touched an instrument, reminding him of his incompetence as a pilot. She scorned him for refusing to bring her the lotus.

By the time Farradyne set the Lancaster down at Sun City on Mars, he had almost arrived at the point where her voice was so much meaningless noise.

He landed after the usual discussion of landing space and beacon route with Sun Tower, and Farradyne found time to wonder whether the word about his affiliation had been spread yet. For the Tower operator paid him no more attention than if he had been running in and out of the spaceport for years.

He pressed the button that opened the spacelock and ran out the landing ramp.

"This is it," he said flatly.

"This is what?" she asked negatively.

"The end of the line."

"I'm staying."

"No, you're not."

"I'm staying, Farradyne. I like it here. You go on about your sordid business, and see that you get enough to spare a couple for me. I'll be here when you return."

Farradyne swore. She had moved in on him unwanted and had ridden with him unwanted. If she wanted to, she could raise her voice and, brother, that would be it. One yelp and Farradyne would spend a long time explaining to all sorts of big brass why he was hauling a woman around the solar system against her wishes. A phenomenal quantity of sheer hell can be raised by any woman merely by making a howl of shocked surprise, putting on a look of wounded dignity and pointing a finger at any man within a pebble's throw. Even men who have been rooked in this ladylike maneuver are inclined to lean the other way and convict the man when a woman plays that trick.

So, grunting helplessly, Farradyne left her in the Lancaster and went to register at Operations. He was received blandly, just as he had been received on Ganymede. Then he headed into Sun City to stall a bit. He went to a show, had a drink or two, prowled around a bookstore looking for something that might inform him about the love lotus and then bought himself some clothing to augment his scant supply. He succeeded in forgetting Norma Hannon for four solid hours.

Then he remembered, and with the air of a man about to visit a dentist for a painful operation, Farradyne went reluctantly back to his ship.

The silence that met him was reassuring. Even if she had been sound asleep, the noise of his arrival should have roused her so that she would come out to needle him some more. He looked the ship over carefully, and satisfied himself that Norma Hannon was not present.

This was too good to miss.

He raced to the control room, punched savagely at the button that closed the spacelock and fired up the radio. "Lancaster Eighty-One calling Tower."

"Go ahead, Lancaster."

"Request take-off instructions. Course, Terra."

"Lancaster, is your passenger aboard?"

"Passenger?"

"Check Stateroom Eight, Lancaster. Your passenger informed us that she was going into town, that you were not to leave without her."

"Aye-firm, I will check." Farradyne snarled at the closed microphone. Willfully abandoning a passenger would get him into more trouble than trying to explain the reason for the presence of his guest. Norma had done a fine job of bolting the Lancaster to the landing block in her absence.

He waited fifty seconds. "Tower from Lancaster Eighty-One. I will wait. My passenger is not aboard."

"Lancaster. Hold-down Switches to Safety, Warm-up Switches to Stand-by. Power Switches to Off. Open your port for visitor."

"Visitor, Tower?"

"Civilian requests conference about pickup job. Are you free?"

"I am free for Terra, Tower."

"Prepare to receive visitor, Lancaster. Good luck on job."

"Aye-firm. Over and off."

Farradyne went below and rode the bottom step of the landing ramp on its way out of the spacelock. He reached the ground about the same time as the arrival of a port jeep, which brought his visitor to him.

"You're Charles Farradyne? I'm Edwin Brenner. I'm told you are free for Terra. Is that right?"

"That's right."

Brenner nodded. He looked around. The jeep was idling and making enough noise so that the driver sitting in the machine could not possibly hear anything that was being said. The driver was not even interested in them; something in the distance had caught his eye and he was giving it all his attention. Satisfied, Brenner leaned forward and in a low voice said, "Let me see what you've got."

Farradyne shook his head. "Who, me?" he asked.

"You. I'm in the market. If they're in good shape, we can make a deal."

Farradyne felt that this was as good a time to play cagey as any. "I don't know what you are talking about."

"No? I hardly think you are telling the truth."

Farradyne grinned broadly. "So I'm a liar?"

"I wouldn't say that."

"Look, Brenner, I don't know you from Adam's off ox. From somewhere, you have the idea that I am a runner and you want to get into the act. In the first place I am not a runner and in the second place you have about as much chance of getting into a closed racket with that open-faced act of yours as you have of filling a warehouse with heroin by asking the local cops where to buy it."

Brenner smiled. "I can see you're cagey," he said. "I don't

ch. ends p. 32

blame you. In fact, I'd not have come out here asking like an open-faced fool if I hadn't been completely out of stock. I'm a bit desperate." He went into an inside pocket and came out with an envelope. "This is a credential or two," he said, "so that when you return this way, we can maybe do business. The usual way, you know. No questions, or witnesses. Okay?"

"I'll be back—maybe, Mr.—er, Brenner."

"You get the idea."

"I'll——" Farradyne's voice trailed away as he caught sight of the object that had held the interest of the jeep driver. It was Norma Hannon, who came around the fins of the Lancaster with the sun behind her.

Her errand had been shopping. The overworn cocktail dress was gone and in its place was a white, silky number that did a lot of fetching things to her figure. She had also taken the complete course at some primpmill. She was another woman. Not even Farradyne, who had seen her for days, could have been convinced that this beautiful perfection was not Norma's usual appearance.

Farradyne was silent. But as Brenner caught sight of her coming around the sunlit tail of the ship, with enough sun shining through her to make the pulses jump he made a throaty discord.

"Hello," she said brightly, as though she and Farradyne were reasonably close acquaintances, but in a tone that indicated that she was paid passenger and he the driver of the spacer. "I've some parcels being delivered in a bit. We'll wait, of course?"

Farradyne agreed dumbly.

Norma nodded coolly to Brenner and said, "I'm going on in," as though she did not want to interfere with any business that might be going on between the two men. She went up the ramp displaying a quantity of well-filled nylon at every step.

The roar of the jeep's engine snapped Farradyne's

attention back to Brenner—or where Brenner had been standing. The jeep was taking Brenner away in a cloud of spaceport dust.

Farradyne shrugged. That was not the man he really wanted. Call it close but no cigar. Farradyne did not want a man to buy love lotus, he wanted a seller of the things, a shipper, a character from the upper echelon. There might be an avenue through Brenner, but he doubted it.

With a sigh, Farradyne went into the Lancaster. Norma rose from the divan[1] along the end of the salon and whirled like a mannequin, her silken skirt floating. She stopped and let the skirt wrap itself around her thighs. "Like it?" she asked.

"It's very neat," he replied flatly. "But where did you get the wherewithal?"

"I figured you owed me something so I took it out of the locker in the control room. You left the key dangling conveniently in the lock."

Clevis had left Farradyne quite a bit of operating money but far from enough to go cutting a silken swath across the average fashion mart. "What's the grand idea?" he asked.

"You're a cold-blooded bird. You don't give a hoot that you and your cowboy-spacing killed my brother and that you and your kind made it possible for some lecher to dope me out of my feelings. I'm told that half-decent gangsters send flowers to a rival's funeral, but you wouldn't part with even a love lotus you aren't paid for. So if you won't give me one, I'm going to force it out of you."

"But——"

"You get the idea," she said, smoothing a nonexistent wrinkle over one round hip. "But I'm honest. You've some change coming." She put her hand down in the space

---

[1] A long backless sofa without arms.

ch. ends next p.

between her breasts and brought forth a small roll of bills which she handed to him. Dumbly, he took them.

They were warm and scented with woman and cologne and would have been hard on Farradyne's blood pressure if it had not been for the anticipatory glitter in Norma Hannon's eyes. There was a small commotion at the space-lock. Farradyne looked to see three men coming in with fancy-wrapped boxes. He groaned and went aloft to the control room. Norma had run the gamut without a trace of a doubt.

4

Farradyne sat before his control panel with his head in his hands and tried to think this affair out to a logical conclusion. There had to be some way out of it all. The only alternative was to go on hauling Norma back and forth, being the brunt of her needling and her viciousness and getting nothing done because of it. The mess had started off bad enough, but had now deteriorated until at the present moment the future looked completely hopeless.

Norma's needling and goading had been hard enough to bear. Her in-between offers of affection had been less difficult because she had not made an attractive picture in the first place and she had not let him forget her attitude in the second. But he realized that she was a smart enough woman; if anything, having her emotional balance dulled had put her in a rather interesting class of intellects. She was able to analyze a situation without being involved emotionally herself in the analysis. She was smart enough and unencumbered enough to realize that playing soft-pedal on the hate theme might eventually get her what she needed.

He was willing to bet his spare money that the boxes she was now receiving contained whatever could be purchased of the most seductive clothing she could find. And included in that basic idea was, most likely, a sharp appreciation of what Farradyne would consider exciting. Acres of exposed skin or rank nudity would pall on him. He knew it and he bet she knew it, too. So she would come out with some little items that might cover her from toe to chin in such a way as to make him wonder about what was underneath: probably simple stuff with a lot of line and fine fit and a semi-transparent quality that compelled the eye. If she coupled this program with a soft voice as she was most likely to do now that she had shucked the sleazy costume, Norma Hannon would be well nigh irresistible. And if she even once got the idea that Farradyne felt protective about her or angry at the man who doped her, she would see to it that she stopped raving at him. It would demolish the barrier completely. Before this happened, he had to park her somewhere that would be binding.

Had she parents? Friends?

He hit the control panel with his fist. He hated to think of it, but he might be able to drop her in one of the sanatoriums that had been set up for love lotus addicts. They did little good for the victims, but did serve to keep them out of other people's hair—and he had to get rid of her.

It should be parents first.

Farradyne's forefinger hit the radio button viciously. "Tower? Connect me to the city telephone."

"Aye-firm, Lancaster. Wait five."

A few seconds later he was asking for the Bennington Detective Agency, an outfit that was system-wide and which advertised enough to make him remember the name. He got a receptionist first and then a quiet-voiced man named Lawson.

Farradyne came to the point. "I want any information you can collect about the family of a man named Frank Hannon who was killed in the wreck of the Semiramide in The Bog, on Venus, four years ago."

"You're Charles Farradyne. The same Farradyne?"

"Maybe, but is that important?"

"It might be but it will be held confidential. I'm asking because we prefer to know the motives of clients. I'd like reassurance that our investigation will be made for a legal reason."

"I'll put it this way. I know Frank Hannon was killed in the wreck. I have reason to believe that he had a sister that disappeared afterward. If this is true, I want to know, but I haven't time to find out through the usual channels. Fact of the matter is, I want no more information than I could get myself if I had time to go pawing through issues of newspapers of four years ago. No more. Is this reasonable enough?"

"It sounds that way. I'll look through our list of missing persons. I suggest that you either call back in a couple of hours or better that you call in person here at my office. There will be no charge for the initial search, but if this evolves into something more concrete—well, we can discuss the matter when you call. All right?"

"It's okay and I'll be in your office at four o'clock."

Farradyne hung up and considered. If Norma Hannon had a couple of grieving parents, he could hand her over to them and that would be the end of that. He lit a cigarette and smoked for a moment and then got up from the control console, snapped all the switches off and started for the spacelock.

He met Norma in the salon. She had changed from her white, silky, wide-skirted thing into a heavy satin housecoat that molded her arms to the wrists, clung to her waist and breasts and throat, and outlined her hips and thighs. Bare feet and painted toenails were provocatively visible below the hem as she sat there with her legs crossed, tossing her foot up and down.

"Thought we were about to take off again?" she asked. Her voice was soft and personal and friendly. She had

ch. ends p. 43

obviously dropped the vindictive tones and was plying the affectionate line as smoothly as she could.

Farradyne shook his head. Having a plan of action made him feel better. "Got a call from the Tower," he said. "More business. I'll be back in a couple of hours."

Norma held up her hand for his cigarette and he gave it to her. She puffed deeply and offered it back. Farradyne refused it. The memory of her needling and her desire for violence had not had time to fade. Another twenty hours of this calmness and he would begin to look upon the sharing of a cigarette as a pleasant gesture of companionship.

Norma shrugged at his wave of the hand in refusal. "I'll be here when you get back," she said comfortably, wriggling down against the cushions, and giving him the benefit of an inviting smile. She looked for all the world like a woman who would be waiting patiently for her man to return to her.

Farradyne left the salon swearing under his breath. If this parking of her did not work, Farradyne was licked and he knew it.

Farradyne walked. He didn't like walking but he preferred it to remaining in the Lancaster with Norma for the next couple of hours. He tried to think, but he could not come to any conclusion because he had all his hope tied on the Bennington outfit and what they might turn up.

He was shown into the office of Peter Lawson, who was a bright-eyed, elderly man with a body surprisingly lithe for his years.

"Now, before we go any further," said Lawson, pleasantly, "I'd like to hear your reasons for becoming interested in this case."

Farradyne nodded. "As I told you, Frank Hannon was killed in an accident on a spacecraft I owned. That was four years ago. Recently I met Norma Hannon in a gin mill on Ganymede and she fastened onto me like a leech as a person to hate. You know the results of love lotus addiction?"

"Yes. Unfortunately, I do."

"Well, it occurred to me that one way of getting rid of Miss Hannon would be to turn her over to some relative or friend who would be deeply interested in her welfare. Does this add up?"

"Quite logical. Miss Hannon is where you can find her?"

Farradyne nodded, with a sour look on his face. "She's sitting in my salon waiting for me to come back so she can bait me some more."

"Why not just turn her over to the police?" asked Lawson, with a careful look at Farradyne.

"Look," said Farradyne testily, "I don't enjoy Miss Hannon's company, but I can't see jailing her. She isn't really vicious, she's just another unfortunate victim of the love lotus trap. Maybe I feel a bit concerned over her brother. Anyway, take it from there."

"Very well. I shall. The facts are these: Frank Hannon was a lawyer with a limited but apparently lucrative practice. Norma acted as a sort of junior partner whose ability with briefs and research made her valuable to her brother. The case history says that Frank Hannon had been on his way to Venus to place some case before one of the higher courts, the nature of which is not a matter for public discussion even at this late date. I don't know what it was myself.

"Then Frank was killed, and afterward Norma dropped her study of law. Her brother's death seemed quite a blow to her. Before, she dated at random, nothing very serious. Afterward she seemed to develop a strong determination to marry and have children, perhaps as a substitute for the gap left by the death of her brother. A man named Anthony Walton became number one boyfriend after a few months and they were together constantly and seemed devoted to one another. She disappeared after a dinner date with Walton, and Walton is now serving a term on Titan Colony for possession of love lotus blossoms."

ch. ends p. 43

Farradyne shook his head. "The louse," he said. "Everybody agrees."

"I don't know as much as I might about lotus addiction," continued Farradyne. "It all seems so quick. One moment we have a well-bred young woman with ideals and ambition and feeling and the next——?"

"It's a rather quick thing," said Lawson. "The love lotus or hellflower is vicious and swift. I've studied early cases. They all seem to have the same pattern. And oddly enough, love lotus is not an addictive drug in every case. It is not only an aphrodisiac; it also heightens the physical senses so that a good drink tastes better and a good play becomes superb. The touch of her man's hand becomes a magnificent thrill. And here is the point where addiction begins, Mr. Farradyne. If the woman's senses and emotions are treated only to the mild appreciation of food and drink and music and a gentle caress, the addiction may take years and years to arrive at the point where she cannot feel these stimuli without a sniff of hellflower. But if she should be so unlucky as to have her emotions raised to real passion during the period of dosage, it is like overloading the engine. You burn her out."

"I see. And there is no cure?"

"Some doctors believe that a long period of peace and quiet under conditions where the mildest of stimuli are available may bring the addict back. I am of the opinion that such a place does not exist. They fasten onto hate as an emotion that cuts through their burned-out emotions and if you should place them among completely bland surroundings they would find it possible to hate those that incarcerated them. It becomes almost paranoiac—anything you do is wrong."

"So I have discovered. But what do I do with Miss Hannon?"

"At the time of Miss Hannon's disappearance, her family offered five thousand dollars for her return."

"I'd be happy to deliver her FOB[1] her own front porch," said Farradyne. "Can I hand her over to you and let you take it from there?"

"She would put up quite a ruckus," said Lawson. "I doubt that Miss Hannon will go home willingly. It is my opinion that her response to Walton's lovemaking was extremely high, so that the result was a quick blunting of her normal capabilities. After this, anger and shame would cause her—a proud woman of education and breeding—to hide where she could not be known, where she could possibly get the hellflower she needed. This would not be in the home of her parents. So she will not go home willingly, and the alternative is an appeal to the authorities. I doubt that such a course would be acceptable to either of us."

"You're right but——"

Lawson smiled. "I heard your offer to deliver her free to her home."

"So?"

"We'll help you. We'll have an operative collect Miss Hannon at the Denver Spaceport. All you have to do is live with this trouble for about fifty more hours. For delivering this information, and for taking Miss Hannon to Denver, we will be happy to divide the reward."

"I'll deliver Miss Hannon to Denver," he said, thinking that for twenty-five hundred he could stick cotton in his ears and sweat it out at about fifty dollars an hour.

"Good, Mr. Farradyne. I'll make arrangements to have our Mr. Kingman meet you at Denver."

Lawson handed Farradyne a few pages of dossier on the case and showed him out of the office. Farradyne took a deep breath and decided that what he wanted was a drink to his good fortune. He could look forward to getting rid of

---

[1] An acronym meaning "free on board": a shipping term used to include or assume delivery without charge to the buyer for goods placed on board a carrier at the point of shipment.

Norma Hannon, at last. He made the street and glanced around. Finding a small bar not far from the office door of the Bennington Agency, he went in to relax and think.

At a small table with a tiny lamp, he opened the papers that Lawson had given him, to read them more thoroughly. The waitress was high-breasted in a manner that invited him to look, but he merely barked, "White Star Trail," and went back to his reading.

"Spaceman?" she asked.

Farradyne nodded in an irritated manner. She flounced off after a moment of futile attempt to beguile a spaceman.

So when a moment later someone slid into the bench beside him, Farradyne turned to tell her to please go because he wasn't having any, thanks. Instead of looking into a vapidly willing face Farradyne's eyes were met by an equally cold blue stare from the face of a hard-jawed man dressed in a jacket tailored to half-conceal the shoulder holster he wore. Farradyne blinked.

"Farradyne?"

"So?" said Farradyne. He tried to think but all he could cover was the idea that someone was now playing games with guns.

"Hear tell you're running blossoms."

"Who says?"

"People."

"People say a lot of things. Which people?"

"Well, are you?"

"Who, me?"

"Can it!" snapped the newcomer.

Farradyne shrugged angrily. "What do you want me to do?" he asked in a mild tone. "You have the jump on me. You slide into my seat and bar my exit and then without introducing yourself you start asking questions that could get me twenty years in poor surroundings with bad company and no pay."

"Call me Mike. Michael Cahill is the name."

"Any identification that doesn't bark for itself?"

"It's usually good enough."

"Probably. But the numbers on its calling cards are always someone else's."

Mike laughed. "That's not bad, Farradyne. But so far as I know your number isn't among those present."

"I'll bet you could change a number fast enough."

"Could be," nodded Cahill. He turned over his shoulder and called to the waitress. "Hey, Snookey, make it two instead of one."

"Mine's White Star."

"That's all right with me. It's easier to drive this rod with a clear head."

"No doubt," said Farradyne. "So now that we are about to drink together let's face it. You had more in mind than to pass the time of day with a nervous spaceman who wanted to be alone."

"Correct. Or as you birds say, 'Aye-firm.' How's the hell-blossom business?"

"That's easy to answer. I haven't any and I am not in the business. See?"

"People say you are."

Farradyne grunted. "Not too long ago someone accused me openly. The story started when someone suggested that the only way a guy could come from down on his bottom to the top of the heap in one large step was to be among the big-time operators. The heavy-sugar know-how. To the limited imagination this meant running love lotus."

Mike Cahill was silent while the waitress brought their drinks. When she left Cahill lifted his glass to Farradyne. "Is you is or is you ain't?" he chuckled.

"I ain't," said Farradyne, drinking with Cahill.

"Or is it maybe?"

"Maybe it's maybe."

ch. ends next p.

"Stop sounding like a parrot. As I heard it that tomato in the bar on Ganymede must have known something. You spent four years as flat on your duff as a musclebound wrestler and then you come bouncing along in a last-year model Lancaster. Since we know damned well that you're no hellblossom runner, where did you get the stack?"

"Thrift and good management."

"Yeah. How'd you do it?"

"I told you."

"Maybe it's a rich uncle?"

"I haven't one. I'm just a capable operator."

"The label is sour, Farradyne."

"Then what do you make of this?" asked Farradyne, handing Cahill his license folder.

"It looks nice and legal but it is as phony as a ten-cent diamond and both of us know it. So how did you get it—and the Lancaster to go along with it?"

Farradyne sipped his drink. "Look, Cahill, it just happens that it's none of your damned business! I am not talking."

"It might make a difference if you did."

"Let's stop fencing. I may be of use to you. Now it might be that you are a SAND agent and it might be otherwise, I still may be of use to you either way. But the first time I start shooting off my trap, you'll begin to get the idea that I'm not close-mouthed enough for whatever job you have in mind for me. So let's leave it this way. I have a ticket that gets me in and out and a spacer that takes me there and back."

"And that's your story?"

"That's my story. *Finis*."[2] Farradyne sipped his drink and then offered Cahill a smoke which Cahill took.

"We've had a rather moist spring," observed Cahill.

"It was moister on Venus," commented Farradyne.

"It's on Terra that the weather is fine," said Cahill. "The

---

[2] Translated from Latin: the end.

crops are coming up excellently, I'm told. Nothing like fresh vegetables."

Farradyne nodded. "No matter how well we convert the planets to Terra condition, nothing grows like on earth."

"Ever enjoy lying on your back in the sun in a field of flowers with nothing to do but get sunburned?"

"Not for a long time."

"Funny how a guy gets out of his kid-habits," mused Cahill. "And even funnier how he wants to go and do it all over again but never quite makes it the same."

"Yeah."

"Farradyne, you're not sold up on this next jaunt to Terra, are you?"

"I've plenty of room. Just one passenger going to Denver."

"Mind if I buy a stateroom?"

"Not at all."

"I want to go pick flowers on Terra," yawned Cahill. "If you like, maybe we can pick some together."

"Maybe we can," said Farradyne, draining his glass and starting to get up. Cahill got up, too, and led the way out of the joint. Farradyne flagged down a taxicab. "Spaceport," he told the driver. "Coming?" he asked Cahill.

"Yeah. Might as well. Nothing else to do this week. I'll go along—for kicks."

5

Farradyne took the Lancaster up and set the ship on its course to Terra. As soon as he could spare the time to think of anything but handling the ship, he began to wonder about Norma and Mike Cahill. She had not been visible when they arrived, but no doubt by now she had made her presence known. It bothered him a bit because he was as certain as a man can be that Cahill was a hellflower operator, and he did not want the man to get cold feet because Farradyne was connected with an addict, if even for a short hop.

So as soon as he could leave the board, Farradyne went down to the salon.

They had met. Norma, for the first time in her trip with Farradyne, was presiding over the dining table. She was wearing a slinky, sea-green hostess gown Veed down to about here and slit on both sides to just below the knees. Her white, bare legs twinkled as she walked and almost forced the eye to follow them. She was giving Cahill all the benefit of her physical beauty, and Cahill was enjoying it. Farradyne had a hunch that Norma was about to start slipping him the old jealousy routine. He wondered about his reaction. He was extremely wary of Norma, but he did feel a sort of responsibility for her. She might make him jealous, but it would not be the jealousy of passion or desire, but the jealous concern that stems from a desire to protect.

Norma's lissome[1] figure slipped out of the salon toward the galley and as she disappeared Cahill wagged a forefinger at Farradyne.

"That dame's a blank," he said in a very low voice.

"I know. She's not my woman, Cahill."

"Maybe not," responded Cahill. "But it sure looks like it from a distance. What are you doing with her?"

"Delivering her to her parents in Denver."

"That all?"

Farradyne nodded. "She latched onto me on Ganymede; she's the dame that made the loud announcement of my being a hellflower runner."

"Maybe she's right."

"She isn't. I'm not."

Cahill grinned. "This much we know," he said.

"You do?"

"Yes. But maybe she'll be right sooner or later. But get rid of her, see?"

Farradyne nodded vigorously. "That I'll do. She has been hell on high heels to have around."

"Looks like she might be fun."

"She hates my guts."

Cahill nodded. "Probably. They usually end up in a case of anger and violence. Tough. But——"

Norma came back with a tray and set food on the table. They ate in silence, with Norma still giving Cahill the full power of her charm. Cahill, who had undoubtedly seen many a hellflower girl, still seemed to enjoy her advances although he accepted them with a calloused, self-assured smile. Once dinner was finished, Norma began to clear the table. This act annoyed Farradyne because he could not account for it, and the only thing that seemed to fit the case was the possibility that Norma was acting as she did

---

[1] Supple and graceful.

ch. ends p. 53

to soften his wariness of her, but she was carrying the thing too far. He did not think she was so unable to calculate; she must know that this act now pointed up her former disdain for any kind of cooperation.

As she left again, Farradyne turned to Cahill and asked, "How can a man tell a love lotus from a gardenia?"

"That takes experience, Farradyne. You'll learn."

"The thing that stops me," said Farradyne, "is that the Sandmen have been trying to stamp the things out for about forty years and they can't even tell where they come from."

"They'll never find out," said Cahill. "Maybe you won't either."

"But I——"

"Better you shouldn't. Just enjoy living off the edges. It's safer that way. Remember that."

"Where are we going after we leave Denver?"

"I'm not too sure we're going anywhere. I'm not too sure of you, Farradyne. You've some holes to fill in." Cahill lit a cigarette and leaned back, letting the smoke trickle through his nostrils. "I don't mind talking to you this way because it would be your word against mine, if you happen to be a Sandman. Some of your tale rings true. The rest sticks hard."

"For instance?"

"Well, let's suppose you are a Sandman. Humans are a hard-boiled lot, but somehow I can't see killing thirty-three people just to establish a bad reputation. So that tends to clear your book. As to the chance of your laying low for four years until the mess blew over, I might buy that except for the place. A guy who can ultimately turn up with enough oil to grease his way into a reinstated license and a late model Lancaster Eighty-One isn't likely to spend four interim years living in a fungus field."

"Maybe I hit it rich?"

Cahill laughed roughly. "Dug up a platinum-plated toad-stool?"

"Maybe I just met up with the right guy."

"Blackmail?"

"That's a nasty word, Cahill."

"Sure is. What did he do?"

"Let's call it maligning. Let's say he played rough at the wrong time and might have to pay high for it at the present." Farradyne looked at the ceiling. "And maybe that isn't it."

Cahill laughed. "Have it your way, Farradyne. Well, tell me, do we have a layover at Denver, or is it better if we take off immediately for Mercury?"

"Cinnabar or Hell City?"

"Cinnabar, if it makes any difference."

"Mercury, Schmercury, I didn't know there was anything there but the central heating plant."

"Isn't much," admitted Cahill. "But enough. The——"

His voice trailed away as Norma's high heels came clicking up the circular stairway, back toward the salon. "I thought I'd have a cigarette and a drink with company before I go to bed," she announced in a tone of voice that Farradyne had not heard her use before. With gracious deftness, Norma made three highballs[2] of White Star and water and handed two of them to the men. She let her fingers linger over Farradyne's very briefly, and over Cahill's longer. She lounged in a chair across from them, all curves and softness, with only that strange, disinterested look in her eyes to give her away.

Farradyne found this a bit difficult to explain to himself. The evening had been a series of paradoxes; Norma's change from vixen to the lady of languid grace did not ring true. He had been aware of her ability to reason coldly, brought about by her burned-out emotional balance which was so dulled that her thinking was mechanically unemotional and therefore inclined to be frightfully chilled logic. But Farradyne's

---

[2] A highball is a cocktail served with ice in a tall glass, usually consisting of whiskey and a mixer such as water or a carbonated beverage.

ch. ends p. 53

grasp of the problem was incomplete. Norma had claimed that she knew the emotions by name and definition, that once she had felt them, but that now she only knew how they worked. Farradyne found it hard to believe that she was so well-schooled in her knowledge that she could put on the act of having them when she obviously did not.

She did not even force herself upon them; when her cigarette and her drink were gone, Norma got up, excused herself and quietly went below.

"Me too," said Cahill.

Farradyne led him down to a stateroom and waved him in. "See you in the morning," he said. Cahill nodded his goodnight and Farradyne went on to his own room to think.

He hadn't done bad. Of course he did not really know how far some of Clevis' other operators had gone, but Farradyne had been on the trail for less than a hundred hours and already had a lead. Obviously the fact of the Semiramide was the tip-off; no Sandman would go that far to establish a shady reputation.

Farradyne was prepared to go as far as he had to. The idea of actually running love lotus was not appealing, but the SAND office had been fighting the things for a half century, watching helplessly while the moral fiber of the race was being undermined by the nasty things and somehow it was far better to let a few more lives be wrecked by hellflowers than to save a few and let the whole thing steamroll into monumental destruction. Farradyne still had to duck a few people who might like to nail his hide to a barn door, but sooner or later he would come out on top of this mess and then he could look his fellow man in the eye and ask him to forget one bad mistake—that wasn't even Farradyne's so far as he himself knew.

Being on his first step eased his mind somewhat. He would be rid of Norma in the morning sometime and on his way with Cahill, and the future looked interesting, if not cheerful. He went to sleep easily for the first time since the meeting with Norma on Ganymede. He dreamed a pleasant dream of freedom and success that ended with the bark of a pistol.

Shocked out of his sleep, he lay stunned and blinking for a moment, and then leaped out of bed and raced to the corridor. The light blinded him first, but not enough to stop him from seeing Cahill.

Cahill came along the tiny corridor listlessly, blood dribbling from under his left arm, running down his fingers and splashing on the floor. On Cahill's face was a stunned expression, full of incomprehension, semi-blank. Blood ran down his leg, across his ankle and left red footprints on the floor.

Through the haze that clouded Cahill's eyes, he saw Farradyne. He stumbled forward and reached out, but collapsed like a limp towel, to stretch out at Farradyne's feet like a tired baby. His voice sighed out in a dying moan that sounded like a rundown phonograph . . . and then the shocking rattle of death.

Steps behind him came Norma Hannon. Her eyes were blazing with an unholy satisfied light and her body was alive and sinuous. A tiny automatic dangled from her right hand. Her lips curled in a sneer as she came up to Cahill and poked at the dead man's hand with her bare foot.

"He——" she started to cry in a strident tone. Then the semi-hysteria faded and she looked down at Cahill again, relishing the idea.

Farradyne shuddered. Cahill probably had not been able to do more than clutch at the deep neckline of Norma's nightgown.

He leaned back against the wall and saw things in a sort of horrid slow motion. Under any normal circumstances, no jury in the solar system would have listened to an attempt to prosecute her. Under any normal circumstances,

Farradyne could bury Cahill at space and report the incident at the first landing. But Farradyne couldn't stand too much investigation. Norma Hannon was a hellflower addict, a "blank," in Cahill's words; she couldn't bear investigation.

Worst of all was the loss of Cahill.

"Why?" asked Farradyne, bitterly.

"He——" Her eyes opened wide again as she relived the scene, relished the violence.

"Have your fun," gritted Farradyne.

"I hoped it was you," she said. "I wouldn't have killed you." Her voice was calm, she might have been saying "kiss" instead of "kill." "Him I did not like."

"And you like me?"

"You I save to hate tomorrow," she said with matter-of-fact flatness.

"Why didn't you save him?"

"What was he to you?"

"He was my source."

"Source?" Norma looked blank. Then understanding crossed her face. "Hellblossoms," she said with a sneer that twisted her face. She stepped past Cahill's body and handed the automatic to Farradyne, who took it dumbly because it was proffered. She went on into the salon and sat down.

Farradyne wanted to hurt her, to reach through that wall and make her feel something besides anger.

"Source," he nodded, following her. "Love lotus. I'd have given you one, Norma."

She made a sound like a bitter laugh. "No good, Farradyne. What good is one lotus?"

"I don't know," he said simply. "I've never had one."

Her laugh was shrill and insane. Then she bawled at him like a fishwife.[3] "What an operator you are. You big,

---

[3] An unruly and coarse-mannered woman prone to shouting.

fumbling boob with your stolen spacer and your forged license, making like a big wind. Fah!"

She got up as suddenly as she had sat down. She paused on her way down the corridor to kick Cahill's leg. Farradyne stayed where he was until he heard her door slam shut. He should be moved, thought Farradyne.

He found himself looking down on the dead man with a strangely detached feeling, as though he were watching a play. He relived the scene although he tried to shut it out of his mind. Shutting out would not work, so he went through it detail by detail minutely, from the sound of the pistol shot to the last dying groan from Cahill's throat. The memory of that dying wail jarred on Farradyne's nerves.

It was a discordant cry.

He found himself making a completely useless analysis, itemizing things that surely could not matter. The cry had been a discord. His mind wandered a bit as he considered the word. A series of atonal notes do not make a discord. A discord comes when atonal notes are sounded at the same time. The former can be pleasant to the ear, the latter not.

And then a chill hit him. He felt like a man who had just been told that he had one more question to answer before winning the prize on a quiz show. Cahill's moan had been a full discord.

With a sudden disconnect of the mind, Farradyne was back in the Semiramide, hearing three voices behind him. They found one skeleton, afterward. Then his mind leaped to Brenner, on Mars, who had emitted an approving grunt when he saw Norma come around the tail structure of the Lancaster with the sun shining through her skirt. He had no proof, no proof. Brenner's grunt had been no discord but nonetheless a mingling of tones. Three voices? Maybe more?

Maybe he was not sure of the first. Brenner's voice had been very brief, maybe he was convincing himself. But

ch. ends next p.

Cahill's death cry was most certainly polytonal. And they were both lotus operators.

It might mean something, or it might not. Farradyne put his head back and tried to hum and say something at the same time. Perhaps the stunt could be cultivated after much practice, and perhaps it was used as a password.

More than anything, Farradyne needed corroboration.

It was a very weak reed, but he stepped over Cahill's body and rapped on Norma's door.

She opened the door after a moment and said, "Now what?"

"Norma, you claim I owe you something, but I think you now owe me something."

She made a scornful sound. "For killing your little chum out there?"

"Maybe," he said as shortly as he knew how.

"Go on, Farradyne, but make it good."

He looked down into her glazed eyes, hoping to see some flicker of expression that showed some interest in anything.

"Norma, you've a good, logical mind. Tell me, did you notice anything about Cahill's last cry?"

"No."

"Nothing odd?"

"I've not seen men die very often. What was strange about it?" The eyes unglazed a bit, but Farradyne could not tell whether this was awakened interest or merely the recapture of the feeling she had enjoyed before.

"It sounded to me like a discordant moan."

"It was discordant."

"Not the way I mean. It sounded to me like there were three or four tones all going at once."

She snorted derisively. "Let me shoot you. I'll make a recording of your death cry and we'll see how well you sing."

"I'm serious."

"Stop beating that dead horse," she told him flatly. "It's

the same chorus you used to sing about the three men in your control room, remember?"

"Brenner made a sound like that, too," he said.

"A pig-like sound," she said scornfully. "Forget it, Farradyne. You've convinced nobody but yourself, and your evidence consists of one man surprised at the sight of a good-looking woman and one man whose throat was coming apart in death. Forget it." She shut the door to her room in his face abruptly.

Farradyne looked down at Cahill's body with regret. Not that Cahill's death touched him in any way but mild shock and distress at the loss of his link to the hellblossom gang. A gunman and a love lotus operator was not likely to have his absence noticed among the kind of people who could afford to start asking a lot of questions of the officials, and there might be a fair chance that Cahill's disappearance would cause the same people to ask a question or two of Farradyne.

He would have liked to keep the body. But hauling a slain corpse—he did not consider it murder—into a doctor's office and asking for an autopsy on the throat could not be done. Nor could Farradyne do it himself. He could perform a fair job of setting a broken bone and he could treat a burn or a cut, but he would not recognize a larynx if he saw it. And although he knew better intellectually, he instinctively considered a vocal cord as a stretched string of some sort that vibrated in the air-stream.

Distastefully Farradyne hauled the body to the scuttle-port and consigned it to space with a terse, "See you in hell, Cahill."

6

The Lancaster came down at Denver. Before Farradyne had the landing ramp out, a spaceport buggy came careening across the field to stop almost at the base of the ship.

"Farradyne?" asked the man.

"You're the Bennington Detective Agency man?"

"Sidney Kingman," said the other, showing Farradyne a small case with identification card and license. "Where is she?"

"Inside."

Kingman handed Farradyne an envelope. He pocketed it and led Kingman into the salon. Norma was there, sitting on the divan, smoking.

"Miss Hannon, Mr. Kingman."

"Another one of your friends?" she sneered.

"No. He's one of yours."

"I have no friends."

"Yes, you have, Miss Hannon. I have come to take you home."

Norma leaped to her feet. "You good-for-nothing bum!" she screeched at Farradyne. "Why did you do it?"

"You wouldn't leave me alone, Norma," said Farradyne softly. "So I've brought you home where they'll take care of you and keep you out of my hair."

"I'll come after you!" she raved. "I'll get you for this!"

"Not if I see you first," he told her. "This is it."

"Why do you hurt everything you touch?" she cried.

"Now who?"

"Me." For the first time, Farradyne saw tears of genuine sorrow. There was anger at him, too, but remorse there was a-plenty. "Why hurt my people!" she asked. "Why can't they just call me dead and let it go at that? I'm worse than dead."

Then her face froze again and she looked at Kingman. "All right," she said in a hard voice. "Let's go and hurt my folks to death. Let's get it over with. You pair of money-grubbing ghouls."

She started toward the spacelock, waving her forefinger at Kingman, who followed. Her face wore a coldly distant expression as she left the Lancaster. Kingman's driver took them off. She did not turn back to look at Farradyne.

And that was that. Farradyne retracted the ramp, closed the spacelock and not long afterward hiked the ship into the sky and headed for Mercury.

7

Cinnabar was inside the sunlight zone by a thousand miles and its sun was always in the same spot of the sky. It was a well-contrived city, built so that the streets were lighted either directly or by reflections. Cinnabar was also one of the show-cities of the system, but Farradyne found that it did not show him the right things. He could have learned as much about hellflowers on Terra merely because New York had a larger public library.

He tried everything he could think of but made no progress. His trail had turned to ice after Cahill's death. He loafed and he poked his nose in here and there and drank a bit and varied his routine from man-about-town to the spaceman concerned about his future. There was only one bright spot—his listing had been tentatively taken up by a group of schoolteachers on a sabbatical, who had seen Mercury and now wanted a cheap trip to Pluto.

Farradyne had accepted this job for about three weeks later. It gave him a payload to Pluto, and when he got there it would be time to do the subcontracting job Clevis had set up as a combined source of revenue and a means of contact. Once each month Farradyne was to haul a shipment of refined thorium[1] ore from Pluto to Terra, a private job that

---

[1] A radioactive silvery-white metallic element that occurs in monazite.

paid well. In the meantime Farradyne could nose around Mercury to see what he could see. Then he could haul his schoolteachers to Pluto and pick up his thorium, which definitely made his actions look reasonably normal to the official eye.

On the end of the drums of semi-refined thorium there would be a spot of fluorescent paint, normally invisible. He was to wash off this spot so long as he had nothing to report. If it remained, then something was wrong with Farradyne; he had not turned up or he had something to report. Clevis would know what to do next.

And so Farradyne watched the date grow closer and closer and his hopes of having something to report grow less and less likely. He felt as though he had been given up, in fact he got to the point where he wondered how a man could get a love lotus if he wanted one. The prevalence of the dope seemed high enough, but as far as Farradyne was concerned it was harder than buying a real gold brick. There did not seem to be any for sale. He thought that perhaps his method of attack was wrong, and yet he did not know how to correct it.

He cursed under his breath at the futility of it, and realized that his curse must have been audible because he felt a touch on his elbow and a voice asking, "Is it that bad?"

He turned slowly, his mind working fast to think of something to say that would not be leading in the wrong direction. "I was——" he started, and then he saw that the voice which had been low-pitched enough to have been the voice of a man had come from the throat of a tall, dark-haired woman who sat beside him at the bar. "Just wondering what strangers do for excitement on Mercury," he finished lamely.

"Spaceman?"

"Yes."

"I guessed it." She laughed in her low contralto.[2] "But spacemen aren't the only ones who drink that watered-down whiskey."

"I know. But this time it is one."

She smiled again. "Is Cinnabar so inhospitable?" she asked.

"To strangers it seems so."

"To me it seems quite normal. It makes the rest of the solar system sound like a very exciting place."

"Born on Mercury?"

"No," she said, shaking her head. "I was born on Venus. I spent four years on Terra before my folks brought me to Mercury. But my last space trip took place when I was nine. Tell me, what is New York like?"

"Buildings and people and mad rushing around. Any change in the last hundred years has been for taller buildings, more people and a higher velocity of humanity. But anybody can find anything he wants somewhere in New York, if he has the money to buy it."

She smiled calmly. "I'll show you that Cinnabar is not an inhospitable place," she said. "You may take me to dinner if you wish."

"I wish," he chuckled. "And since we haven't a mutual friend to introduce us, I'm Charles Farradyne."

"How do you do?" she said solemnly, putting a lithe hand in his. "I'm Carolyn Niles." She took a little step out from the bar and made him a slight curtsey. He saw that she was almost as tall as he was, and he grinned as he thought that her figure was far better than his.

"How shall we meet?" he asked.

"We shall not meet," said Carolyn. "We shall play it very bright and very interesting. You shall drive me home where we will have cocktails with my folks and you will meet them.

---

[2] The lowest female voice or voice part, in range between soprano and tenor, and often shortened to "alto."

You will be an old friend of Michael's, who is a sort of school-chum of my brother. After cocktails I will run upstairs to change and you will make polite conversation with my family—none of whom eat personable young men, though they may scare them to death by having Father show them the fine collection of Terran shotguns he owns. Then we will go out to your spacecraft, and you will change while I roam around and investigate the insides. This I will like because it's been some time since I have seen the insides of a spacer."

"Done," agreed Farradyne.

Something rapped him on the elbow and he had to look down before he saw a boy of ten or so with a green-paper lined box containing flowers. The young merchant had an eye for business; he eyed Farradyne knowingly and smiled at Carolyn fetchingly. "Corsage? One dollar."

Farradyne grinned and then almost recoiled before he realized that nowhere in the solar system could a love lotus be purchased for a dollar. These were definitely gardenias. He bought one to cover up his confusion, and handed it to Carolyn. She pinned the gardenia in her dark hair as she smiled her thanks, then led him from the bar to an open roadster almost as low and long as the curb it was parked against. Carolyn handed him her keys and Farradyne drove according to her directions until they came to a rather large rambling house just outside the city limits.

She introduced him, and he was received graciously. Her father was a tall, distinguished man with a dab of gray at the temples and a rather stern face that became completely unstern whenever he smiled, which was frequently. Carolyn's mother was tall and dark with only a sprinkle of gray. The brother was not present, which made it completely easy for Farradyne who could not have given any account of his friendship for the unknown Michael, stated friend of Robert Niles.

Mr. Niles mixed a pitcher of martinis and inquired about

the spaceman business. Farradyne explained how it was. Mrs. Niles laughed at his story of fish one day and fins the next and said that she thought it couldn't be quite that bad, really. Farradyne grinned. Mr. Niles observed that a man who can operate a spacer and pay off a mortgage on the craft must not be entirely penniless or without prospects.

Mrs. Niles countered with, "I suppose it takes money to operate, Mr. Farradyne."

"A fair amount. A spaceman begins to think in large figures so much that he wonders how he can get along on a more humanly reasonable amount. To clear a reasonable standard of living, a rather staggering amount of money comes in one hand and goes out the other. Operating expenses are high, but so are charges."

"But do you land on Mercury often, Mr. Farradyne?"

Farradyne smiled. "Perhaps less frequently in the past than in the future."

"Now that's sheer flattery," laughed Carolyn.

"Better enjoy it," observed her father with a chuckle. "Charles, you are welcome here any time you land."

"Thank you," smiled Farradyne. "But all things considered, I should think that you'd take a dim view of any man that brought your daughter home wearing a gardenia."

"Gardenia? Oh. You mean that it might be——" Mr. Niles laughed. "I think that Carolyn has enough judgment to take up with the right kind of young man, Charles."

"Of course," said Mrs. Niles. "Robert and Michael wouldn't stay friends with the wrong kind."

"So you see?" laughed Mr. Niles.

"By the way," asked Mrs. Niles. "How is Michael?"

"Quite well, the last time I saw him," said Farradyne, quite sure that this was the right thing to say at any time.

"You're sure?"

"Of course."

"I'm very happy to hear it," said Mrs. Niles. "We knew he was with you, but we didn't know how long he stayed."

Farradyne gulped imperceptibly, and he hoped that they did not notice. "You did? Then he must have mentioned me."

"Oh, he did. Tell me, Charles, what happened to Michael?"

"Did something happen to him?"

Mr. Niles eyed Farradyne rather pointedly. "Mike took off with you from Mars. He did not land at Denver, Mr. Farradyne. So what happened to Mike Cahill?"

Farradyne gulped, and this time it was a full-throated gulp that left him with his Adam's apple high in his throat.

Carolyn cooed, "Yes, Charles, what happened to Michael Cahill?"

A shiver crossed Farradyne's nerves and he felt the muscle-loosening tingle of fear. His thinking mechanism stopped functioning. His mind buzzed with a frenetic insistence that he say something, but he was completely unprepared. And he dimly knew that his long speechlessness was as damning as any story he could have prepared after such a pause. He thought all the way around in a circle, coming back to the fact that he should say something but that his mind was so busy insisting that he fill in this bizarre event that it did not furnish him with anything to say.

Then it occurred to him that he need not say anything. The die had been cast and he stood accused, twice; once by the Niles family and once by his own shocked reaction. What he must do was act for the next moment because the passed moment was irreparable. One of two things was evident: either Cahill was a double-dealing rat or the man was hand in glove with the Niles and that meant——

Farradyne laughed at his own simplicity. It was a sort of brief, scornful bark.

"What is funny?" asked Mr. Niles.

"It just occurred to me—the brilliant concept that you people are either innocent or guilty."

ch. ends p. 69

"Very sage," commented Niles dryly. "You don't seem quite that bright, Mr. Farradyne. Not even that bright. Now, what happened to Cahill?"

Only for a fleeting moment did Farradyne follow the possibility that Niles was innocent. There had been no attempt on Cahill's part to contact anybody from the time Farradyne met him until he saw him last alive. Ergo, the Niles must have been forearmed with Cahill's plan. This was the place that Cahill would have brought him; it had just taken him a bit longer to get here without the proper guide.

He leaned back, trying to relax. He took a sip of his martini, not that he wanted it, but to see if his hand were still trembling. It did not seem to shake.

He said, "If you knew Cahill and his whereabouts, you also know quite a bit about me. You'll have heard that I was recognized in a bar on Ganymede by a woman named Norma Hannon, who is a hellflower addict. She hated my guts because I am Charles Farradyne and her brother was among those present when I had the accident in The Bog. She hung onto me for the emotional ride it gave her. I succeeded in locating the home of her parents and was going to take her home when I met Cahill, who offered to come along after a bit of talk. Then during the night, Cahill made a pass at Norma, and she shot him. I put his body out through the scuttle port."

"Cahill was always a damned fool," nodded Niles. "He was a dame-crazy idiot and it served him right. Some men prefer money, power, or model railroads. Women are poison."

"I seem to have followed one of them like a little lamb," said Farradyne. "But I was picked up and brought here for a purpose, so let's get down to cases."

"You're a rather quick-on-the-trigger man, aren't you? What makes you assume that this purpose was anything beyond finding out about Cahill?"

"Because you have tipped your hand," said Farradyne

feeling more at ease. "You could have accomplished the same thing by tipping the police and waiting for the case to be newscast. If Cahill admitted to hellflower running, it was for a purpose, too. I call the same logic in you, Niles."

"Please. *Mister* Niles. I'm a bit your senior."

"All right. Mr. Niles. I've learned one thing so far: I can tell a love lotus operator from the rest of the system."

"How?" They all leaned forward eagerly.

"Because it is the real operators that take an amused view of my alleged machinations. They know the facts."

"Very sage. You are a bit brighter than you appeared a moment ago."

"May I ask why you let me cool my heels for almost a month before you hauled me in?" He looked at Carolyn with a wry smile. "I would make a mild bet you weren't more than a few hundred feet from me all the while?"

"You are a blind man, Farradyne," she said calmly.

Mr. Niles smiled knowingly. "There are a lot of unexplained items in your past, Farradyne. We never could be too sure that you were not a Sandman. Of course, it does seem a bit hard to believe that a government operative would crash a spacer and kill thirty-three people just to establish a bad reputation, especially when his own neck was involved in the affair. Still, such a deal might have been managed. So we have been checking on you and from that angle you are clean. Then comes the question of Cahill. It might be that you thought turning in a hellflower operator would help to smooth your lot in life, mayhap get you a bit of a reward. So we waited. No Cahill. Cahill started to bring you here; he would either have turned up with or without you. Or he would have gotten in touch with us. Unless Cahill was dead. You would know the answer. Norma Hannon is keeping her mouth shut, so far as we know. Of course no one would believe a blank anyway, and she probably knows that. So it stands to reason that you know more about Cahill than anybody else."

"No more than I've told you. Cahill came and made me a sort of sidelong offer."

"That much of it rings as true as the other. But there are still holes in your story."

Farradyne nodded. "Let's put it this way: there are ways of getting money and things. I found one way, which is an obvious fact. But I have been told time and again that the entering wedge to a full confession is a willingness to talk. Do you follow me?"

"I do. But——"

Farradyne smiled. "I don't care to face it. Not in company, Mr. Niles." Farradyne's emphasis on the "Mister" was heavy with sarcasm. Niles looked at him piercingly.

"You are a bit belligerent and a trifle sure of yourself. Close-mouthed and apparently able to get along. You'll be out on a lonely limb for some time, Farradyne, but we can use you."

"I can use the sugar," said Farradyne.

"Naturally. Anybody can use money. In fact everybody needs money. What visible means of support have you?"

"I've a subcontract. Once each month I'm to lug a load of thorium refines from Pluto to Terra."

"It's a start but it isn't enough."

"I'll pick up more, doubtless."

Niles leaned back and put the tips of his fingers together pontifically. "One of the hardest jobs in this business is to justify your standard of living. The financial rewards are large and the hours involved are small. It is patent that a man who has not been granted a large inheritance or perhaps stumbled on a lucrative asteroid, cannot live in a semi-royal manner without having to work in a semi-royal fury. One of the great risks in this business is the accep- tance of a recruit whose appearance causes discussion. The day when a man can build a fifty-thousand-dollar home on a five-thousand-dollar salary without causing more than a raised eyebrow has gone. If a man has a hidden income, he must appear busy enough to warrant it—or at least provide a reasonable facsimile."

"This I can understand."

"For a job like this," explained Niles, "we prefer the natural-born spaceman, with sand in his shoes or space dust in his eyes. Because the man with a bad case of wanderlust always looks busy even when he is idling. You seem to be that sort, but we never can tell until it is tried. Unless, of course, you turn out to be woman-crazy."

"I'm a normal enough male," said Farradyne. "I'll remind you that Cahill was the guy that tried and failed."

"How normal are you?" demanded Niles. "We'd have less liking for a misogynist than for a satyr[3] here."

Farradyne smiled serenely. "I have enough sense to keep my hands off Norma Hannon, but I have enough red blood to come home with Carolyn. That good enough?"

Niles thought a moment. "Could be. Anyway we'll find out. For one thing, Farradyne, you'll be in no position to hurt anyone but yourself if you're playing games. Once we're really sure of you, it won't matter anymore because you will be in a position to get hurt plenty. We'll try it, and see. Now, when do you go to Pluto?"

"I've some schoolteachers to haul out there tomorrow. I've taken them on——"

"Good. Gives you a good background without much labor. Now, when you land on Terra, you'll not bother posting your ship for a job because you have already contracted for a job. Carolyn will be there on a business trip for me and will have chartered your ship for a hauling job back to Mercury. During this trip you will get some more details on how you

---

[3] A licentious man; one with strong sexual desires.

are to operate. This much I can tell you now, Farradyne: you will be an inbetweener, in fact almost the operator you set yourself up to be. But with one difference, we'll inform you just who is and who is not to be trusted. In other words, you'll have your regular customers and you will sell to no one else. They'll take your entire supply, pay for it and you will take your profit. The remainder you will use to purchase your supply from the upper source. Advancement may come slow or fast, depending on you. You'll get the details later, as for now——" Niles leaned back in his chair and smiled. "Farradyne, you met my daughter in a cocktail lounge and several people heard the two of you planning an evening together. So you will go dancing and dining and have a drink or two and maybe a bit of lovemaking, which is an entirely natural performance. And from this moment you will be Charles and I shall be Mr. Niles and we'll have no nonsense. Understand?"

"I do."

"Good. Now have another martini while Carolyn dresses for dinner."

Niles poured. Carolyn disappeared. Mrs. Niles leaned forward and asked, "Charles, why did you become a spaceman?" Her tone of voice and attitude made her seem like all the other fathers and mothers who have asked the same question. For the moment he forgot about her position in this odd scheme of things just because she looked precisely fitted to the role she played for public consumption. Almost mechanically, Farradyne began to explain. He knew the story by rote[4] because he had told it so often in the same manner and to the same sort of person. This gave his mind a chance to consider them, partly.

Mr. and Mrs. Niles appeared to be the successful businessman and his wife. The aura of respectability extended

---

[4] Mechanical routine or habitual repetition.

to include the house and its spacious grounds, so that Farradyne burned with resentment at any proposition whereby he, who had not committed anything more than a few misdemeanors and some rather normal fun and games which are listed on the books but are likely to be overlooked, should be less cultured, less successful and less poised than this family of low-grade vultures. If anything, the attitude of Mrs. Niles shocked him more than the acts of her husband. Men were the part of the race that play the rough games and run up the score, according to Farradyne. Women occupied one of two positions: they were patterned after Farradyne's mother who had been a poised, mature woman of education and breeding, if a trifle puritanical; or they were slatterns and sluts and they looked as well as acted the part. So instead of Mrs. Niles presiding over the mansion as a gracious lady, she should be loud and cheap. That she was poised and gracious offended Farradyne's sense of fitness.

As for Carolyn, who was equally engaged in this loathsome game, Farradyne felt annoyed because there was nothing about her outward appearance that would permit him to scorn her. Like her parents, she gave the impression of success, as though the business they were all engaged in were both honorable and beneficial. Farradyne yearned for the moment when he could pull the pedestal out from under them and dump them into the mud where they damned well belonged.

Farradyne became, in those few moments, a more mature man. He understood Clevis' attitude. Always before, he wondered why a clever man would work for peanuts at a thankless job which included anonymity when he could have put his efforts into some sort of business and emerge wealthy and famous. Now Farradyne was beginning to understand the personal satisfaction that could be gained by following in the footsteps of a man like Clevis. In Niles' own words,

ch. ends next p.

some men like money, others like power, and still others build model railroads. Well, some achieve their personal gain by rooting out the lice that undermine the moral fiber of the race, and this gives them the same satisfaction that amassing a billion dollars gives a man whose ambition is wealth.

Money had never been Farradyne's god. He had not wanted more than enough to exchange for the fun and games he preferred, and these did not come high. He found himself elated to have discovered a new outlet for his nervous energy and his urge to do something. Performing a thankless job in anonymity could provide for Farradyne a deep satisfaction in proving that he was smarter than people like Niles and family.

He smiled as his mouth got to the point in his story where he was telling about the time he had landed the training ship perfectly—but nine feet above ground, so that the ship dropped the nine feet and nearly flunked him out of spaceman's school. He knew that his smile was hypocritical and he enjoyed this sort of thing. If Niles could play the hypocritical game, so could Farradyne. But Farradyne could play it better because his own kind of hypocrisy was—he hated to call it righteous but could not find a better word to describe it. He could play Niles' game, and he could even go along with Mrs. Niles, although he wondered how a woman that looked as honorable as Mrs. Niles could justify her willingness to have a daughter engaged in the vile game of hellflower running. He could play their game because he would have little contact with them.

But he wondered whether he could play the game Carolyn expected. He did not know exactly what she expected but his guess was that anybody amoral enough to run dope would hardly cavil[5] at anything else. He knew that many a

[5] Make petty, annoying, or unnecessary objections; to argue or find fault over trivial matters.

man could lie in his teeth and play the role of spy convincingly, but when the role included making love to a woman whose background was distasteful to a man, Farradyne believed that this distaste would show through anything he did.

And then Carolyn came down the stairs in a white strapless evening dress and Farradyne knew that he was going to have trouble remembering that she was worthy of only shapeless, gray prison denim. "You have to dress, too, Charles," she said in a soft voice, reminding him of their plans for the evening.

Farradyne nodded and got up. He wondered how she could possibly act this part of a young, marriageable woman pleased with a date when at the same time she was engaged in a hellishly illegal operation. He realized at the same time that Carolyn had most likely spent her entire life this way and was attuned to it. Such was her natural way of living, and there was not going to be any possibility of weaning her into a life of honorable struggle.

Then she put her hand into his elbow and gave a little squeeze and Farradyne found it not too hard to put his personal attitude into a small compartment in his mind and half-close the door. The bait was very attractive and only the image of Norma Hannon and her dulled eyes remained with Farradyne to keep that compartment of his mind open to the character of Carolyn Niles.

8

In the salon of the Lancaster, Farradyne smiled knowingly. "The plan was to let you investigate this ship while I dressed, but I gather you have seen your share of spacers."

"I admit it," she replied. "For that I am sorry, Charles. But I couldn't very well have played the know-it-all, could I?"

"I suppose not. Well, park yourself somewhere while I get into whites."

She sat down and stretched. "A highball and a cigarette?" she inquired.

"The cigarette is easy," he said, handing one to her and flipping his lighter. "But the highball may be more difficult. I've nothing but White Star Trail aboard."

She nodded at him. "With water," she said. She relaxed into the cushions. Farradyne went and mixed her highball. She sipped it and nodded approvingly. "Charles, please go dress but fast—I am rather more hungry than curious about the insides of a spacer."

"Of course." He turned to go.

"Charles?" She rose and came forward, lifting her hands to put them on his shoulders. He stood woodenly. "Charles," she asked in a soft voice, "are you unhappy because I am not the girl you hoped I'd be?"

Farradyne wanted to hurt her. "How many men have you played this role for?" he asked.

A wry smile twisted her face. "I should slap your face for that," she said. "Because when I tell you the answer you won't believe me."

Caution came to him. He was the rookie hellflower operator, not the young man who has discovered that his girl has been playing games behind his back. He tried to fit himself into her picture and decided that according to her code of loused-up ethics she might possibly be thinking of a future: a pleasant home with rambling roses and a large lawn and a devoted husband and maybe a handful of happy children all creating the solid-citizen facade for dope running, just as her parents were doing. If this were the case, Farradyne was to play the suitor. He must carry roses for his wife in one hand, toys for the kids in the other and his hip pocket must be filled with hellflowers.

He played it. He relaxed and put his hands on her waist. "I admit to being a bit of a louse," he said with a brief laugh. "But that's because I'm a bit new at a very rough game."

She leaned forward a bit. "Even rough games have their rules."

"I'll play according to the rules as soon as I learn them."

She looked at him. "You know them," she said quietly. "All men and women learn them at home, in school, in church. They're sensible rules and they keep people out of trouble, mostly. If you adhere to the rules, people will have nothing to which their attention can be directed. That's what Father was trying to say when he suggested that you provide a visible means of support for yourself. Play by these rules and we'll get along. It's especially important when we must not have people looking in our direction, Charles."

She sighed and leaned against him softly. "You asked me a question, Charles. The answer is three. One of them preferred a blonde and they are living quietly and happily on Callisto. The second couldn't have jelled because he

ch. ends p. 75

was the kind of man who would work eighteen hours a day. Some men are that way and some women like it that way, but not me. The third, Charles, was Michael. Mike didn't last long. Only long enough to prove to me that he was a woman-chaser. The fourth could be you, and maybe there mightn't be a fifth."

"Three men in your life," he said.

She smiled up into his eyes. "Three men in my life," she said with a happy little nod of her head, "but, Charles, it isn't three men in my bedroom." Carolyn cocked an eyebrow. "The only way the fourth will get in is to make sure there won't be a fifth. So now you know. You can play it from there."

His arms did not slip around the slender waist, but the hands pulled her close to him. He kissed her gently, and for a moment she clung to him with her body. Her response was affectionate, only bordering on passion. Then she leaned back and smiled into his face. "You need a shave," she told him. "So let go of me until you can kiss me without scratching my skin off." Then to prove that she didn't really mean it, Carolyn kissed him again briefly, and ended it by rubbing her forehead against his chin.

Farradyne went to his stateroom and showered. He shaved, and dressed carefully in white slacks and shirt, and the last remaining holdover from a Victorian period, a dark necktie. He returned to the salon to find Carolyn waiting for him calmly and patiently. She looked him over and nodded approvingly, then got up and rubbed her cheek against his, cooing pleasantly, but moved away again when he tried to kiss her.

Then she tucked her hand under his elbow and said, "Dinner, man-thing."

Farradyne chuckled. "Dinner," he repeated.

She hugged his arm. He led her down the landing ramp and into her car, and at her direction drove to her preference in a dinner spot. The food was good. Carolyn was a fine dancer with a high sense of rhythm and a graceful body. Farradyne decided that if this were a thankless job that gave no chance for fame and fortune, there were plenty of very pleasant facets to it. . . . Her shoulder rubbed his as he drove her home hours later.

He handed her out of the car and walked to the front door with her. She gave him her key and he opened the door; she walked in, to wait for him just inside. She came into his arms as the door closed behind them and she clung to him, returning his kiss and his embrace; matching his rising fervor with a passion of her own. They parted minutes afterward. Farradyne moved her slightly, settling her body into a more comfortable fit against him.

"It's late," she breathed.

Farradyne chuckled. "With the sun shining like that?"

She kissed him, amused. "It's always like that, silly. You're on Mercury, remember?"

Farradyne held her close and kissed her again. A minute passed before he came up for air. He looked at her, leaning his head back so that he could see her face without looking cross-eyed. "I'll bet you are a real hellion in the dark."

Carolyn laughed, and shook her head. "Like all the rest of the women on Mercury, I'm scared to pieces of the dark. But it is late, Charles, and you've just got to go." She hugged his head down so that he could look at her wrist watch on the arm about his neck. "It's five o'clock and you are to take off at nine. Charles, please don't crack up just because of lack of sleep."

"Okay," he said regretfully, "okay."

She held him close. "It's been a nice evening, Charles. So kiss me goodbye, and remember that it won't be long until I see you on Terra."

ch. ends next p.

"It gets dark on Terra," he told her. He tightened his arms and she pressed against him.

Against his lips she murmured, "I might not be afraid of the dark, Charles."

The promise of her last embrace stayed with him. There were only three hours of sleep between the time he left her and the time of awakening for the take-off, but dreams of Carolyn filled them all. They were pleasant dreams and they were unpleasant dreams; he saw Carolyn coming to him with her past renounced, he saw her coming to him as a secret agent who was in the hellish business for the same reason he was. And he dreamed of her waving him a good-bye with her dark eyes filled with tears as she was taken off to the Titan Penal Colony. He even entertained notion of joining her, justifying himself by thinking that people who fall in love with love lotus addiction are the weaklings of the human race and could be eradicated to the advantage of the general level. This he recognized as sophistry.[1]

But, be it as it may, Carolyn was a pleasant, attractive companion, and if her presence could only be known for a very short time, it was nonetheless pleasant. It was a rough game they were playing and many people were bound to get hurt. More people—innocent people—would get hurt if he called it off. So by the time Farradyne and his dreams came to the conclusion that he could afford to take what pleasure out of life this situation offered for the moment and let Tomorrow exact its tribute, it was time to get out of bed and start the pre-flight check-off.

He had work to do. Schoolmarms[2] to haul to Pluto and some refined thorium ore to bring to Terra. He would make no signal this trip, he was still far from being on the inside.

---

[1] A plausible but false, misleading, or fallacious argument.
[2] Schoolmistresses or female teachers, especially those who are regarded as prim, strict, and old-fashioned.

Maybe the next. Or the one after that, depending upon his progress. But in the meantime he would be seeing Carolyn Niles on Terra.

Farradyne began his check-up, already anticipating the reunion which was at least ten days away.

9

They came aboard a half hour later and Farradyne saw at once that this trip would be free of trouble and danger. They were all mild and wide-eyed curious. They obviously knew their place and how to go about in life with a minimum of friction.

Their leader was a Professor Martin, an agile gentleman of about sixty years who led them up the ramp and then stood there introducing each and every one of them to Farradyne as they came in. They became a sea of faces and a sound of disconnected names except for a few of the more vivid ones. Miss Otis, who giggled like a schoolgirl but hadn't been of schoolgirl age for at least thirty years; a Mr. Hughes, dark of skin and smiling, who tried to convey the impression that he knew his way around in space; a very prim dame named Miss Higginbotham who probably had every kid in her class scared of her; a Mrs. Logan who was far too beautiful to be part of Farradyne's narrow pattern for schoolteachers. Miss Tilden seemed to know something about spacing, and her friend, who was old enough to be Miss Tilden's mother, Miss Carewe, knew more about spacing than Miss Tilden. And a Mr. Forbes who seemed completely impressed by everything he laid eyes on.

And so they came, a prim and strait-laced lot, the like of which Farradyne had not seen in a long, long time.

Certainly nothing of the hellflower flavor among this group. It made Farradyne feel easier, and after a bit he began to smile at their innocence and their wholehearted interest. He came to understand that this trip was to be a bit different for them, or it could be if he cared to make it so. It was obvious that their previous hops had been made under pilots who treated them with the usual aloofness that spacemen hold for their passengers. Farradyne felt more sympathetic about them; he wanted to help, wanted to show them what could be seen.

Part of this desire to help them have a good time was born in the idea that someday Farradyne would probably be looking for some character witnesses and if he treated these schoolteachers with cordial interest and a willingness to explain and demonstrate his spacecraft, they would be inclined to accept him as a man of understanding, honesty, and ability.

They took off after Farradyne delivered a very short talk on the rigors of take-off maneuvering and the necessity of staying strapped down whenever the spacer was about to cut didoes.

It was even less of a strain than Farradyne anticipated. They helped. Miss Carewe was a home economics teacher and she took care of the galley in a highly efficient manner. Mr. Forbes taught manual training or something of the sort; he requisitioned an oilcan and removed the squeaks from a couple of doors and took care of some of the minor details that Farradyne was inclined to ignore because he had other things on his mind. Someone, Farradyne never found out who, made beds and policed the ship, cleaning the salon and passengers' quarters until the rooms and hallways shone. Whoever it was did not recognize the faint stains of blood apparently, because there were no questions asked about the evidence of Mike Cahill's death.

Miss Tilden spent quite a bit of time making a small oil

painting for the space above the bar which she said looked vacant. The degree of their tolerance was high, too. None of them cared for drinking, but they approved of Farradyne and his White Star Trail.

In return, Farradyne took them into the control room and showed them how the ship was run. Professor Hughes toyed with the computer by the hour[1] because he was a mathematics teacher, and Miss Tilden listened to Farradyne by the hour as he recounted some of his adventures in space because she was a teacher of modern history.

The beautiful Mrs. Logan taught science, so Farradyne took her below to explain the atomic pile and how it worked.

With a pre-recorded tape from the course computer running through the autopilot, Farradyne pointed out the motion on the control rods that regulated the activity of the pile. Above the pile, he explained, was a huge tank of water that was used as a reaction-mass. Water was fed through the pile and its energy was raised to some tremendous degree, then hurled out through the throat of the reaction motor.

Mrs. Logan then pointed to the series of little ports in the hull.

Farradyne explained, "Now and then it is necessary to replace the control rods because they become transmuted into metals that have too little absorption factor. To get rid of them on a spaceport would mean the trouble of disposing of quite a bit of metal that is dangerously radioactive. So we take the convenient method of tossing them out in space where they can't harm anything."

"But where do they land?" she asked. "Isn't that dangerous?"

"Not at all. We use discretion. Look. In a few hours we will be halfway to Pluto. Our velocity will be tremendous

---

[1] "By the hour" means continuously.

because we have been accelerating all the way from Mercury. To land on Pluto we'll have to make a turn-over at halfway and start decelerating. If I wanted to replace control rods, I'd do it just before turn-over. The velocity of the ship and the rods would be a good many times the escape velocity of the entire solar system, so the rods would continue on and on, and actually they'd pass out of the solar system beyond Pluto in a matter of hours. Long before we got there."

"But supposing one did land on Terra, for instance?"

"It would make an interesting looking meteorite; it would melt in mid-air. Then the total radioactivity would spread thin and do no damage."

She was satisfied, and Farradyne led her back to the salon.

For the first time in years Farradyne began to feel at ease with the universe. His mind, previously busy with his main problem, found time to consider other things. And, like the rest of the spaceman breed, Farradyne was something of a gadgeteer.

Spacing, in a sense, was very much like the manning of a sailing ship of the nineteenth century. When something needed attention, in space it was during maneuver for landing, take-off, or turn-over; on sea it was coming about on a tack[2] or setting sail, a full-time attention was necessary. Between periods of activity, the spaceman sat on his duff and waited for one of the silent twinkles to detach itself from the stellar curtain above his observation dome and become a planet or destination.

Some spacemen reverted to the point where they built spacecraft in old bottles, others spent their time in tinkering.

Farradyne had always been one of the latter. And so as his mind felt at ease, he began to tinker with the gear down in the repair shop. It was a small room below the

---

[2] A nautical term for the act of changing a vessel's course by turning into and through the wind, so as to bring the wind on its opposite side.

ch. ends p. 84

passenger section hardly large enough to hold the machinery it contained. But Farradyne, like many of his fellows, enjoyed making things, repairing things, and generally experimenting. Every spaceman hoped to come up with something that would make him rich and famous, and some of them had done it. They had plenty of time, a good grasp of things scientific, as well as manual dexterity.

So Farradyne tinkered happily.

The shop was silent; the usual milling around of his passengers stopped as they went to bed. Now there was only the occasional groan of metal-upon-metal or the faint whine as a motor somewhere wound up to do some automatic job. The click and clack of relays were just barely audible; they would have been unheard by someone whose training had been other than that of a spaceman. In the background was the muted sibilant[3] of the reaction motor, a sound like the shush of a distant seashore. Farradyne heard these sounds unconsciously. They were as pleasant to the ears of the spaceman as the sounds of a sailing ship were to the old-time seaman.

But another faint sound came to disturb him, rising up into the level of audibility very slowly.

It was a ringing in Farradyne's ears.

Ringing in the ears can come from too much alcohol, or a shot of dope, or a slap on the side of the head. Or a change in air-pressure. Farradyne had not been drinking nor taking the needle, but he had spent many years in an environment where the supply of air was important. He had become oversensitive to it. He sniffed automatically, the gesture of a man who has reason to suspect the quality of the air he is breathing. He shook his head. He did feel a bit light-headed. There was the bare trifle of a dull pain above his eyes and

---

[3] Hissing sound.

a sting in his nose. He sneezed and brought forth a dribble of blood.

Farradyne raced aloft; he could settle nothing standing in the workshop. The bulkhead door between the hold of the Lancaster and the passengers' section was closed. He pushed it and it opened with slight difficulty to let a blow of air hit his face. He grunted in puzzlement. Any change in air-pressure in any part of the ship should have started a clangor of the puncture alarm, a racket loud enough to waken the dead.

He went through the stateroom corridor and listened carefully as he went. Some rooms were silent and others sounded like the song of the cross-cut saw working its way through a burl of maple. There were gradations of snores between these extremes. Nothing that a suspicious man could put his finger on. He did not pause in the salon, which was silent and darkened, but not completely black. There was nothing out of the way here.

In fact the only thing that was out of line was the queer fact that the ship was silent when the alarm should have been sounding. He went up to the control room.

Lamps told him the story in a series of quick appraisals, because of some long-forgotten genius that had insisted that whenever possible, warning devices should not be fused, should not be turn-offable, and should not be destructible. The Lancaster was a fine ship, designed well, but a frontal attack on a panel with metal cutting tools made the exception to the "whenever possible" part of the design of warning signals.

The ship's bell-system had been opened like a tin can.

But the pilot lamp system was strung here and there behind the panels and it would have taken a major overhaul to ruin it; the saboteur would have spent all night opening cans instead of doing his dirty work. Farradyne should have

ch. ends p. 84

been asleep, then he would not have noticed the blaze of lamps.

They told him the tale in a glance. The low-pressure portion of the ship was down in the pile-bay, and the reason was that one of the scuttle-doors was open. The pressure in the reaction-mass bay was low, and now that Farradyne had come aloft, the pressure in the upper levels was as low as the reaction-mass bay. As he watched, another one of the scuttle ports swung open and its warning lamp flared into life.

Farradyne went into action. He ripped open the cabinet that held his space-suit and clawed the thing from its hook. He started down the stairway on a stumbling run, getting into the suit by leaps, jumps, and pauses. He realized that he could have moved faster if he stopped to do one thing at a time, but his frantic mind would not permit him to make haste slowly. So he stumbled and he fell against the walls, and the tanks of his back rapped against his shoulder-blades, and the helmet cut a divot out of the bridge of his nose. Luckily it did not make him bleed, but it hurt like the very devil.

He zipped up the airtight clotures[4] by the time he reached the little workshop and he ducked in there to get a weapon of some sort. He reached past the hammer, ignored the obvious chisel because it was not heavy enough, even though it was sharp, and picked up a fourteen-inch half-round wood-working rasp.[5] He hefted it in his gloved hand and it felt about right.

The air-break on the topside was open, and Farradyne closed it. He fretted at the seconds necessary to equalize the pressure, and to check the workings of the space-suit. He also located the cause of the air-leakage; normally the

---

[4] Closures.

[5] A coarse file with sharp points instead of raised lines forming the grating surface.

air-break doors were airtight. A sliver of wool or cotton string lay in the rubber gasket and produced a channel for the escape of some of the air into the pile-bay. Farradyne stopped, his attention attracted by this trifle of evidence. It was neither wool nor cotton, but a match torn from a giveaway book and used to light a cigarette for Mrs. Logan a good many hours before.

He threw it aside and went in, his attention once more on the important business before him. He ran along the curved corridor. And there, a figure in a space-suit was quietly levering one of the control rods out of its slot and preparing to hurl it into the void.

Farradyne understood the whole act in that one glance; it was the sort of thing that he would do if sabotage were his intention. The single scuttle-port had been opened first by hand. Then the saboteur had scuttled the stock of spare control rods, and since the Lancaster was reasonably new, there had been quite a batch of them. Furthermore they were long, unwieldy, heavy things that took time to handle. Naturally this was the first act, because the next act would cause the ship's acceleration to rise. The rise in acceleration would make the rods too heavy to carry and would also cause investigation as soon as people became aware of the increasing pressure.

Then the working rods would be hurled out, leaving the ship heading toward some anonymous star at about eight gravities of acceleration. The passengers and crew would be helpless—and dead long before they got within any appreciable fraction of a distance to any planet.

Maybe two or three of the rods had been scuttled already. The rest, functioning on the automatic, would have been shoved in farther to compensate; Farradyne could feel no change in the acceleration pressure. But once the working rods were all the way home, the removal of the next would cause the ship to take off, literally with the throttle tied

ch. ends next p.

down. Farradyne was willing to bet the rest of his life that the safety-valve that furnished the water-mass to the pile was either welded open or damaged in such a way that the supply could not be stopped.

Then—and Farradyne had to admire the vandal's precautions—he would make his way to the escape hatch and let the helpless passengers go on . . . and on . . .

Victims of another case of "Lost in Space."

The saboteur was well prepared. His suit was a high efficiency job capable of maintaining a man alive for a long time in space. It had a little radio for calling and a small and expensive chemical motor for mild maneuvering, even though it would not be strong enough to permit planetary landing. The man had friends, obviously, lying in wait out there, who would pick him up.

A parcel of ice-cold-blooded murderers.

Farradyne saw the man through a red haze that clouded down over his eyes. His evaluation of the act was made in a glance, and in the bare instant that it took for Farradyne to see the man he got his feet in motion. He plunged forward with a bellow that hurt his own ears.

10

The man whirled and sent a heavy-gloved hand back against Farradyne's face glass. Farradyne lifted the file for a second swing and caught the gleam of a heavy knife just as it swung upward at his face. The blade jabbed at the face glass and blunted slightly before Farradyne's eyes, splintering the glass and sending a shard or two against his cheek.

Farradyne's second swing caught a shoulder and sent the man staggering back; the knife came up and the gleaming edge sliced close to Farradyne's arm. The man stumbled and fell, and Farradyne came forward to take advantage of the opportunity. The long lever used to handle the radioactive control rod chopped against Farradyne's shins and cut his feet out from under him; he landed on his face and the other man kicked out with heavy space boots. The heels rammed Farradyne's helmet hard down into his shoulders, and the top of his helmet hit the top of Farradyne's head, stunning him.

The other scrambled forward and landed on Farradyne's back. He pulled up and back on the fittings of Farradyne's helmet until the pilot's spine ached with the tension. Then the man thrust forward and slammed Farradyne's face down on the deck. The splintered safety glass cracked further and there came the thin, high screech of air escaping through a sharp-edged hole.

Farradyne lashed out and around just in time to parry a slash of the knife. Blade met file in a glint of metal-spark and both weapons were shocked out of the gloved hands to go skittering across the deck.

The man left Farradyne to scramble across the floor after his knife. Farradyne jumped to his feet, took three fast steps and leaped, coming down with both feet on the man's back. The other collapsed and Farradyne fell, turning his right wrist underneath him. The other made a kick that caught Farradyne in the side, turning him over. And as Farradyne rolled, the bent hand touched metal and he came out of the roll clutching a heavy pair of repair pliers. He could cut bolts with them, and had.

He faced the killer, standing again; armed again, space-man's pliers against assassin's knife. He plunged forward and felt the knife bite against his suit, he swung the pliers as a club and caught the killer's upper arm; he opened the jaws and bit down, twisting and pulling.

A three-cornered tear ripped and came away with the point between the jaws until the heavy outer cloth gave way. The knife came up and bit through Farradyne's suit across the knuckles of the hand that held the pliers. Farradyne kicked, sent the killer staggering and followed him probing at the tear to get at the thin inner suit. The other man struggled, hurled Farradyne back, but Farradyne staggered back with the thin lining between the jaws of the pliers. The suit ripped and there came a puff of white vapor as the air blew into the void.

The struggling killer stopped as though shocked by an electric current; he stood there stiffly, his hands slowly falling to his sides, limp. Farradyne took a step back, breathing hard. He could see now that his head was not jerked back and forth behind the cracked glass. He peered, in time to watch the froth of blood foam out of Hughes' nose.

Hughes! The math professor. The wise guy who had created the part of dumb bunny by making sounds of knowing too much, who pretended to know his way around in space.

Farradyne wondered whether Hughes had cried out in a polytonal voice—then he hauled him into the air-break and slammed the door shut. He felt for a pulse and found one fluttering; he turned him on his face and pumped the ribs in, out, in, out, wondering whether he was wasting his time.

Hughes groaned painfully. His groans echoed and reechoed in the tiny space, but Farradyne could not hear more than the wreaking moan of a man hurt very deeply. Hughes stirred and opened one eye. Then he closed it again and sobbed under his breath. Farradyne checked the heart and found it beating weakly; the pulse was not fluttering any more, and the breath was coming naturally, even though the man's chest heaved high and dropped low and there was a foghorn sound in the throat as he gasped huge lungfuls of air.

Whatever, Hughes would give Farradyne no trouble for some time. Farradyne carried the unconscious man to his stateroom and dropped him on the bed. Then he went below and closed the little hatches, reinserted the control rod, and wondered whether missing a few would louse up his landing.

He went up to the control room and replaced the wiring torn out of the audible-alarm system. The phalanx of warning lamps had winked out and the clangor of the alarm did not come.

Farradyne went back to Hughes; the man was in a semicoma.

"Can you hear me?" demanded Farradyne.

Hughes roused slightly and looked at Farradyne through heavy eyes, mumbling unintelligibly.

"You dirty louse!" fumed Farradyne. "I'd have let you die

if it hadn't occurred to me that you might be good for some information. What makes, Hughes? Or should we have an accident below?"

Hughes mumbled something that sounded like defiance.

"Think your friends will give you a raise for this fumble?" jeered Farradyne.

Hughes roused a bit more and looked at Farradyne more directly. "Smart guy," he said in a toneless voice, "you can't——"

Farradyne smiled cynically. "Yes, I can and I have," he snapped. Then he leaned down and put his face close to Hughes' and said carefully, "Hughes, sing me a trio."

Hughes' control was good. His eyes widened only a sliver and the catch in his breath was faint; anybody not watching for these signs of sudden alarm would not have noticed anything amiss. Then the eyes dimmed again and Hughes said, weakly, "Sing nothing."

"What's your pitch, Hughes?"

"I don't know what you're talking about."

"The hell you don't," said Farradyne harshly. "And if you won't talk without it, I can make you yelp real loud. First I break all your fingers, one by one, and then your toes, and then if you're still playing stupid, there's always the trick of slipping a soldering iron under your armpit and then plugging it in. Between the time the current goes on and the time you really start to feel it burn should be long enough to make a lot of gab."

Hughes looked at Farradyne directly. "You'd better kill me," he said flatly. "Because you can't hold me."

"I'll make you a bet," sneered Farradyne. "I'll bet that I can hang onto you, and if I do, you'll pay off by talking. Even-steven, Hughes."

Farradyne went to his small medicine chest and came back with a hypodermic, which he loaded with deliberation. He made a dramatic scene out of pushing the plunger, watching the droplet form on the end of the needle and then adjusting that dose against the scale on the side of the cylinder.

"Marcoleptine," he said conversationally. "A fine pain-killer, Hughes.[1] Just the thing a man would do to help a very ill comrade. It'll keep you quiet until we can discuss the situation without having your screams disturbing the passengers. Slip me your arm, old man. This won't hurt much."

Hughes mouthed a curse, but Farradyne paid no more attention to the man's objections than he would have to the objections of a child. Farradyne caught Hughes' wrist and brought the man's hand up under his armpit, then braced his forearm under Hughes' elbow. Then he lifted an arm-bar, which raised Hughes' shoulder from the cot; Farradyne slid the needle into the elbow easily with his free arm, probed for the vein and discharged the hypodermic.

"I wonder," mused Farradyne aloud, "whether marcoleptine is really non-habit-forming." He sat there on the edge of the bed watching Hughes very carefully. Hughes struggled to keep his eyes wide, fighting off the narcotic. But then the eyelids grew heavier and started to close.

In a weakened, drugged voice, Hughes mumbled, "Easier to slip under—now—can't do anything—will . . ." and he was gone. His breathing grew regular and his body was completely flaccid. Farradyne waited until Hughes was well under the dope and then he stopped watching the man critically and began to plan his next move.

Hughes was going to be a sick man. Therefore the marks of battle should not be visible to his companions when they wanted to look in on the ill professor. Farradyne got a wash-cloth, soaped it well and went to work. He let the hot cloth soak into Hughes' face for a minute or two massaging the

---

[1] Marcoleptine is an invention by Smith.

face under the cloth with agile fingers. Then he began to scrub.

The caked blood came away. And so did some dark pigment that stained the cloth. The dark-complected Hughes lightened in color; the lines in his face seemed to become less deep as the shadowing pigment was washed away. Schoolteacher Hughes came off into Farradyne's washcloth and what was left was the would-be hellflower trader, Brenner.

"Brenner," breathed Farradyne in astonishment.

But the dope had taken effect and Brenner was out cold. Farradyne bemoaned his enthusiasm for doping the man because questions would fall on deaf ears. Then Farradyne took a more rational view. There would be plenty of time to question the hellflower operator after the schoolteachers left. Meanwhile, Brenner would be kept doped, quiet, and nailed-down for the duration. He left Brenner and went to his own bed where—to his surprise—he went to sleep at once instead of lying awake with myriad questions in his mind . . .

He carried his book on Medicology with him to the breakfast table the following morning, and at the questioning looks, Farradyne made his announcement, "We have a sick man aboard. Hughes."

Professor Martin asked, "What happened, Mr. Farradyne?"

"It must have been about midnight, I was working below. I heard a rather strange noise up in the passengers' section and went up to find out what was going on. I found Mr. Hughes coughing and sneezing in the passageway, obviously in distress. I inspected him as best as I knew how and we got out my Medicology and compared symptoms. I'll read this section:

"'Coryosis, one of the nine allied infections which are frequently grouped under the ambiguous term "Common Cold," is extremely contagious but fatal only in cases of extreme sensitivity. Treatments consist of isolation amounting to a formal quarantine, and frequent injections of MacDonaldson's Formula 2, Ph-D3; Ra7. The patient is to be kept warm at all times and must remain quiet.'

"So we went to his cabin and I slipped him a shot and he went to bed. Now I'll read a bit more:

"'Contagion measures: Since the source of infection is a filterable virus, care must be taken to remain outside of the twenty-foot range of water droplets resulting from a cough or sneeze. All things touched by the patient must be either sterilized or burned. It is suggested that only one person tend the patient and that this person be immunized with MacDonaldson's Formula at regular intervals. Visiting should be discouraged, and if necessary must be carried on at a distance and for a very few minutes only. The incubation period is very short; the duration of coryosis is approximately fourteen days. It is, however, possible for a re-infection to take place which often resembles the initial infection, thus giving rise to the six-week cold.'

"There's more along this line but I think we have the picture well enough," Farradyne concluded.

Professor Martin's face was grave. "What must we do?" he asked anxiously.

"Nothing," said Farradyne firmly.

"But he shouldn't stay on Pluto."

"That is correct. Pluto is very cold, even with the Terra conversion program going on. Mr. Hughes should be returned to Terra."

"But——"

Farradyne smiled. "I've got to make a freight pickup on Pluto for Terra," he said quietly. "I'll take Mr. Hughes back home."

"That would be very considerate of you, Mr. Farradyne."

Farradyne shook his head in disclaimer. "It's only what

any man would do," he said. "What do we know about Mr. Hughes?"

Miss Tilden said, "Not very much, I'm afraid. Mr. Hughes teaches Ancient History in Des Moines, Iowa. He joined us on Mercury, you know."

"No," said Farradyne, "I didn't know. I thought you were all together."

"Apparently Mr. Hughes was traveling alone until he heard of our group," offered Professor Martin. "He was, he said, seeking a reduced-rate trip to Pluto—as we were— when he noticed our flight-plan filed on the bulletin board. He got in touch with me and offered to join."

Farradyne nodded. "There's really plenty of time," he said. "No use getting excited. I'll contact the Des Moines Board of Education later—after we've made our landing and take-off, and are close enough to Terra to make the radio effective. It'll save us some money that way." The latter, he thought, would appeal to these people.

It was left that way. Farradyne did not assume for one moment that Hughes was a complete fake. One of two ideas was certainly true: either there was a real schoolteacher named Hughes who looked like the made-up Brenner, or Brenner had been masquerading as Hughes and really taught school in Des Moines when he was not peddling hellflowers.

There were more important things to be considered, too. Was there another hellflower operator in the ship? Farradyne watched them all like the proverbial hawk but he could see no evidence of another hellflower man. He decided to take no chances; it would be very much like the higher-ups in this racket to have put a second operator aboard the Lancaster to take over in the case of Brenner's failure; the second undercover man could escape as easily as could Brenner and in the same way as soon it became evident that the Lancaster had been properly sabotaged. To forestall this possibility, Farradyne built a small photoelectric alarm and put it across the stairway that led from the passengers' cabin to the below-deck section of the ship.

Some of Hughes' friends went with Farradyne to watch him tend the stricken one. They stood in the doorway while Farradyne gave Hughes his shot of marcoleptine out of an ampoule[2] carefully labeled "MacDonaldson Formula 2, Ph-D3; Ra7." There was no doubt in their faces; Farradyne was a fine man, doing all he could to relieve the illness of another man.

The rest of the trip was uneventful. Farradyne was asked periodically about Hughes' condition and he replied carefully and cheerfully, once going so far as to remark with a slightly bitter laugh, "Hughes will probably feel fit as a fiddle by the time I get back to Terra, and he'll then hate me for lugging him home. But we couldn't leave him on Pluto with that coryosis, could we?"

Since none of them cared to have a man coughing and sneezing in their midst, they all agreed solemnly.

Then, inevitably, the trip wore to a close. Pluto loomed large in the sky, and Farradyne went below to see Hughes-Brenner about an hour before they were due to land.

---

[2] A small glass or plastic capsule or vial in which liquids for injection are hermetically sealed.

11

Farradyne found Brenner awake but logy.[1] "How do you feel?" he asked Brenner.

"I feel dopy," admitted Brenner dully.

"Good. You've been a very sick man, Brenner. Or should I call you Hughes? Which is your name?"

"What difference can it make?"

"I like to know these things," said Farradyne. "I seem to collect a lot of information, one way and another, and I admit a lot of it is useless, but I find it interesting. For instance, Brenner, can you make that triple-tongued sound?"

"What triple-tongued sound?"

"Come off it, Brenner. You know what I'm talking about."

"Do I?"

"You do and I intend to find out," said Farradyne. He loaded his needle and approached Brenner with it. "This is for the last time, Brenner. And I've ideas on how to make a man talk—or sing a trio."

"You're a devil from hell," Brenner snarled.

"And you're an angel from heaven, ripping out the control rods to give us the Long Ride? Brenner, I owe you a lot that I'm going to collect. You'll wish you had died, Brenner. And

---

[1] Lethargic; sluggish.

you probably will die not long after your friends find out that you've talked."

Brenner eyed Farradyne wearily. "You haven't won your bet yet," he said. "And even if you do, there's the problem of extracting payment."

Farradyne shrugged. "You'll talk," he said flatly. Then he reached for Brenner's arm, imprisoned it so that Brenner could not move without dislocating the shoulder, and slid the needle home. "Just to be sure," he told the man, who was showing all the defiance that a man in a weakened condition could display, "I gave you a slightly larger dose. The Medicology says that this is accepted practice with marcoleptine, when the patient is in some danger of an excitement-crisis."

He waited until Brenner's eyes closed and the breathing became deep and regular. Then Farradyne left Brenner, went aloft and made contact with Pluto Spaceport. He came down with one hand poised above the power lever; at the first glimmer of any hanky-panky, Farradyne was going to slam the power home and take off for space at full power. Questions could be asked afterward.

The landing was as good as any that Farradyne had ever made, but he was almost a nervous wreck worrying about the possibility of a recurrence of the Semiramide incident. He relaxed only after he had peeked, unobserved, at Hughes, still doped, and then led the covey[2] of schoolteachers down the landing ramp.

It was a happy parting, with just the right tone of regret and a large amount of congratulations as to his ability, helpfulness, and willingness to explain things to them that other pilots brushed away. They shook his hand and Miss Carewe permitted him to kiss her cheek and called him "Son" and Miss Tilden giggled and lifted her face for a chaste

---

[2] Small group.

peck. Mrs. Logan's lips were warm and soft but completely uncooperative.

Then Professor Martin made an "ahem" in his throat and said, "Young man, we've all decided that you should have something to show our gratitude. Unfortunately it cannot be expensive or exotic although we have all agreed that an appropriate gift should be both. So since we cannot go to the high extreme that we all feel, we have decided that the next best thing is something completely valueless except for its sentiment."

He fumbled in his side pocket and brought out a small piece of slate, broken from some outcropping, somewhere.

"On this slate we've signed our names with a sharp instrument. I hope you like it, Charles."

Farradyne took the bit of slate. It said, "To Charles Farradyne, Pilot First Class, in memory of a very pleasant flight." It was signed by all of them.

"Thanks," he said, shortly. A lump hit his throat and his eyeballs stung. He felt ashamed. He had been playing games and holding high intrigue almost under their noses and they had responded with this very simple gesture of sincerity: Pilot, First Class—with a forged license and a record of hell-raising. "Thanks," he said again.

"It's signed by everybody but Mr. Hughes," said Professor Martin. "But you can ask him to sign it before you leave him. He will be happy to, I know."

There was a sound at the spacelock. "I'll sign it now!" said Hughes.

They all whirled. Hughes, eyes alight, the smile on his pale face eager, came down the ramp with his suitcase in one hand.

"But you——" said Professor Martin.

Hughes laughed and his voice was hearty, "I kept telling Mr. Farradyne that he was too heavy with the medicine." Hughes poked Farradyne humorously on the shoulder.

"Coryosis, Mr. Farradyne, is nowhere near as violent an illness as you have been led to believe. Our ancestors called it the common cold and most of them spent a few weeks each year fighting one form or another, frequently several forms at the same time. Sleep and isolation cured me. I'm quite all right now."

"You're certain?" Farradyne managed.

"I'll let any doctor on Pluto look down my throat," promised Hughes. "And I'll go back with you if he doesn't say I'm fit. I'm a bit pale, I admit, and I won't regain my color until we get back sunward, but I'm telling you that I am quite cured of my brief encounter with coryosis."

The spaceport bus came to a stop at that moment and Hughes, pausing to scratch his name on the plaque, thanked Farradyne for the thorough medication that had kept him quiet, got on the bus, waved, and was whisked away.

Farradyne, stunned, could only wave like a reluctant schoolboy.

So Hughes-Brenner disappeared again, wandering away under the protection of a group of honest, unsuspecting human beings who would have been aghast at the first cry of villain against one of their number.

Farradyne felt like a seven-year-old who had just been trapped into admitting that he has been a naughty boy. But out of the maze of items one thing was obvious.

Hughes or Brenner or whatever he called himself was a very extraordinary man. He had been able to walk off the ship with his eyes bright and his system hale, when he should have been flat on his spine with a brainful of marcoleptine. And marcoleptine was one of the most completely paralyzing drugs that had ever been synthesized. Hughes had feigned his doped slumber and his helplessness because he had known that Farradyne would not attempt to ask questions until he had Hughes alone. He had also lulled Farradyne into thinking him drugged so that he could come

ch. ends p. 101

out nice and easy to join his fellow-travelers in such a way as to turn Farradyne's own explanation against him. Then he had walked away without a murmur of dissent from Farradyne who had no legal right to raise a cry against him.

Hughes-Brenner was a very remarkable fellow.

Farradyne watched the truck bringing out his shipment of refined thorium ore. Outpointed, outsmarted, outnumbered, the evidence he had was so very meager. He sneered at himself. Evidence? It was more a mere belief.

But what was a case history but snippets and bits of inconclusive evidence that somehow fitted together like the sections of an interlocking jigsaw puzzle? What did he have to fit together? A common pattern of love lotus background. A man who died with a discordant moan. A man who grunted in a polytone when surprised, and who could take a paralyzing dose of marcoleptine and then walk out jauntily. A family of apparently well-to-do formality with a proud place in the community, and a girl who worked hand-in-glove with hellflower manipulators but who obviously had never had her delicate nose near one of the hellish things. Or maybe she was immune, as Hughes was immune to marcoleptine? And did *she* make multiple-toned sounds when she was startled?

A few very remarkable people . . .

●

Farradyne took off for Newark with his cargo, still trying to think the matter out. Two things were certain: Farradyne himself was afraid to take a needleful of marcoleptine because he knew damned well that he was not immune; Farradyne could not make a polytonal sound with his vocal cords.

He sat in the salon, alone and quietly thinking, and

finally realized that he was completely isolated from everyone else in the solar system. He could sing crazily or go to bed, and no one would know which he did.

He essayed a sound. It sounded like the croak of a Terran tree-frog. He made the whimper of a cocker spaniel and succeeded in getting a cramp in his throat trying to get down an octave below his normal register. He hummed and he spoke in a falsetto that made his tongue ache way down deep in back, and he tried humming and speaking and groaning at the same time and the result of that was a toneless croak.

It struck him funny after a bit, and while he was laughing at himself, he concocted a ludicrous picture of himself kissing Carolyn Niles, and she responding in a three-toned moan.

Alone and lost in his own thoughts, Farradyne slipped deeper and deeper into his daydream, until he answered her throaty little sound with an audible reply.

"I love you," he said, straining at his vocal cords. It sounded like an over-age choir boy whose voice was not ready to stay in one key yet. Soprano and baritone and tenor sounded the words, but they came out in sequence instead of all at once. A bit sing-songy, like Chinese.

The sound, at discordant odds with the smooth, pleasant daydream, jarred Farradyne's mind into wakefulness. The chances were that if he had been able to create a three-toned reply he might have gone on with the pleasant reverie. But now aware, Farradyne tried it again.

"I love you," he said aloud. He was not particularly aware of the meaning of the words, they had just been appropriate to the dream. If Farradyne had been daydreaming about dinner he probably would have been trying the strange triple tone on, "Please pass the mashed potatoes."

He tried it again. What Farradyne wanted to do was to say "I" in *F*; "Love" in *A Natural*; and "You" in *E Flat*, which would have been a nice chord in *B Flat Minor* and somehow appropriate to the context of the words. "I hate you" would have been just as likely.

Old Brenner-Hughes might have said, "That's very neat!" when he had seen Norma Hannon with the sun shining through her skirt. Or its equivalent, all coming out in one surprised grunt.

Carrying this line of thought still farther, Farradyne considered the original saboteur, who might have said, "That takes care of you, Farradyne," as he clobbered the relays in the Semiramide. And Mike Cahill, who might have cried, "I've been shot!" or more probably something completely unprintable.

Farradyne sat bolt upright. As a countersign to tell another hellflower operator your own identity it was a fine job. But could a whole language be constructed out of this three-tongued hodgepodge?

Or was his entire trend of thought based upon the ultimate hope of discovering something that would absolve him from the responsibility of the wreck of the Semiramide? Actually, what did he have to go on? An exclamation, a surprised grunt, a death cry. Absolutely nothing but his own suspicion. That plus the fact that Farradyne's ship had been subjected to some intercepted sabotage, by a hellflower operator, who had made a sound that might have been polytonal.

If nothing else, the fact that the dope-running gang was trying to clip him was enough for Farradyne to seek Clevis' help. He went down into the hold and started to wash the ends of the thorium drums.

Then he spent a lot of time tinkering with a little semi-circle of soft plastic material across the opening of which he stretched two, thin, flat strips of hard-surfaced waterproofed paper. As a boy, Farradyne had been bilked out of fifty cents for a gadget advertised in a cheap magazine that purported to give the user the powers of ventriloquism.

It hadn't enabled Farradyne to throw his voice into a trunk but it had made a rather interesting bird call. Such a gimmick now might enable him to make a multiple tone.

Farradyne spent the remaining time of his trip from Pluto to Terra building the gizmo and practicing with it until he could make a very odd moaning cry in three notes. Meanwhile he wondered whether Carolyn Niles would actually be on Terra to meet him.

12

Farradyne wondered how soon the fuss would start once the drums of refined thorium went under some hidden beams of ultra-violet light. He watched the drums being trundled off, and they disappeared, and Farradyne waited and watched until it was evening in that part of New Jersey, but no one came on the double-run to ask him leading questions.

He took off about nine o'clock, finally, and made the looping run from New Jersey to Los Angeles in time to get him there just about dusk.

He checked into the control tower.

"Regular listing?" asked the registration clerk, looking at the license without turning an eyebrow.

"No, I've a charter run," said Farradyne.

"Then why register here?"

Farradyne thought fast. "This is one of those things," he said. "A darned good hope but no down payment. I was told to land here this evening and if nothing had changed while I was on the run to Pluto and back, I could have a rider to Mercury. But if this passenger does not show up, I want to be registered for anything heading Mercury-ward. I'll be going there in two days anyway, but I'd rather go loaded."

"Reasonable. Tell you what, Farradyne, I'll make yours a tentative listing. If your passenger doesn't show by tomorrow morning, you'll go up on the board as having registered tonight."

"Thanks," said Farradyne. He took the opened license back and slid a finger into an inside slip-pocket. "Got a picture here you might be interested in. A portrait of one of our early presidents."

"I'm a bit of a collector," said the clerk.

"Well, in that case, you can have it for the favor. I just keep it around for a curiosity."

The clerk pocketed the bill easily and Farradyne went over to the mail-listing window. "Anything for Charles Farradyne?"

"Expecting something?"

"At least one, a payment voucher from Eastern Atomic. Come yet?"

The mail clerk disappeared; came back with one envelope. "Nothing from Eastern Atomic," he said. "But here's a letter for Charles Farradyne, Pilot of ship's registry Six-Eight-Three, a Lancaster Eighty-One. That must be yours."

"It's mine. But keep an eye peeled for a landwire payment voucher, will you? I had to leave Newark before it was ready and the guy at the shipping office said he'd notify the company that the stuff was received at port, and that I'd be in Los Angeles. Okay?"

"Aye-firm."

The letter was from Carolyn. A brief note telling him that she would be ready for the trip on the morning of the fifth. This suited Farradyne; he had been afraid that Carolyn might be waiting at the spaceport for him, and that they'd be taking off before Clevis had a chance to find out about the washed drum-ends.

She also suggested as a postscript that she might possibly be at her hotel and free about nine any evening, and there was some reference to her being a bit squeamish about the dark. Farradyne was half-inclined to believe her.

ch. ends p. 112

Carolyn Niles lived on Mercury—a planet that knew no night.

He looked at his watch, he had a couple of idle hours left. He started to wander the streets of Los Angeles, wondering just how a man went about buying a hellflower. He had done that before, but that was on Mercury where such things might be more difficult to find. There were two places in America where, for generations, a man could get anything he had enough money to buy and knew where to look. He was in one; the other was three thousand miles across the continent, in New York. All that remained was the problem of finding out where to look.

Farradyne had to admit he had a difficulty. He was in a position similar to a teetotaler[1] in a prohibition area who suddenly decides to buy a drink and cannot, from lack of experience, locate a speakeasy. And dope, which had been with the human race ever since the first caveman took a bite out of a bit of saw-toothed weed, and was sold on the street by peddlers, was singularly hidden from the clutch of a man who just casually wanted to collect a packet.

So Farradyne spent some time wandering. He went into a florist shop and tried to buy a corsage. He could buy a corsage for a few dollars, but not for fifty. At least, for fifty he could get nothing smaller than a garland.

In one place Farradyne tried his tonal throat gadget. The florist eyed him curiously and asked him if he had something wrong with his throat.

And then, about fifteen minutes before he reached Carolyn's hotel a man sidled up alongside him and said, "Say, Jack, lookin' for somethin'?"

"Who isn't?"

"Might be able to fix you up, Jack. Got five?"

---

[1] A person who never drinks alcohol.

Farradyne knew that this was not the price, so he looked at his watch and said, "I've got fifteen."

"Won't take that long. Try the stand in the Essex Lounge."

Farradyne blinked. The Essex was no more than six years old, right in the middle of the city, and considered one of the plush joints of Terra. Selling hellflowers at the Essex was like selling the things on the steps of the Terran Capitol Building.

"Yeah?" he asked sourly.

"Yeah. Tell 'em Lovejoy sent you to pick up his flowers. Cost you fifty, Jack. Willin' to pay?"

"I've got it; and I'm willing."

"See ya, Jack."

The character sidled away, leaving a slight scent of decaying cloth mingled with a faint fragrance of gardenia. It was, according to Farradyne's standards, one god-awful mixture.

Farradyne went to the Essex and into the florist shop. A girl who was undeniably beautiful came forward. Farradyne smiled knowingly.

"I'm a friend of Mr. Lovejoy," he said. "He asked me to stop by and pick up his corsage."

"Of course." The girl disappeared and returned with a transparent plastic box containing a gardenia—or a love lotus. "That will be five dollars," she said with a piercing look at Farradyne.

Farradyne took a fifty out of his wallet and handed it to her. She rang up five on the register, and Farradyne walked out, wondering if anybody ever considered that Mr. Lovejoy must have a number of peculiar habits and rather easy-going friends that could be imposed upon.

At Carolyn's hotel a few minutes later, the desk clerk informed him that Miss Niles was expecting him and he should go right up.

Carolyn greeted him warmly, took him by the hand and

ch. ends p. 112

drew him into the hotel room. Once the door was closed she came into his arms and kissed him, not too fervently, but very pleasantly, with her body pressing his briefly. Then she moved out of his arms and accepted the flower. "Lovely," she said.

She opened it and breathed the fragrance deeply. She held the white flower at arm's length, admiring its beauty. Then she held it to her nose and took a deep breath, letting the fragrance fill her lungs.

Farradyne's mind did a flip-flop. First he felt like a louse, as she smiled at him over the edge of the flower and then took another sniff of the fifty-dollar blossom. "Maybe," she said archly, "I shouldn't do this."

Well, she was immune—or she wasn't. Could be that it wasn't even a hellblossom. But she should know. He hoped his smile was honest-looking. "You are stuck already," he grinned wolfishly.

Carolyn took another luxuriant breath and tucked the blossom in her hair. She came into his arms and kissed him sweetly. Then she relaxed, leaning back in his arms to look into his eyes. "I'm not afraid of you, Charles," she said in a low, throaty voice.

"No?"

She laughed at him and then turned out of his arms. She went to a tiny sideboard and waved a hand at glasses and a bottle of Farradyne's favorite liquor. He nodded, and she mixed. "Don't disappoint me, Charles," she said.

"How?" he asked, wondering what she was driving at, and feeling that this had nothing to do with hellflowers.

She handed him the highball.

She sipped at her drink and flirted with him over the top of the glass for a moment. "I don't think anybody will call me overinflated if I admit for a moment that my family is a long way from poverty; if, for an instant, I admit that I know that I am very well equipped with physical charm.

I also flatter myself that I have a mind large enough to absorb some of the interesting factors of this rather awesomely beautiful universe."

"I will grant you the truth of all three."

"Thanks," she said with a sly-looking smile. "But the point is, Charles, that a girl with a bit of money in the top of her stocking—and a brain in her head—wonders whether the gentleman is interested in the money, or the shape of her stocking. She is more interested in having the man want her for the aforementioned brain, I think. She'd like to feel that the gentleman in question would still be interested if the shape of the stocking changed for the worst with age and the money disappeared."

Farradyne looked at her and wondered again what she was and what she was after. If nothing else, Carolyn was a consummate actress. He wanted very much to take his face in his hands and ponder this problem deeply, but there was no time. He had to reply at once or have the appearance of a man who must make a careful answer. He walked across the room and took Carolyn by the shoulders and shook her gently. He bent down and kissed her and he found that the warm and eager response was back again, even though he touched her only with his lips and his hands on her warm shoulders.

"Let's leave it just that way," he told her. "Sooner or later something will give me away—and then you will know whether I am after your body, your money, or your mind." Farradyne kissed her again, and again lightly. "Until you know, nothing I say will convince you of anything."

Farradyne still had her shoulders under his palms; Carolyn moved forward into his arms and rested against him. She put up her face for his kiss, and held herself against him, close. Then she said dreamily, "You're a nice sort of guy, Charles, and I'll be very happy to leave it that way. Maybe you'll be the one who stays."

ch. ends p. 112

Farradyne recoiled mentally and hoped that his instinctive revulsion was not noticed. It was too easy to forget what Carolyn represented when Carolyn went soft and sweet and eager. He wanted to be a male Mata Hari;[2] he wanted to lure her on, to caress her into breathless acquiescence and then walk out with a cold smile to show his contempt.

Then he relaxed—and hoped that the muscles of his body had not undergone the change that his mind had—and decided if this were part of the game he had to play to cut the hellblossom-hellflower-love lotus ring out of the human culture, it was nice work. He recalled reading in history, as a child, another, but mild drug, marijuana, had multiple names . . . His job would have been infinitely more difficult if Carolyn had been a gawky ugly duckling with buck teeth and a pasty complexion.

"Charles," she breathed, "take me out into the dark?"

He laughed lightly. "Where?"

She leaned way back, arching her fine back. "I want to go out to some dark gin mill and dance among the smoke and the natives and the throbbing of tomtoms."

Their evening was a repetition of the evening on Mercury except that on Terra it was dark outside. They danced and there was a steak dinner at midnight, and there was Carolyn relaxed in his arms in the taxi on the way back to her hotel at three.

He took her up to her room, and Carolyn came into his arms again, soft and sweet. Her response was deep and passionate in a mature way that Farradyne was not prepared for. The woman in his arms was all woman and there could be no mistaking the fact, but there was also the mysterious

---

[2] Generally, a beautiful and seductive female spy. Specifically, Margaretha Geertruida MacLeod (1876–1917), better known by her stage name Mata Hari, was a Dutch exotic dancer and courtesan who was convicted of being a spy for Germany during World War I, and was executed by a French firing squad in 1917.

ability of the woman to know when to call a halt. She smiled softly and put her head on his chest.

"It's been wonderful again, Charles," she said quietly. "I hope it always is."

Farradyne rubbed his chin against the top of her head. Then Carolyn swirled away. "It's incredibly late again. I'm going to come aboard your ship at seven tomorrow night so we can take off before the crack of dawn. This much I'll tell you and no more, now."

"But——"

"Easy, sweetheart, easy. Take it slow and lovely. Tomorrow night. Tonight I need my beauty sleep."

He eyed her humorously.

"Think it doesn't help?" Then she laughed happily. "Charles, do me a favor. Put this gardenia in your refrigerator for me. Please?"

Farradyne nodded dumbly. He watched Carolyn put the thing into its plastic box, he watched her tie it up in the original ribbon. She handed it to him, and then, chuckling because he had one hand full, she came into his arms again for one last caress.

"Go," she told him with a wistful smile. "Go and dream about tomorrow night."

Farradyne went, half-propelled by her hands, his reluctance partly honest and partly curious. But he went.

On the street he hailed a taxi and spent the time on the way to the spaceport wondering whether sharpers had clipped him for fifty for a five-dollar gardenia. He wanted to toss the thing out of the cab window, but he did not because Carolyn would ask for it tomorrow. He even cursed himself for being willing to save it for her.

Farradyne walked into his spacer feeling like a man who had put his last dollar on the turn of a card, and lost. Lost at least until he could get somewhere and draw another stake from the bank. Futility and wonder confused him;

in one moment he was on top of the world with everything going according to plan and the next his world was kicked out from underneath him and he was dropped back into the mire of fumbling, helpless ignorance again.

Farradyne walked into the salon of the Lancaster and stopped short. The last peg had been pulled out of the creaky ladder of his success.

"What's the matter, Farradyne? Aren't you glad to see me?"

There was plenty the matter and he was not glad to see her.

Her eyes widened a bit and she came up out of her chair and toward him. "Farradyne," she said, with more eagerness in her voice than he had ever heard before, "you've brought me a love lotus!"

He let her have it, and watched as her rapid fingers tore away the ribbon.

Norma lifted the flower from its nest in the box, buried her nose deep in the center of the blossom and inhaled with a deep shuddering sob. Her eyes closed, then opened serenely to look up at Farradyne from beneath half-closed lids. She relaxed. The tension went out of her body and she sank back against the cushions. She put her head back and rested. And now Farradyne could see her face more clearly. Her features had lost their chiseled immobility and her eyes had lost the glassy stare. Her face became alive, and pleasant color flooded it. Her muscles took on tone and Norma became alive and young-bodied and beautiful. She was a new person.

Her lips parted slightly and curved into sweet lines. The hand that held the flower lay idly on the seat beside her, the other lay palm up on the other side. She looked like a young girl who had just been kissed. Slowly, Norma lifted the blossom to her face and inhaled again the fragrance from the center of the flower.

"Thanks, Farradyne," she said softly.

Farradyne's mouth was open and his mind refused to work on any but the single thought. It was a hellflower. It had had no visible effect on Carolyn—why? Then the attitude of the woman sitting on the divan forced the other thought from his mind.

Not that Norma's attitude had changed in the past minute or so. She was still relaxed, alive, and obviously at peace with both the world and herself. But Farradyne had been expecting much more; he had expected an onslaught of passion, of hate, of violence, of emotion. It might be either a demanding lust or the pleading languor of a woman bereft of her defenses. Or . . . But in any case Farradyne expected passion, of a wanton depth.

He was wholly unprepared for this calm return to young and healthy womanhood.

He wondered whether Norma would react normally to a gesture of affection and absently he took a step toward her. He felt once again that flush of pity for her and righteous anger for the rotten devils that had done this to her; he wanted to comfort her. She had changed visibly from a hardened woman whose beauty was stiff and unnatural to a girl whose loveliness was vivid enough to shine through the hard facade of heavy makeup.

"Norma," he said.

She smiled at him warmly but shook her head. Her arms raised as she tucked the hellflower in the heavy hair over one ear. The gesture slimmed her waist and raised her breasts, and through the triangle of her arms he could see her eyes. They were sultry as they contemplated him, but she shook her head.

"No," she said and Farradyne stopped. "You are a nice sort of fumbling idiot, Charles, and I've stopped hating you for the moment, but that doesn't mean I want any part of your caresses."

ch. ends next p.

"I——"

She smiled at him knowingly. "You were, Charles. You were. But don't." The odor of the love lotus, identical to the heady perfume of a gardenia, permeated the room and Norma sniffed at the air, lifting her face as she inhaled. "The smell of this is all I want."

Farradyne looked down at her and swore under his breath. This was the story then. The future under such conditions must be insufferable. He contemplated a man with an addicted wife; he would go on slaving night and day to buy this damnable and beautiful hellflower for her just to see her make this swift, sweet return to the normal woman he had once known, only to discover time and again that she had no use for him.

A smile crossed her face and Farradyne realized that Norma had dozed off in an ecstasy of relaxation. He wondered what to do next; his mind was mingled with the desire to protect her by letting her sleep the effects of the love lotus off, and the certain knowledge that if he did, Norma would never leave him in time for his meeting with Carolyn Niles. Of the two, the latter was by far the more important.

13

As Farradyne stood there wondering what to do, a knuckle-on-metal rap came at the spacelock and he turned to see Clevis standing there. He waved Clevis in.

Clevis came through the inner lock and caught sight of Norma. He stopped stock-still and looked the woman over from head to toe and back again. His eyes were bleak, his face bitter and hard as he turned away from Norma to face the other man.

"Farradyne, is this the contact you've managed to make?" The tone was heavy with sarcasm.

Farradyne shook his head sourly. "She's the one that got me started on the road to find out——" He was about to explain but Clevis cut him off with a scowl.

"You do seem to have started," said Clevis. "That's a real hellflower she's doping, you know. If I'd known——"

"Oh, for God's sake, listen!" snapped Farradyne. His shout rang through the salon and echoed up and down the ship's corridors. Norma stirred and came awake. She looked at Farradyne happily first, then her eyes settled on Clevis.

"Company? Hello, Howard," she said cheerfully.

"How do you do?" said Clevis, coldly.

"Not bad, thank you. In fact, I'm feeling in very topnotch shape, thanks to Mr. Farradyne."

"You're——"

"I must admit. A shame, too, but there it is."

"There's a reward out for you, Miss Hannon."

Norma's eyes twinkled a bit. "I know. He tried to collect on it. In fact, I think he did collect on it. But I couldn't sit around and watch a couple of fine old people tearing their hearts out over the ruin of their daughter. That's a hell of a way to end an otherwise happy existence—a son killed, a daughter doped. So I left."

Farradyne looked at Norma and Clevis sharply, he was lost; he could only wait for Clevis' next move.

Clevis shrugged, Norma nodded and relaxed again. She said, quietly, "If you gentlemen want to talk business, do it somewhere else. Or better, Charles, may I have my old room again for the night?"

Farradyne nodded, speechless in his furious bewilderment, and led Clevis up into the control room. Here, in a low voice, he explained how Norma had announced his connection with the hellflower racket, how Cahill had been killed and how he had picked up Carolyn Niles and the subsequent sabotage by Brenner, sometimes called Hughes, and the rest of it. At the end he spread out his hands and said, "This isn't hard work and good management, Clevis. But here I am. It isn't even good thinking, but I have a couple of questions that I'd like to have answered."

"Yes?"

"Carolyn Niles wore the hellflower for six or seven hours without turning a corpuscle.[1] Norma Hannon proved that it was no gardenia. There is something fishy here. Does medical history indicate any immunes to the love lotus?"

"Some. Not many. Some doctors have even gone so far as to claim that the hellflower is no more dangerous than tobacco."

---

[1] Any cell or similar minute body that is suspended in a fluid, such as a blood or lymph cell.

Farradyne swore. "Not according to Norma Hannon, it isn't," he said harshly.

Clevis eyed Farradyne carefully. "You're not a bit soft-headed over Norma, are you?"

"I doubt it," said Farradyne honestly. "She's a poor kid that got clipped and it makes my blood boil, and I want to go out and rap a half-dozen scum-brained heads together for what they did to her. Norma, she'd be the kind of woman I could fall in love with, Clevis, but Norma is a real blank. You know, if you doped up enough women with hellflowers, the birthrate would take a decline that would alarm a marble statue."

"It's something to think about," nodded Clevis.

"Of course, I've never seen a woman after she has just taken her first sniff so I don't know what it really adds up to, and I don't know how long after the first sniff a woman's libido is still capable of being excited, or even how high the libido can get under hellflowers. But by the time they get to Norma's state, a love lotus only changes their attitude from a completely scar-tissued emotional system to something barely normal whose only desire is to sniff the flower." Farradyne shook his head roughly. "Anyway," he said, after a moment of thought, "you can get a couple of ships to follow me day after tomorrow morning. We're going out somewhere—destination unknown—to make a rendezvous with someone who is high-up. And no matter what, Clevis, I think it wise for you fellows to keep on my trail, because at least one faction of their gang is out to clip me hard. Sooner or later—if my luck holds out as it has—they'll be sending someone of large proportions to clobber me and then I'd like to have your gang move in fast. Preferably before the clobbering gets too thick. And there's more to it——"

"Give," said Clevis in a flat tone.

"All right, you asked for it." Farradyne took the

throat-whistle out of his pocket and tucked it back against the curve of his tongue. He tried it and produced a three-toned sound, brief and musical.

"That's the sort of thing I was telling people about," he said. "At the Semiramide's crack-up. Three voices, I thought—then."

"That's the sort of half-witted story you tried to use at your trial."

"That's the sort of noise that Cahill made as he died. It's the sort of noise made by Brenner-Hughes. Clevis, could it be the rudiments of some odd new language?"

"How could you use it?"

"I don't know. Maybe a polysyllabic word like 'manifest' might turn out to be a single chord with certain articulation spoken in three distinct tones."

"How would you articulate?" asked Clevis.

"Well, you'd have to utter the same vocal sound sequence for all registers of the word. The word I just used for an example is a rather complicated series of sounds, with definitions I am not familiar with, like dental fricative,[2] and sub-dental stop. Regardless of the names of the tongue-flappings," said Farradyne, "the word itself would have to be revised in pronunciation."

Clevis shook his head. "With a gizmo such as you are choking on," he said, "you'd have a hard time making a tone other than the one it's tuned for. You're asking a lot, Farradyne. Furthermore, I gather that you have a fair-to-middling ear."

"It isn't absolute pitch by a hell of a long way, but it is good enough to make my face turn sour when the third violinist hits a crab on his strings."

Clevis leaned back in the chair. "I'd be in bad shape,"

---

[2] A fricative, or spirant, is a consonant, such as f, s, or z in English, characterized by audible friction produced by forcing the breath through a constricted or partially obstructed passage in the vocal tract.

he said. "I'm tone-deaf. Someone would say, 'Clevis, have a drink?' and I'd shake my head because it sounded like 'Do you like radishes?'"

Farradyne eyed Clevis for a moment. "Supposing for the moment that this odd evidence I have——"

"Based upon a grunt, a cry, and an exclamation."

"——is true. Then mightn't they prefer to let people into their organization who, they know, have a good pitch sense?"

Clevis looked back at Farradyne. "We've spent years following less rational will-o-the-wisps than that. Perhaps we should follow this crackpot idea for a couple."

"Well, let me toss you one more. During the next few days I am going to startle Carolyn Niles, and I hope she cries out or whatever in three notes. Then I'll have a tie-up."

"How so?"

"She has a hellflower-operator background. She'll have a three-noted cry. And she'll be immune to the God damned flowers her gang deals in. And there is something more than money in this."

"Okay, for the time being that's your game. But in the meantime, what are you going to do with Norma?"

Farradyne eyed Clevis carefully. "You are going to drive off with her."

"What makes you think I'm going to drive off with a doped-to-the-eyes hellflower addict?"

"Because one of the games I'm playing is nosey-nosey with Carolyn Niles, and there's going to be no addict cluttering up my spacer. She'd crumb up the whole deal for fair. You obviously know her, know where she belongs. Take her to a sanatorium. That'll keep her out of everyone's hair, especially mine, and she's on my trail."

"I guess this move is up to me. I hate to drop her in a sanatorium."

"What else can anybody do?" asked Farradyne, wistfully, spreading his hand.

ch. ends p. 125

"Not much, but I feel that I owe her more than that kind of handling. Not much more than a jail, you know." Clevis sighed.

"I can imagine. But what can you do for people cursed with a disease that no one knows how to cure?"

"Segregate 'em," growled Clevis. "Well, let's see what we can do about carting Norma out of the ship. When you ship out you will be followed at extreme military radar range. You'll have hard-boiled company watching you, Farradyne."

They went below and found Norma stretched out on the divan. She was sleeping, relaxed as a kitten, with one leg drawn up to uncover the other shapely leg. Her hands were outstretched over her head and open. Her breathing was regular, and normal. The hellflower still cast its heady perfume through the room, and Norma was smiling.

Farradyne plucked the flower from her hair. "This I'll need," he said quietly.

Clevis nodded. "I'll carry her," he said. The Sandman picked Norma up gently as she sleepily protested, but put her arms around Clevis' neck and her head against his cheek and let herself be carried from the salon.

Watching from the port, Farradyne reflected that they looked like a happy party-couple, leaving after too many cocktails, with the girl dozing on her man's shoulder.

Farradyne shrugged. Clevis had bought himself a bundle of trouble—when she awoke, with Clevis, and without the love lotus . . . He smiled cynically, and went to bed . . .

Carolyn came aboard that evening and her first request was for her "gardenia." She put it in her hair and stood there inviting him with her eyes. Farradyne kissed her briefly and waved her to a seat.

"Tired of me, Charles?"

"I've had no time to get used to you, let alone tired of you," he told her. "But I'm more than a trifle curious about this trip we'll be taking in the morning."

"Why not let it wait until then?"

Farradyne looked at her boldly, made no attempt to hide his careful appraisal of her figure and face. She accepted his brazen eyeing and colored a bit. Then he said, "Let's admit it, there's nothing I'd rather do than spend the night making love. It's my favorite indoor sport. It's fun outdoors, too. But there are at least two things against it."

"Two?"

He smiled. "You've made affectionate noises and a few statements regarding your previous affections which lead me to believe that you would not applaud me if I slung you over one shoulder and carried you down to your stateroom. The second item is that the way to get ahead is to marry the boss' daughter, not make her your mistress. Also if you think for one moment that I have enough ice in my spine or hardening in my arteries to make with happy-talk from now until six ack-emma,[3] you're wrong."

Carolyn leaned back and laughed.

"Carolyn, have you ever heard of *noblesse oblige*?"[4]

"What has that to do with me—and you?"

"It applies. You are a damned attractive female, and as such you should not use this attraction unless you want the man you are luring. Follow?"

Carolyn nodded. "I'll behave," she said. "I like you, Charles. No other man has ever talked to me like that."

"Well, be careful or I'll prove to you that I am just like all the rest. Now, how about this other deal? Or should we talk about the weather—or chess, tiddly-winks, astronomy?"

"Astronomy. We see no stars on Mercury, you know."

"So it's up to the telescope. Come on."

Farradyne shook his head in amused concern. It was apparent that Carolyn liked to play with fire; either that

---

[3] Military parlance for A.M., or in the morning.

[4] The inferred responsibility or moral obligation of privileged or noble people to act with generosity and honor toward those less privileged.

ch. ends p. 125

or she wanted to show her own superiority to herself. She could hardly have known about the visit of Norma Hannon, so she would not be aware of the fact that Farradyne had been able to establish the validity of the hellflower. Mentally Farradyne kicked himself. All he had done was to put the woman on her guard. She knew it was a hellflower, she must know it. So this nice little game she was playing was known to be a game.

So that made it even—both of them knew it was the real thing, both of them knew she was immune.

This might be cricket, but it was not good management. This was not a contest for the Glory of Good Old Siwash[5] or to win the Golden Fleece.[6] This was a game where the loser never came to bat again, and once he was out, started polishing the Golden Gates or riding gain on the servo-amplifiers for Mephisto's atomic hellfire. He had to pull a part of this play back out of danger.

He had pulled a fluff—the obvious way to remove it was to admit it.

In the darkened control room, Farradyne reached forward and removed the love lotus from her hair. He threw it into the chute that eventually led into the incandescent reaction blast.

She turned and her face was dim in the starlight.

"Why did you do that?" she asked.

Farradyne lied calmly, "Because when I give you your next corsage, it will be a bona fide gardenia if I have to get a pedigree from the guy who grew it."

---

[5] Likely a reference to the writings of George Helgesen Fitch (1877-1915), an American author, humorist, and journalist best known for a series of popular stories set at the fictional "Good Old Siwash College," which first appeared in the Saturday Evening Post in 1908.

[6] In Greek mythology, the fleece of the golden-woolled, winged ram Chrysomallos was known as the Golden Fleece and it was stolen by Jason and the Argonauts with the help of Medea.

Her smile was a trifle bitter. "What would you have done if it had worked?"

Farradyne laughed. "I didn't expect it to work."

"But——"

He went on swiftly. "Like several million other people I've been wondering how you can tell a gardenia from a hellflower. Honestly, I expected that you would take one look at the thing and then coldly inform me that you knew the difference. Then I was going to ask you to prove it. I was even going to be indignant over your thinking that I would do such a thing. Upset, fraught with unrequited love and all that bosh. I was prepared to maintain that I had bought the corsage in good faith and that some joker like Cahill had played a gag on me, just for kicks. Sooner or later you'd have told me how one could determine the difference." He laughed bitterly and it was not hard when he thought of Norma Hannon.

"Then," he went on, "you accepted it and put it in your hair, and I know damned well that you can tell them apart. That made me think, and I remembered that there are cases of women being immune. So I found myself sheepishly afraid to explain, and let it go at that. Carolyn, I just couldn't explain last night. But I do want to be honest with you."

He waited, hoping he had done a good job.

Carolyn put a soft hand against his face and then looked down. He reached for her chin and lifted it. She blinked a few times, and then smiled faintly. "Of course I knew what it was," she said. "And I know that I am immune, so I took it and wore it. I wanted to see how you would react. I wanted to find out why you did it. If you had done it for the usual reason, I was going to lead you on until you were incapable of control and then I was going to laugh at you and send you packing." She looked up at him shyly. "I didn't want to think it was for the usual reason."

She leaned toward him, but he took her by the shoulders

ch. ends p. 125

and turned her to face the telescope. At this, Carolyn put her head back against his shoulder and rubbed her cheek against his.

"None of that," he said with a sharp laugh. "Hell, woman, you do fine without a hellflower."

She turned in his arms and melted against him. He held her close for awhile and then pushed her away from him. "We're running by the rules, remember?" he said softly. "No fair, Carolyn. Think of my poor, broken-down blood pressure, woman. Let's get back to astronomy. I may live longer that way."

Astronomy is a fascinating hobby. Besides, this study required quite a bit of close proximity, with his arms loosely around her so that he could handle the setting-wheels on the telescope or Carolyn leaning back against him as he looked over her shoulder to set the piece on another object in the sky.

At midnight Farradyne showed her to her stateroom, and it was only after he was in his own room that he remembered that she had carefully ducked the explanation of how he could tell a love lotus from a gardenia. He wondered at that. Maybe she thought he had not noticed the careful steering away from the subject—and maybe a man who was going into the business for what it was worth would not have noticed the evasion.

Then there was the question of his own moral sense. So far as he had appraised himself he had damned little such sense and most of this was a matter of personal taste rather than observance of a set of rules. More strange was the moral sense of the Niles family. It seemed to be high except for their completely amoral disregard for what happened to the hapless victims of their racket.

He went to sleep murmuring a line from a poem many hundreds of years old that he had read as a youngster:

"... their honor rooted in dishonor ..."[7]

Take-off was scheduled for six o'clock and Farradyne barely made it. Fortunately there was only an Albemarle Seventy-One coming in on a landing beam and he could take his Lancaster up with his eyes closed. The Tower signed him out with a few remarks about sleepy people who just got up and a yawn over the near-at-hand bedtime. Then the contact was closed and Farradyne was a-space on the next leg of his journey.

Free from the control board, Farradyne had two choices. In his role of lover he could rap on her door because he wanted to be near her, or he could let her sleep because he did not want to disturb her. He listened at her door on his way to the galley but he could hear nothing; apparently she did not snore. He went on down and built himself a plate of ham and eggs and a large pot of coffee, and thankful for the quiet and the solitude and the freedom, he ate his breakfast and then loafed in the salon, trying to plan his future course.

Carolyn made her appearance at ten o'clock and reproached him. He gave her the stock answer, against which there could be no rebuttal, and offered her breakfast. He was solicitous and gentle. He felt that with four hours of nerve-soothing quiet behind him, he could play it with a bit more relaxation.

"Where are we?" she asked.

"About a half-million miles out from Terra, I can figure it out for you if you want it precisely."

She smiled at him. "It's important. How close is that 'about' a half-million miles?"

Farradyne leaned back in his seat and closed his eyes as

---

[7] A line from *Idylls of the King*, a cycle of twelve narrative poems published between 1859 and 1885 by the English poet Alfred, Lord Tennyson (1809–1892), which retells the legend of King Arthur and the rise and fall of his kingdom.

he went through the familiar formula, tossing out the figures beyond three significants. It took him half a minute of plain mental arithmetic to come up with the answer, "Four hours at one gravity makes it six hundred sixty thousand miles. There's some error there, caused by the fact that our apparent gravity just at take-off was not much more than one-point-three, and the pull of the earth was replaced by true accelerations as the Terran gravity diminished. But those figures should be close enough."

"I didn't think you could guess that close."

"That was no guess, it was a practiced estimate. I can come closer than that with some thought. After all, a shoe salesman should be able to call off the sizes of the shoes he sees on the street, and you know the Classical Chinese Carpenter?"

"No."

"The Chinese Carpenter is an oriental who comes in and takes a careful look where the plaster fell out of the ceiling, and then goes away and cuts a hunk of plasterboard that exactly fits the holes without any cutting or even shaving."

Carolyn laughed politely.

"But this is neither here nor there. There are two things to consider: one is breakfast and the other is that we are on our way, but your pilot does not know where he's going."

"Can you strike a line between Terra and Polaris at a distance of three hundred million miles?"

"Duck soup," replied Farradyne. "But how fast?"

"Zero with respect to Terra at three hundred million."

"Let's go up and start computing," he suggested. "I'll construct you some grub after we get the first approximation and we get the ship on the preliminary correction course."

He led her up to the course computer in the control room where she added the time of rendezvous to the rest of the figures. He plucked at the keyboard steadily for a minute, then sat back while the calculator machine went through the program of arithmetical operations for which it was designed. He took the punched paper strip from the machine and fed it into the autopilot, and then said, "Now we'll go below and eat."

"You haven't been waiting for me?"

He nodded, hoping that he looked a bit lovesick.

"You shouldn't have."

They went below and she eyed the dirty dishes with womanly amusement. "You are a sweet sort of liar, Charles," she said, turning and coming into his arms.

He returned her kiss, thinking, these are the "dames" that try men's souls.

14

Carolyn's eyes were fastened on the telescope, her attention was rapt. There was a tiny signal pip at the extreme range on the long-range radar that controlled the telescope, but the object was still too far away. The range was closing slowly, but they would meet somewhere out there, three hundred million miles above Terra to the astronomical North.

Farradyne knew his instruments and his attention was therefore free to think of other matters. Carolyn was busy at the "scope," so Farradyne carefully and quietly slipped a long fluorescent lamp from its terminals and stood it carefully on one end beside him. He balanced it carefully and took a couple of silent steps toward Carolyn before the tube lost its balance and fell to the floor with an ear-shattering explosion.

It even shocked Farradyne, who knew it was coming.

Carolyn reacted like a person stabbed with a red-hot spear. Every muscle in her body tensed as her nervous system twitched and she stood there for a full ten seconds as stiff as a figure of concrete while the shock gripped her. Then adrenalin poured into her veins and she started to bundle up muscularly at the same time that she realized that there really was no danger. Farradyne could see the relaxation of her body taking place almost inch by inch.

The tension crept out of her silently until her breasts began to fall in a shuddering exhalation. Then she sighed, and her tuneful voice was a wordless trill of relief.

Farradyne's attention snapped into full awareness and he felt a thrill of exultation run through him. Carolyn Niles' voice was a quavering trill in *three lilting tones*.

Then the spell was gone and she relaxed against a brace holding one hand under her left breast and breathing heavily. "What on earth——?"

"Lamp fell out of its moorings," said Farradyne. "My fault. That's one of the pre-flight check-ups that I didn't have time to make this morning. Stay where you are and I'll clean up this mess."

"Do you mind if I sit down? I haven't been that startled in years. I thought the ship had exploded."

"Park yourself in the pilot's seat," he said. "But be careful. Broken fluorescent tubing is doubly dangerous. The gook they put on the inside is as poisonous as hell and the glass is as sharp as a razor."

She nodded and picked her way through the glass. She looked up at him and said, "You don't seem to have been startled at all."

"I had a few millionths of a second to get my nerves in readiness," he said. "I saw it come down. You took a beating."

"I guess I did," she admitted weakly.

Farradyne laughed; it was a forced laugh but he hoped it was convincing. "Someone told me once that when a person is excited he always reverts to his native tongue." Her eyes widened and her mouth started to open, but Farradyne went on as though he hadn't been watching avidly for some sign. "But I didn't think your native tongue was Upper Irish Banshee."

Her eyes half-closed and her mouth snapped back from slack wonder to toned self-control. "What did I say?" she

ch. ends p. 133

asked with a half-humorous smile, which Farradyne knew to be false.

"It sounded like, 'I am slain to pieces' but I don't know Upper Irish Banshee very well."

"You're making fun of me," she complained pettishly.

"No I'm not. Not really. Anyone can be scared right out of his skin when something like that happens unexpectedly."

"All right," she said, and the humor was gone from her voice. "So you are not making fun of me. You've been playing a very serious game with me, haven't you?"

Farradyne thought fast but came up with only, "What makes you think——"

"Let's drop our masks, Charles."

"Masks? Look, Carolyn, I'd rather go clean up this glass."

"Sweep it up, then. But while you're cleaning up, we'll talk seriously."

"About what?" He got a brush from the locker and a square of cardboard from the bottom of a ream of paper, and started to collect the debris.

"What do you know about our language?"

"Damned little. Frankly, I'd had only a very insecure suspicion right up to the moment that you admitted it that there was any language involved."

"So I gave it away myself?"

"Yes."

"I knew you were smart, Charles. But none of us thought that you were smart enough——"

"Thanks, m'lady."

"Stop it!" she cried. "What do you want of me?"

"What do I want of anybody?" he whispered in a voice thick with anger. "I had four brutal years clipped out of the middle of my life by a three-voiced unknown party who wanted to commit suicide bad enough to take thirty-three innocent victims along with him. They blamed it on Hot-Rock Farradyne, the spur-wearing spaceman." His voice came back and he was half-roaring. "I've seen the results of the hellflower in a ruined personality that might have been a brilliant and gracious woman. I've seen a man plugged through the middle, to die at my feet. And on top of that, I've seen a family of prosperous stability calmly making their place in 'society' by dealing in the stinking things that brought the ruin and the death to millions." His voice calmed to a cold, brittle determination. "What do I want of you? Your lovely, flawless hide skinned alive and spread seductively before a fireplace. That's all."

She shrank away from him; looked wildly at the stairway and back into his face as she realized there was no place in the spacecraft where she could hide.

He sneered at her fear. "I'm not going to hurt you, now." His voice was heavy with derision. "You're beneath my hurting you."

Carolyn drew herself together; somehow her self-confidence was returning; perhaps it was the realization that he was not going to do anything violent. "Why take your hatred out on me?" she asked. "Have I done anything but—"

"You?" he asked. "You? How in hell should I know what slimy game you are playing? You're all painted out of the same can, and the color is black. I know that I am not the guy responsible for the Semiramide affair, but who's to prove it? Who's the character that started tossing the conrods out of the Lancaster? What was your former boyfriend doing on my ship? Setting me up for another kiss-off? Jesus Christ, woman, you'll be asking me not to take these things personally next!"

"You shouldn't. They're the fortunes of war."

Farradyne roared, so loud that his voice echoed and reechoed up and down the ship. "Fortunes of war be damned!" Then he stopped suddenly and looked at her again. "War?" he asked. "Between whom or between what and where? Who and what are you and your ilk? I——" He sat down and put one hand to his head. Carolyn started to speak. "Charles——" but he looked up and said, "Shut the hell up and let me think!"

"But I——"

"Shut up or I'll slap you shut!" Farradyne meant it, and Carolyn must have understood that slapping her senseless did not conflict with his aversion to violence. Not now. Not anymore.

He had enough evidence to make a shrewd guess if he could only sort out the hodgepodge, throw out the dross, hang the material end to end, and then take an impersonal look at it to fill in the gaps.

Some of it had to do with a combined suicide and wanton mass-murder in a wrecked spacecraft; he should study that incident with the view of discovering why it was done, and *not* why it had been done to Charles Farradyne. There were the Nileses who probably went to church on Sunday, belonged to the Chamber of Commerce and the Ladies' Aid and the Civic Welfare and considered running hellflowers a proper business. And the daughter, Carolyn, who wanted marriage and a home and a bunch of kids to bring up into the same hellish business so well run by their grandfather— just as she had been raised. Something important hinged on the triple-toned voice which now had become more than a hasty impression made under stress and excitement. Women who were immune to the solar system's most devastating narcotic and used their immunity to deal in the things with safety, bringing ruin to other women. It was more than jealousy between women, it went farther than that. It was a form of warfare, and this idea indicated an organization large and well-integrated; capable of out-maneuvering capable and brilliant men who had dedicated their lives to stamping out the racket—and who died under the juggernaut instead of destroying it.

Well, there it was and what could he make of it?

No, there was more to be added. Brenner-Hughes, who tried to remove the control rods of the reaction pile, and who was immune to marcoleptine. That was an oddly shaped piece of the puzzle that suddenly dropped into place with a click and coupled up two isolated chunks to make one solid corner.

Farradyne put himself in the position of Professor Martin, who might have been a survivor of the Lancaster foundering. Martin might ask why someone had tried to kill him, just as Farradyne had so often asked himself why Party X had tried to kill Farradyne in the Semiramide. The answer was that Brenner-Hughes had not directed his efforts at Martin, but at Farradyne, who had some knowledge that was dangerous to the hellflower ring. Martin would have been the same sort of innocent victim to the second episode as Farradyne had been to the first. Party X had wrecked the Semiramide because there was someone aboard with dangerous knowledge. There was a coldly operating group of persons, immune themselves to drugs, who were efficiently undermining the rest of the human race by preying on weakness, lust, and escapist factors that lie somewhere near the surface in the strongest of human characters.

He raised his head and looked at Carolyn Niles.

She faced him squarely and asked, "Have you figured it out?"

"I think so," he said coldly. "There are a couple of gaps yet which you can fill in."

"What makes you think I'll do it?"

"You'll do it," he said in a brittle voice. "For instance, what are you, real or artificial mutant?"

Her laugh was strained and cynical. "Brilliant!" she said. "*Homo Superior*, Charles."

"All right then, keep it clammed. But we'll find out."

"You haven't found out yet," she remarked pointedly.

"We didn't always have electric lamps, either."

Carolyn shook her head in a superior manner. "You did not discover this thing either," she said calmly. "You were shown most of it deliberately."

"Indeed?" His voice was sarcastic.

"We knew that someone high-up and undercover had furnished you with a spacecraft and a forged license and set you to running into us, hoping that your reputation would establish you as a racketeer. He used you efficiently, so we used you more efficiently. There are two ends to a fishline, Charles, and the fish and the fisherman never meet until one pulls the other in. We caught Howard Clevis on the wrong end of the line, so to speak. We also——"

"You caught Clevis?"

"As soon as we knew who your contact was we pulled him in. So if you are expecting a flight of military craft to come racing up in time to intercept the rendezvous ship we have out there, forget it. The military are still on the landing blocks at the spaceport."

Farradyne whirled and peered into the radar. The single pip was close and closing the range swiftly but there was nothing else on the "scope." It was a huge ship, if the size of the radar response meant anything and Farradyne peered into the coupled telescope.

Nothing like it could ever have been built in secret anywhere among the habitable planets of the solar system. The size of it was such that the metal alone, even if one piece were placed with each manufacturer to conceal the process, would have attracted notice, and the rest of the project would require the resources of a planet to feed it and the men that built it. It would be like trying to build a four-hundred-inch telescope in secret; the very least that could happen would be some avid press agent taking note of a massive casting and using it in an advertisement, and that would start the parade.

Farradyne turned away from the telescope. "Baby, what

a sucker you played me for!" he jeered. "So I was to be your lover, your husband? Together, hand in hand we go to cement the first interstellar union. The mating of a jackass and a triple-tongued canary, that the fruit of such union will be half-assed and bird-brained." Farradyne's voice went hard. "Well, if it's war your people want, we'll give it to you!"

Farradyne strode across the room toward the controls and as he came, Carolyn's hand moved swiftly, catching up the microphone in a single swoop and bringing it to her mouth. She had had the radio turned on all the while, obviously, and Farradyne's tirade had been going out.

Carolyn cried a sing-songy rhythm into the mike. It reminded Farradyne of an exotic trio chanting a ritual celebration of some heathen rite of sacrifice.

He slapped the microphone out of her hand; the thing hurled out to the end of its cord and jerked free, to crash against the far wall leaving the cord-ends dangling open like a raw sore.

He caught her by the hair, lifted her out of the seat and hurled her across the room. She fell and went rolling in a welter of arms and legs until she came up against the wall beside the mike. She scooped it up and hurled it at Farradyne's head, but he caught it in one hand and dropped it to the floor.

He dropped into the seat and hit the levers with both hands. The Lancaster surged upward, throwing Carolyn back to the floor in a painful heap. The acceleration rose to three gravities, then to four.

"This trick we take," he gloated.

Carolyn moaned; it sounded like attempted laughter.

He looked into the radarscope and saw that despite his four gravities of acceleration the monstrous spacecraft was matching him and closing the range.

15

Farradyne watched Carolyn uncaringly as she fought herself out of the crumpled position and succeeded in flopping over on her back where the four gravities were not making her body press against her arms and legs. She spreadeagled on the floor and her chest labored with the effort. Then she relaxed, because four gravities are not too uncomfortable when lying on the back, even though the floor below is hard.

"Forget it, Charles," she said slowly, and with some difficulty. "You can't run away from a ship—that can go—faster than light."

"I can try."

"You can't win."

The radio speaker came alive, "Surrender, Farradyne! Stop and submit or we fire!"

Farradyne's lips tightened as he fought the controls so that the ship slid sidewise,[1] putting another vector in its course. He twirled the volume knob to zero on the radio with a violent twist of his wrist. "They're your friends, and they don't mind killing you," he sneered.

"I'm not afraid to die."

"I am," grunted Farradyne. "I have some knowledge that I don't want to die without telling."

---

[1] Sideways.

"That's why I'm willing—to keep you from telling."

His hands danced on the levers and the Lancaster turned end for end and sped back at the huge craft almost on a side-swiping course. Out here intrinsic velocity meant nothing, the only thing that counted was the Lancaster's velocity with respect to the velocity of the spacecraft from the stars. He had one advantage, his ship was smaller and therefore it must be more maneuverable. Furthermore he had the advantage of surprise. He could go where he pleased, and the other pilot must follow him. Since Farradyne's changes of pace and course would come without warning, each switch would take a few fractions of a second to follow. On land a few fractions of a second mean little, but in space they mean miles. On land a quartering flight meant closing of the range; in space where the pursuer could not dig a heel into the ground and turn on a dime, quartering flight meant adding another vector to the course.

He widened the gap.

Somehow Farradyne realized that because a ship could exceed the speed of light, it did not follow that the ship would be able to catch an elusive quarry.

He looked at Carolyn, plastered against the floor by four gravities and realized that her race could be no more hardy than his, and therefore four gravities was about all they could take over an extended period of time. Maybe the more hardened space-dogs could take five or six, with training and special seats and wearing equipment. His outfit protected him more than the flimsy stuff she wore.

Here at least he was on an equal footing with the other spacer. It was obvious to Farradyne that interstellar velocities did not depend in any way upon reaching that speed by plain acceleration. A force field of some unknown kind was needed, and this force field must not be one that permitted the body to stand, say a thousand gravities or this force field would go on and the other ship would catch him as easily as a greyhound could catch a rabbit—and here in space there were no brambles in which to hide.

He snapped his Lancaster around and crossed behind the course of the other ship. Again he widened the gap.

He had only one thing to worry about. To the present moment and until it became evident that he would get free of pursuit, this new and sudden enemy was hoping to take him alive. So until it became evident that he could make his escape he had nothing to fear. Once he was free of them, he would have to face the terror of target-seeking missiles capable of several hundred gravities of acceleration and equally capable of turning in midflight if he managed to make them miss him.

He wished desperately for a cargo of bowling balls or steel castings that he could strew in his wake. He cursed his lack of foresight in not having the control rods replaced, because a few of them might have done the trick.

Farradyne stopped cursing. He struggled to the computer and played a long tune on the keys, ignoring the fact that the enemy had finally lined up on his course from behind again and was closing range. Recollection of Brenner-Hughes and the depredations in the pile-bay had started a train of thought that Farradyne followed with growing interest. It was long and involved and it depended upon a large amount of luck, good planning, and ability. He hoped all three were with him.

The Lancaster made one more complex turn as the end of the punched tape entered the autopilot. Then, if Farradyne's computations were correct, the Lancaster's nose was pointed at Terra.

The spaceliner behind, fooled again, made a turn and began to pick up the space that had been lost.

Farradyne saw that he had plenty of time. He waited until the punchings on the tape cut the drive a bit, and then he went below and came back into the control room with

Brenner-Hughes' space-suit. He got out patching material and carefully repaired the triangular rip. He cleaned out the strong-locker, putting the greenbacks into one of the many pouches of the suit. Then he set about checking it, testing the air-supply and purifier, filling the food pouch and the water tank. Men had been known to last seventy-two hours in a suit like this without any discomfort other than the confinement. The primary danger was running out of oxygen and the secondary danger was thirst. How much longer than the three days depended upon the character of the man and when he had last eaten and taken his fill of water.

The suit was checked to Farradyne's satisfaction and he started to put it on. "How handy are your friends with that big spacer?" he asked.

"Good enough," she said.

"You'd better pray for them to be better," he said. "Because your life depends upon how handy they are."

"Charles, you can't possibly make it."

Farradyne paused; he wanted to take time for a last cigarette. He lit one and puffed before he said, "Honeychild, I could outguess that gang until Sol[2] freezes over, except that sooner or later they'll get sick and tired of the chase and end it by launching a target-seeking missile and that would be that. I have no intention of sitting here and letting them catch me, either."

"So what are you going to do?"

Farradyne reached up and stopped the clock. "I've punched a very interesting autopilot tape. It'll dodge and swoop along at about four gravities and lead your pals a long and devious way after you and I part company. Four gee[3] is enough to keep you flat on your attractive behind so you can't louse it up. Since you can't measure time too

---

[2] The sun.
[3] Short for gravities.

accurately, when they grab you, you won't be able to tell 'em just when I took off and they'll have a fine time combing space for a man-sized mote, making his course to Terra."

"Charles?"

Farradyne snubbed his cigarette out and dropped on his hands and knees so that he could look down into her face. "You've pitched me many a low, soft curve to the inside," he told her quietly. "Now you are lying there looking helpless, with those big eyes telling me that I am leaving you here to die. Good act, Carolyn, but this time you didn't think it out far enough. By now you should have known Farradyne well enough to realize that staying here will kill us both because I won't be taken alive! By scramming, maybe we'll both live. This is one battle you lose. And the last. But maybe we'll meet somewhere again to take it up later."

He bent down with a cynical smile and kissed her on the lips. To his surprise he found her lips responsive, but he had neither the time nor inclination to carry the emotion any further.

"So long, Carolyn," he chuckled. "Some of this has been a lot of fun."

He finished donning the space-suit and then with a careless wave of his hand he went down the stairs. She was not looking at him, but at the ruined microphone and the raw cord-ends, and the radio equipment far out of her reach. Panic showed in her face and it gave her some strength, but not enough to fight the four gravities that held her flat.

Then as Farradyne lost sight of her, his jaunty self-confidence faded. Up until not too long ago he had been complimenting himself on being able to find out more about the hellflower operation than the Sandmen. Now he knew the hellflower gang had been using him in a more efficient manner than Clevis and the Solar Anti-Narcotics Department. It became obvious to Farradyne that fighting a gang of cut-throats and fighting an enemy race of intelligent people were about as different as he really was from the brilliant operator he imagined himself to be.

It also required that he change his plans for escape. He knew that he could flee the big ship and had a fine chance of being picked up by a Space Guard scooter as soon as he could get within calling distance of Luna.

But the chances were high that the hellflower people would have their entire undercover outfit alerted and at the first touch of radio call they would be swarming the neighborhood to pick him up. He would call and several ships would answer; there would be a lot of calling back and forth with the result that some "commercial spaceliner" would pick him up, reporting the incident to the Space Guard, who would not even take off from the station on Luna. Then Farradyne would be delivered right back to the place he was leaving now.

He paused by the spacelock and cracked the big portal, and stood there eyeing the huge starship, a tiny dot in the distance below, visible only because its reaction flare limned[4] the ship, making an annular object against the cold twinkling stars. He kept the spacelock open long enough to make it look like a real escape to Carolyn, who would be watching the indicator lamp and marking the time.

Then he closed the spacelock and went down and down in the Lancaster until he found the lowermost inspection cubby. He crawled in and closed the hatch behind him. He settled down to wait with about the same amount of wondering concern as the school boy summoned to the principal's office without being told why.

Even the small amount of evidence that he now could use had been given to him as bait to catch the one man who would be willing to listen to him. He groaned and swore

---

[4] Illuminated.

aloud and the sound of his voice echoed and reechoed within the confines of his helmet.

Time creaked past and the Lancaster turned and curved according to the punchings on the autopilot tape. Farradyne had only one prayer—that the enemy would not get tired of the chase and fire a missile that would end the whole game with a wave of intolerable heat and indescribably bright light. Only Carolyn's presence aboard might prevent that until the last moment.

Then the hour-period ended with the Lancaster pointing up and a quartering course from Terra and Sol and a long, long way from the point of supposed escape. Not long after that Farradyne felt the clink of the magnetic grapples.

He tensed again. Would they fine-comb the Lancaster? Or would the inevitable question and answer session that must ensue, once they found Carolyn alone, convince them that he had abandoned ship? Would they take her off and blast the Lanc' or would they deem it of value and keep it?

His mind went on and on—how good was the radar? How alert was their radar operator? Were both good enough to state unequivocally that there had been no minute object leaving the ship on a tangential course, or would there have been the usual clutter of noise and interference and lack of anticipation so that someone could assume that he had left the ship? Someone was going to get chewed for it in any case. Then assuming that the enemy considered the ship valuable, where would they take it and what would they do with it?

Far from feeling gratified at his maneuver, Farradyne was only satisfied to be alive and temporarily out of the hands of the enemy. What happened from here on in must be played by ear against an unknown score for three voices.

The drive of the Lancaster dropped from four gravities to about one, and Farradyne could hear, dimly, the clumpings of heavy feet coming in through the rooms above him.

Then the drive diminished again, remaining at about a quarter-gravity or maybe less, and there were sounds of feet above his head. He tensed and he tasted the acid in his mouth; he found his heavy automatic and clutched it clumsily in the heavy space-glove. Capture might be preferable to death, except that Farradyne was fairly well convinced that the enemy could not permit him to stay alive with what he knew about them, even though it was precious little and unsupported.

The cubby he was hiding in was angularly shaped; to one side was space beyond the hull-plates. Inside was the water-jacket that cooled the throat of the reaction motor. Farradyne moved quietly around the central pillar until he was on the opposite side from the inspection hatch and settled down again.

On the plates above his head there were footsteps and the scraping of something heavy being hauled across the deck.

He heard the sound of triple-tongued voices barking musical and discordant sounds, distorted and muffled by the deck and the helmet he wore. One fiddled with the inspection hatch and Farradyne found the scuttlebutt[5] and valved the air out into space knowing the enemy would have a hard time cracking the hatch against the pressure of one atmosphere. They gave up after a moment; then came the sound of drilling on the deckplates above him. A cloud of whitish vapor spurted downward and the sound of alien voices rose sharply as the drill came through. Three more spurts of escaping air blasted downward and skirred around the room to go in a fading draw toward the scuttlebutt.

Plugs filled the four holes and Farradyne turned his head

---

[5] Traditionally, a scuttlebutt was the nautical term for the cask used to serve water to the crew; much like a modern day office water cooler. Here, Smith has appropriated the term to mean a valve.

ch. ends next p.

torch on them. They were heavy self-tapping bolts being turned in from above.

The maneuver was repeated three times, ninety degrees apart. Then there was a softer sound of scraping and gradually the clumping of feet and the sound of men at work faded away.

Farradyne took a deep breath and realized that his skin was itching from the cold perspiration of fear that bathed him. The taste in his mouth was brackish and his heart was pounding, his breath shallow and rapid. He opened his mouth to gasp and discovered that he had been clenching his teeth so hard that his jaw ached and his molars hurt.

He closed the scuttlebutt, but did not valve any air into his hiding place. He put the top of his helmet against the deckplate above him and listened. Far above he could hear them, still at work but they were going higher and higher in the ship. He relaxed, waiting . . .

Three more hours passed, as nerve-wracking a three hours as Farradyne had ever spent. Then, with absolutely no warning the drive went off completely. He floated from the deck and scrabbled around to grab a stanchion.[6] He held on, finally getting his magnetic shoes against a girder where they held him at an odd angle.

The drive went on to a full one gravity and hurled Farradyne flat against the bottom of the cubby, wrenching his ankles slightly. The drive went off again, on, and finally off. This time it stayed off.

Floating free, with only his feet for mooring, was like resting in a tub of body-temperature water, and as the lulling muscle-freeing sensation went on and on, Farradyne dozed. From the doze, which was fitful for quite some time, he dropped off into a deep slumber.

---

[6] An upright or vertical post or support.

16

Farradyne awoke to the pressure of about one gravity and he consulted his watch. Either fourteen hours had passed, or thirty-eight, but he could not believe the latter. A full clock-around was hardly possible for Farradyne, even when he was dead tired, so one clock-around plus fourteen hours was unthinkable.

He put his slumber at fourteen hours and then set his mind on other, more important things.

The ship was silent. His suit hung from him limply, indicating that air had seeped into the cubby again. He tried the scuttlebutt but no hiss of air came. The Lancaster was a-planet.

It might be Terra, Venus, or Pluto according to the pull of gravity, but Farradyne did not think it likely to be any one of the three. He suspected that whatever the gizmo was the enemy had installed on the deck above him, it had something to do with transcending the limiting velocity of light. He was probably grounded on enemy soil . . . somewhere.

For a moment his mind grappled with the problem of interstellar travel and lost the fight. It was possible, proven by the starship of the aliens. But to come aboard with a gadget under one arm and install it, like putting in a radio set, seemed entirely too simple. On the other hand, Farradyne was sufficiently aware of basic physics to understand that anything that could be used to create a condition where gross matter could exceed the velocity of light would be something that did not have to perform in conjunction with a matter-operated reaction motor. He remembered, dimly, some fanciful theories written by some of the white-tower boys in one of the big universities. These had been experiments in field-theory and group-theory which had indicated that under certain conditions, some rather minute spherical volumes of space could be made to misbehave.

The difference was that with the physicists and their operations, a vast room full of gear had been used to make a five millimeter sphere, and the contrast was marked.

The meat of this matter was that the gizmo that made it possible to travel faster than light must be some sort of field-generator, and such a field-generator might well be packaged in small form for installation. Whatever the science and whatever the location, Farradyne could not hope to learn anything penned up here.

Again he listened. The ship was silent as the proverbial grave. He cracked the inspection hatch and peered out. It was dark as the grave, too.

Boldly he opened the hatch and stepped out. Under the light of his headlamp, Farradyne inspected four rectangular metal boxes, painted a nondescript gray. Cables led from one to another, terminating in white metal connectors. The boxes were bolted to the deck by the self-tapping bolts that had come through his ceiling.

From one of the boxes ran a cable that led to a wall-connector.

Like all other Solarian spacecraft, the Lancaster was well supplied with a network of cables running up and down the length of the ship to serve as test connections and spares for this or that equipment. This made it possible to install some bit of gear for pleasure, comfort, or added maneuvering without having to tear half the ship apart to run the necessary wiring.

The enemy had re-connected their multi-line cable to one of the standard Terran connectors and plugged the cable into the Lancaster's cable-plate.

Farradyne could see nothing about the metal boxes that would tell him anything, so he left them and went aloft, cautiously. He doffed[1] the space-suit at the next level and hung it in a suit locker, and continued to walk up the stairway that would lead him to the spacelock and the salon.

Out of one porthole he could see the spaceport. It was broad and dark except for a bouquet of searchlights that drilled into the sky around the rim, a wash of floodlamps that surrounded one of the vast starships many miles distant, and the far-off blur of bright, red light that probably read "Spaceman's Bar" in whatever the natives used for a printed language.

He left the viewport and went higher in his ship until he came to the salon. He peered into it from floor level, but it was dark and untenanted. The spacelock was open and Farradyne looked out of the large round opening across the field to another starship standing a few hundred yards from the Lancaster. The other ship was just as dark as his, except for one small porthole that gleamed like a headlight in the darkness.

The problem of where he was called him to the control room.

He looked into the sky, hunting for familiar constellations. The Pleiades were there, but warped quite a bit and Farradyne found that, while he knew they were distorted as an aggregation of stellar positions, he could not remember their proper relationship. Orion was visible, but the hero had hiked his belt up after a swing of his sword at

---

[1] Removed.

the mythical enemy. The Great Bear was sitting on his haunches instead of prowling and the smaller Bear had lost his front feet. Cassiopeia had gained some weight, enough to squash her throne and Sirius no longer blazed in Canis Major. Procyon had taken off for parts unknown, while several other bright stars dotted the skies in places where no stars had been on Terra. It was likely that some of these were merely displaced stars, but no one could tell Sirius from anything else without a set of astronomical instruments and a few years of study unless he knew which way Sirius was from this position.

Coldly and calmly Farradyne scanned the skies. Providing they had not traveled more than forty or fifty light years, the constellations before and behind the direct line of flight should be reasonably undistorted, except for those stars that would have been bypassed en route. This would only add a star or two to a constellation behind and subtract the same from a constellation dead ahead. The ones to the side of the line of flight would be misshapen and warped.

It would have been easier if he could have viewed the entire sky, but he had to be content with one hemisphere. If he could find an undistorted constellation with a few stars missing he had come in that direction and, conversely, if there were stars added, he had gone away from it past some of the stars between Sol and this enemy system.

He tried to recall visits to the big stellartarium in New York where the lecturer displayed the skies as seen from various well known stars that were within half a hundred light years of Sol. Certain sky-marks and their displacement would be very helpful, if he could remember them. But he found that he had not been as visually attentive as he might have been, or that he had seen and been entertained and then discarded the data as interesting but useless in a scientific culture that firmly believed in the limiting velocity of light.

Finally he gave up hoping to establish his whereabouts by visual inspection. He found a small pad of paper and began to make layouts of the familiar constellations as he saw them. Someone among the planets of Sol would be able to measure the angles and changes and come up with the right answer within a few light years, and stars were sufficiently separated so that the chances were good for a reasonable identification.

He put a dozen small pages in his pocket and then took his first look at the control room. He could see nothing changed at first, but then he found a small auxiliary panel beside the pilot's seat which contained a bar-topped toggle switch and three pilot lamps that were different in appearance from the rest of the Lancaster's standard equipment.

He felt an urge to try the toggle, but fought it down. It was too much like playing with toy building blocks made of sub-critical masses of plutonium, and Farradyne wanted to stay alive long enough to watch the downfall of the enemy, not participate in the explosion. Curbing his human curiosity to fiddle with strange gadgets, Farradyne turned away from the board and went to the cupboard where he took out his binoculars.

He was astonished to find out how far away the starship really was, and how big it was when it leaped into closer view in the glasses. It was still as dark as an untenanted building except for that one lighted porthole, but the angle into the cabin beyond was too steep. Farradyne could see nothing more than the corner between the opposite wall and the ceiling. He toyed with the idea of trying to lift himself to the top of the dome, but gave it up because he realized, once he removed the binoculars from his eyes, that the additional few feet of height would not change the distant angle enough to make it worth his while.

The question of what to do next perplexed him. Obviously there was no answer. There could be no plan. He would have to play it by ear again, with the other guy calling the moves. He grunted unhappily; he could not even smoke because he feared to show even the smallest light. But——

Farradyne went down to his galley and opened a can of mixed space rations which he shoveled in cold. It filled him adequately but not tastily and he realized that the best of fine food would have been stowed away in a frenzy of nervous listening for the inevitable sounds of the enemy's return. With haste, Farradyne cleaned up the evidence of his presence, thinking how ridiculous it was to be stealing from his own spacecraft.

He was finishing up this job when the faint glint of a distant flash of light caught his eye. He hurried to the porthole from which the glint had come, and peered out. A large caravan of heavy trucks was snaking around the corner of a distant building and turning onto the spacefield. Their headlamps cut forward like scythes of light, cutting a brilliant path toward the Lancaster.

Farradyne did not deem it wise to sit this out. They might have been heading for the other side of the field, but if they weren't he was trapped. He went aloft to the salon and scuttered down the landing ramp, around the back side of the poised spacer and away from the direction of the trucks, running in the shadow cast by the Lancaster. Five or six hundred yards away was another spacer, and it was completely dark. Farradyne scurried around the widespread tail fins of the monster and stood there, peering at the caravan from between the angle made by the tail fin and the in-curving body of the spacecraft.

The trucks came around the Lancaster, surrounded it in a circle, and then a blaze of lights came, lighting the Terran ship from dome to reaction funnel. Ladders were sent aloft and a huge crane lifted. The calls of workers and the directions of their superintendent came to Farradyne clearly. He wondered what they were doing and saying; except for the three-toned voices that added an audible complement of women and children to the gang, it sounded like any work party on earth yammering in a strange tongue.

He watched for an hour, and then he saw that the distant sky was beginning to show a very faint glow of gray. Sunrise—or perhaps a false sunrise, he could not tell.

He scuttled like a human spider away from the direction of the work party until its flood lights were a distant miniature stage setting. He wound in and among silent, dark spacecraft, avoiding those with lights even though he had to detour wide for the sake of this safety. Eventually he came to the far side of the spaceport.

He cased the place warily from behind the fin of a spacer, looking at the dark, silent buildings and wondering if this gang of aliens had ever heard of night watchmen. He did not trust the quiet darkness of the apparently uninhabited spaceport because he was suspicious and he knew that other people were as suspicious as he was. He was glad that he did not barge in brashly, for along about the first glimmers of real graying sky, a man came out from between two of the buildings waving a searchlight. He sauntered along in front of the nearest building and disappeared between it and the next.

Farradyne skipped across the space and went into the gangway the watchman had just come out of. He walked warily through and came to a high wire fence. Keeping to the building side of the clearance-way between fence and building, Farradyne skulked along in the direction opposite to that taken by the watchman.

He needed a minimum of two items: A set of Planet X clothing and a way out of this rattrap.

He found the way out a few minutes later.

A dim striking of a bell alarmed him until he realized that it was tolling, rather than clamoring an alarm. He followed the tolling for seventeen bongs and came upon

ch. ends next p.

a small sentry house perched beside an open gate. As the tolling stopped, the man in the house stretched, yawned and got up, picking up a searchlight. He stepped outside and looked around in a bored manner.

The watchman took one look at the open gate some ten feet from his position and shrugged. He turned his back on it and disappeared between a couple of buildings not far from Farradyne's place.

Farradyne grinned. Obviously it had been so long ago since any trouble had been this way that the guard-system had become lax. Farradyne praised laziness and complacency highly as he sped across the open space on silent feet and passed the gate on his way to the outside.

Dawn was breaking and the chill of the morning nipped at him. He had broken free, but it was just as dangerous for him to remain in front of the open gate as it might have been for him to be roaming around the spaceport in the full light of day. He turned to the right and started to walk along the road toward a group of small buildings a few hundred yards from the spaceport.

The second item Farradyne needed came later. He had sauntered along several deserted streets in the gray of dawn and down a couple of alleys and through a vacant lot or two until he was quite some distance from the spaceport. Here, in a dimly lighted district Farradyne met his Planet X clothing.

The stranger did not have a chance. He had been drinking or sniffing whatever the enemy used for celebration and he had used too much. Farradyne's hard fist came out of somewhere and the stranger went down like a log, silently. Farradyne dragged him into an alley and stripped him to the skin.

His own clothing Farradyne stuffed in a trash barrel, pushing the bundle down below the rest of the rubbish in the hope that the barrel would be collected by a couple of hard-working and uncurious men who would never note the alien cut to the cloth.

He left the fellow naked to suffer both a hangover and a lot of embarrassment.

Then in the pleasantly bright dawn, Farradyne walked boldly down the city street jingling a bunch of native coins in the side pocket of his costume and feeling just a trifle silly, like an introvert at a fancy-dress ball. The trousers were striped gaudily and the loose jacket hugged his waist a bit on the too-tight side. There was a widish hat and a pair of shoes that could have been put on either foot. He looked like a character out of an old-time musical comedy and he hoped that his costume was not the kind worn by Planet X-ians as formal evening wear because then he would look silly to them wandering around in the morning light like a man caught far from home at six ack-emma in a tuxedo.

Eventually he passed a shop window and saw other garb like the junk he was wearing and he felt better.

He had every faith in the belief that people are disciplined against striking up an acquaintance with a total stranger, and so he turned into what was obviously a main thoroughfare and strolled along it until the streets began to fill with people.

17

There was no doubt about the alien quality of the city. But in its functional qualities, it was very familiar. These, he realized, were developments that had been found to be effective over a long time of sheer operation; functions that would have been mechanically similar on any planet no matter how alien, so long as its inhabitants breathed air, ate food, and perambulated.[1] Buildings were mostly squarish blocks cut with windows and doors; shops had broad windows for displaying their wares and even the wares were not too exotic. Clothing stores and gewgaw[2] stores and food shops and now and then one that sold stuff that was not to be identified by a stranger.

The streets and alleys and gutters and sidewalks were normal. Traffic ran to the left, however, which gave Farradyne some trouble because he had been used to stepping from the curb and glancing to the right. Drivers squawked at him with their horns and swore at him in their multi-tongued voices. Farradyne forced himself to learn this left-handed traffic problem; he did not want to be handed a traffic ticket, nor did he want to be asked by some policeman for an explanation of his stupidity.

---

[1] To walk about; to roam or stroll.
[2] Something gaudy, useless, and worthless.

By now the sun was well above the horizon and the streets began to teem. The air began to sing with the noise of people chattering, greeting one another, and generally making a racket resembling a Chinese laundry in an air-raid. He heard the clash of metal on metal and turned to watch a couple of drivers arguing over their dented fenders. As he walked with his head turned, Farradyne bumped into someone and the man chittered something at him angrily. Farradyne nodded humbly and grunted under his breath and hurried on. So did the other man, who merely replied to Farradyne's grunt with a single three-toned discord before veering off and away.

He had to be careful, he told himself; he had found this city so closely resembling a city of his own system that he had become careless. He knew by now that if he conducted himself without attracting attention and if he walked without cringing, no one would think to stop him for questioning.

What had Carolyn said? Something about their springing from the same basic stock some fifty thousand years ago? Well, anyway, these were of the same family of curious apes who were gregarious enough to band together and still individualistic enough to resent any intrusion upon privacy. There would most certainly be three-toned hell to pay if he opened his own trap, but so long as he kept it shut, they had no way of telling him from any of their own kind.

And so he walked among them for hours, until the crowd thinned and the traffic became less boisterous and frantic and the city settled down to the quieter routine.

Farradyne found it hard to place this cosmopolitan culture in the same niche with the society that appeared to be systematically undermining the Solarian civilization. It was quite similar to the paradox he had found in the Niles family. It was as though murder was an honorable enterprise and that the dope-sales were listed on the daily stock exchange under the commodities section.

ch. ends p. 161

Farradyne had expected to find some monstrous ugliness here. A police or slave state would not have surprised him; it was such a culture that usually fostered villainy. Instead he found a city much like his own and it was hard for Farradyne to shake off the feeling that the only misunderstanding between them was the age-old barrier of tongue.

Eventually he came upon an ornately carved building that stood with the doors open. People were sauntering in and out with no obvious barrier, and so Farradyne followed one group at a little distance and went into the building.

It could have been any museum on Terra, for the life-forms displayed were as bizarre as any of the stranger bits of artwork on the earth or other of Sol's planets. He came upon a quiet hallway that had a non-scale model of the solar system; it was a working orrery[3] that told Farradyne nothing other than that this system had eleven planets and a batch of satellites. None of the planets had rings like Saturn. He looked for something that could identify the parent sun for him, but he found nothing familiar about any of the displays, except one.

There was a small model of Sol and its planets on a pedestal, and while the sight was familiar, the lettering below the display was not. If the legend said anything about distance and direction, it was not only in the alien's terms, but in the alien's written language.

To find out where in the sky he was, Farradyne needed a fast course in Planet X-ian language, and then a six months' concentrated course in uranography.[4] He began to understand that the matter of being lost is only a dislocation of your own frame of reference. Cities do not have large signs around the streets saying "This is Chicago" because any man in his right senses knows that he is not in Detroit, and

---

[3] A mechanical model of a solar system.
[4] Also known as celestial cartography; the branch of astronomy concerned with mapping the positions of stars, galaxies, and other celestial bodies.

if he does not, there are better places for him than either city.

He shunned the opportunity of visiting the enemy planetarium. Having some lecturer explain the heavens as seen from Planet X in a trio-voice would get him nowhere.

He left the museum and began to trudge back toward the spaceport. He was hungry again, and the morning and early fore-afternoon had been frustrating, even though it had been enlightening to find that the aliens lived and breathed and enjoyed themselves like people instead of the cold inhuman monsters he had expected.

Again Farradyne watched his fellows carefully. It seemed that one medium slug would buy him a wad of paper that could be nothing other than the afternoon news, after which he would get two smaller slugs in change. He strode to the newsstand with a what-the-hell feeling and tossed down one of the medium slugs. He scooped up one of the papers and two of the smaller slugs and walked away without saying a word. The newsman watched the transaction without turning an eye. Then Farradyne folded the paper through the middle and tucked it under his arm and sauntered along like the absent-minded professor until he found a quick-grab joint that opened on the sidewalk.

He stood at the counter scanning the wall-menu as though he knew what it said until the waitress sounded off at him. He looked down at her with a frown of irritation, and then waved two fingers at a hot plate full of flat square things floating in an oily sea of juice. He unfolded his paper and immersed himself in a page while the waitress scooped two of the flat things from the plate and slid them between folds of something like a bun. She shoved them beneath the lower edge of Farradyne's paper on a flat plate and stood there mewing at him like a trio of alley cats.

Acting in an absent manner Farradyne took two of the larger slugs from his pocket and dropped them on the bar.

The waitress took one, deposited it in a register with a shrug, as if she had seen oddly absorbed characters before, and returned with three of the smaller slugs which she piled on the bar beside Farradyne's remaining coin.

He munched his greasy God-knows-whats and while he mentally complained about the flavor and the greasiness, he was forced to admit that they were more satisfying than his earlier cold can of mixed space rations.

Then he folded his paper (wondering whether he had been absorbed in a lonely hearts column, the local stock market, or a nice lurid sex-slaying) and sauntered off toward the spaceport. He made it in easy steps, angling this way and that and wandering like Haroun al Raschid,[5] but feeling more like that other fabled Arabian who was forced to remain in the body of a stork because his bird's mouth could not pronounce the magic word in the proper language.[6] No one paid him any attention.

The sum and substance of his adventure was the feeling that a hyena can walk through a monkey cage so long as the hyena has enough sense to wear monkey clothing and keep his big bazoo shut, and an opinion that it was a damned shame that such nice-appearing folks could be such lice.

By the time Farradyne returned to the vicinity of the spaceport it was getting along toward late afternoon. It was a long day on Planet X and if Farradyne's judgment of time were anything worth mention, the day had still some hours to go until the real darkness came. He had no watch. A watch would have come in handy for time estimating even though there stood an excellent probability that the length of the day did not match anything like the Terran standard

[5] Abu Ja'far Harun ibn Muhammad al-Mahdi (c. 763–809), famously known as Harun al-Rashid, was the fifth Abbasid caliph of the Abbasid Caliphate who reigned from 786 until his death, and whose reign is traditionally regarded as the beginning of the Islamic Golden Age.

[6] *The Tale of Caliph Stork* is one of the most popular fairy tales by German poet and novelist Wilhelm Hauff (1802–1827).

of time. He had dumped his wrist watch along with his own clothing because it was obviously alien; the watch he wore was his victim's but it was calibrated in Planet X time and Farradyne had not had a chance to compare times, nor to sit quietly and observe the relative motions of the several hands around the dial.

He was too early, but he had no other place to go. He could see across the spaceport to the Lancaster, where the cranes still poised high and the work went on, but still he had no more urge to return to the city.

Farradyne observed the entry of others carefully, and discovered that there were a couple of smaller ships taking on passengers, and that a number of people were coming along to watch them off. It looked like the operations on the average civilian spaceport, where people were not herded around nor treated with suspicion. It caused Farradyne to think that obviously the people of Planet X were all in accord on the plans of their undercover attack on Sol. Farradyne smiled sourly, on the planets of Sol any such venture would have been greeted with every shade of reaction from eager applause to outright hostility.

Farradyne was more than willing to take advantage of their obvious self-confidence or lack of concern over the possibility of sabotage, espionage, or enemy action. He was fitting himself unobtrusively into a group of people who were entering the main gate of the spaceport when he heard the raucous toot of an automobile horn.

Like all the rest, Farradyne turned to look. An official looking limousine was slowly coming up that broad drive. In it were driver, three guards, and——

"Norma Hannon!" he said with astonishment.

Then Farradyne felt the cold chill of fear crawl down his spine because he knew that he had made a hideous mistake. He turned away slowly, hoping that the others were turning as slowly to go about their own business. He started toward

ch. ends p. 161

the spaceport, only to find a uniformed guard barring his way.

The guard chimed at him tersely.

Farradyne took his guts firmly and eyed the guard with a contempt that he did not feel. "Talk Terran," he snapped.

The guard blinked and chimed some more, less tersely but no less demandingly.

"Talk Terran," snapped Farradyne firmly. "Or I don't hear you. I know too many who've let down too often and relaxed into their own tongue. They aren't alive."

"I don't speak Terran very well."

"Well, damn it, learn it!" roared Farradyne. "You'll be needing it soon enough. Now, what did you have to say to me?"

"You heard me, but I'd rather——"

Farradyne relaxed with a grin. "No, I didn't. You could impugn my wife's virtue and I wouldn't listen to you. So now let's start over again."

"I was going to ask——"

"No," said Farradyne shortly. "Not that way. I said 'start' and I meant that we'd start *thinking* in Terran, like I've learned to do. Now, you addressed me properly and I said, 'Talk Terran!'"

"Oh. Er, look, you're not going to make me repeat it?"

"Why not?"

"I'd feel like a fool. After all, a mistake is a mistake, isn't it? I could hardly know that you were one of the Terra group, could I? After all, you're not dressed in Terran clothing."

Farradyne saw a glimmer of doubt in the guard's face; Farradyne should have been in Terran clothing if his intention was to stay as Terran as possible until the bitter end. He merely smiled, thinking fast. He said, "Don't want to attract any more attention here than I do on Terra. Frankly, I'm masquerading here. See?"

"I guess you're right. You can speak to your own group,

but others can see you. Tell me, sir, what is it like? On the planets of Sol?"

"Pleasant enough."

"Is that so? I've heard they were rich. But the people? Are they as bad as I've heard?"

"Worse," said Farradyne, thinking that propaganda was as universal as anything could be. He began to itch. How could he break this off before he really did give himself away? The cold sweat that had been running down his spine at the time of the guard's first hail, which had dried in the exultation of knowing that he had succeeded in turning the guard's suspicion away, now started to itch again as another sweat came out to wet the dried salt.

Farradyne was saved the trouble. The car tooted for attention again and Farradyne turned to see it coming back from the spaceport.

"There goes the other one," said the guard, nodding at the car. It passed them and Farradyne saw, with less astonishment this time, that the new one was Howard Clevis.

"Sure does," chuckled Farradyne. "And now so do I."

"You've plenty of time before they hop off for the colony. But go on, and good luck! I'll remember what you said about thinking in Terran."

Farradyne waved and went into the spaceport. He was walking on wobbly legs, because he did not know whether the guard would suddenly begin to suspect him and let fly. But as he passed beyond range around the fantail of a big spacer he relaxed once more.

Farradyne walked slowly out across the field, feeling let down. He had learned nothing from the day's wandering, but while he dawdled all over town, Norma Hannon and Howard Clevis had been within a shout of his Lancaster. Not that he could have done anything, but just being able to talk it over might have brought something out of meeting up with them.

Night was slow in coming, but Farradyne loafed along on his mile and a half walk through the tails of the parked spacecraft until darkness was well on its way.

Two things he noted:

The work-crew around the Lancaster were polishing off the last bits and some of the trucks were folding down their ladders and preparing to take off for home. The other item was the position of the lonely lighted porthole in the big starship. It had changed. To Farradyne this meant only one thing. Clevis had been in one stateroom from early that morning or late last night, but Norma had been missing. Now Norma was back to her own stateroom and Clevis was off, possibly being questioned.

Could he—should he—? Questions raced through his mind. And if he did, would Norma be able to tell him anything? He had his own plans; to hide back in his Lancaster and wait out developments. At least long enough to throw a hard hammerlock on whatever pilot came to drive the Lanc' and twist information out of him.

Norma, he thought then, might know one thing: Their location. It would be a help to know. For if push came to shove, Farradyne was going to enter the Lancaster and take her up and then he was going to experiment with that auxiliary drive. He might die, but he was going to try the thing as soon as he knew that he could never find out without taking the long gamble.

One of the work trucks made up his mind for him. It turned from the Lancaster and its headlamps cut a swath across the field, swinging toward Farradyne. It took Farradyne less than the proverbial half a jiffy to come to the conclusion that bamboozling a guard at the gate was one thing, but to be found slinking around either near the Lancaster or the big starship was something else again.

He avoided the lights of the truck by scooting up the landing ramp of the starship and into the spacelock. It occurred to Farradyne as he went that the lack of people, including guards, out in this region of the spacefield was in a way its own protection. Any distant watcher seeing a figure out here would know automatically that the person was an intruder; perhaps the only reason Farradyne had not been hailed down was due to the known presence of workmen.

Farradyne lay with his chin on the sill of the spacelock and peered out as the truck went by. It would be some time before they were all finished, he concluded, and so he decided to kill the time in action.

Feeling his way along the dark corridors, Farradyne made his way aloft, up the stairways, and around the circular floors until he came upon the one door with a streak of light coming underneath it. The light helped him see; the door was secured with a single bolt of the sliding variety, easy to open from the outside but impossible to move from within.

Farradyne slid the bolt and pushed open the door.

Norma was standing inside, poised defiantly with her hands on her hips, waiting. For a moment she did not recognize him, then her face twisted and said, "Well! If it isn't our interstellar man-about-space, Charles Farradyne!"

18

"Now see here," he said shortly, "Clevis must have told you about me."

"I knew that you and Clevis had something cooked up together the first time I saw him come into the Lancaster without a blazing gun in each hand," she said sourly.

"Well, then you ought to know that I'm——"

"You're a damned idiot, Farradyne! You bumbling fool!"

"But look, I'm here——"

"Where?"

"I was hiding in the inspection hatch. I couldn't see out. Don't you know where we are?"

"They didn't think I'd find it necessary to know," she replied bitingly. "You fancy pants!"

Farradyne swore in his throat. "Now I'll ask you whose side you're on," he snapped. "I came here to——"

"Whose side I'm on?" she laughed harshly. "Whose side are *you* on, Farradyne? I hope you're on their side; you're bound to louse them up sooner or later."

"Look, Norma——"

"So you come bubbling home with the bait in your mouth, unable to feel the hook, and hand it to Howard to get caught on. Go back where you got that monkey costume and die."

"Norma, answer me one thing. Who was Frank Hannon?"

"Frank? Frank was Howard's right hand undercover man,

Farradyne. He had the goods on a man whose name no one knows; he didn't say because he didn't have the chance. He had it all with him when you dumped the Semiramide."

Farradyne eyed her coldly. "There's one thing you've got to admit," he said. "That tale of my three-tongued people was no lotus-dream."

Her silence was as good as a grudging affirmation.

"So part of the pattern is clearing up," he went on. "But if Clevis found me because I'd had four rotten years mucking toadstools on Venus, I'm not above wondering if this was not part of some master plan. Could someone have wrecked the Semiramide and saved me to act someday as bait for Clevis?"

"Isn't that just a bit far-fetched?"

"Maybe and maybe not. Just think. We're not merely fighting an apparently well-integrated mob of dope-runners. We're fighting a blind battle against a whole culture that is calmly and maliciously undermining the moral fiber of the whole race so they can move in and take over with little or no opposition. Doesn't that make sense? Such a program has plans that extend for years; I may be only one small angle, although mine happens to be the angle that worked. Don't tell me you expect warfare to be run like a football game, complete with referees and penalties for kneeing a fallen contestant in the kidneys."

Norma considered it a moment. "I suppose it does make sense. Any formal declaration of war is an openly expressed intention of committing suicide. But you explain yourself if you can."

Farradyne shrugged. "Maybe for the first time I out-guessed them," he said hopefully. He went on to explain how he had done it in a few quick sentences. "Then," he finished, "the big ship didn't even try to find me—the little man that didn't escape. I also doubt that they knew where I was, or they'd not have let me run free all over town." He went on and finished the tale of his peregrinations.[1]

"We saw them catch the Lancaster," she said. "We wondered just why you suddenly went dead at the stick after giving them such a chase. Well, I guess that's it. I'll go on the assumption that you aren't a hellflower devil."

"Thanks," he said bitterly. "And, why the sudden change?"

"I've heard this three-toned language that everybody was so scornful about. I've heard a lot of it. I know that a full-scale organization such as this bunch can and will pull some rather complicated capers, so I am no longer sure that it was your inept handling of a spacecraft that caused the death of my brother. He was on someone's trail and I've assumed it was you. Maybe it wasn't. And if it wasn't then the Semiramide affair was not even an accident on your part. So, damn you, I can't hate you anymore."

"You can't hate me?"

"Not unless you turn out to be one of this outfit. And for the life of me I can't see just what you hope to learn from me that I didn't spill during their questionings."

"Did they——" he let the rest of the sentence hang because he didn't know just how to express it.

"They know everything I know," she said. "I've been filled to the gills with something they shot out of a needle that made me as happily loquacious as a babbling marmoset."[2]

"Did they explain why they brought you back here? It seems to me they'd imprison you."

"That's for later. They're now comparing my tale with Howard's and after they get done comparing notes they'll bring Howard back and we'll take a little jaunt to what they call their 'Detention Planet' where I'll meet a certain number of other Solarians who have gotten a bit too sharp for their liking. It's in another stellar system, I believe,

---

[1] Journeys; travels.
[2] Monkey.

completely safe and far from home and as a last lever in this war they'll hold the lives of a few hundred thousand men and women over the heads of Terra."

Farradyne swore. "The stinking bastards!"

Norma shook her head coolly. "That's emotion, Charles. I don't know exactly what their purpose is, but I do understand that this is a conflict of eventual survival, and rule of an economic empire."

"But——"

Norma shook her head. "Try the shoe on the other foot, Charles. Suppose you had come upon these people with the rest of your kind—how would you see them?"

"As possible allies and friends."

"Balderdash! You'd have seen them as possible customers and people to be exploited and maybe enemies after you'd seen their history. Their attitude is as arrogant as ours and their personal justification as high. By some obscure luck of science they got to interstellar travel before we did and they automatically place us in an inferior position, but they also know that this inferiority is not so great as to make us a pushover. We are scientifically capable of discovering their interstellar drive at any moment, and why we have not is probably just a matter of our not combining the right sciences. Our knowledge of medicine is far vaster than theirs, for instance."

"How can you know this?" he asked.

Norma opened a few buttons at her throat and slipped her dress down over one shoulder. There was a small circular bandage stuck to one spot. "They took a sample of me," she said. "Because I seem to be immune to several diseases that should give me trouble. When I asked about this, they told me that they hoped to discover just what cell change took place when we take our anti-cancer immunization. This thing they have yet to discover. Oh they use our immunization," she said, slipping the dress up but forgetting to rebutton it, "but they use it as an African witch doctor might use a typhoid serum."

She nodded as she went on thinking, "This thing you have to remember, Charles, that if Terrans had arrived there first there would have been the same conflict, but conducted from the other side."

Farradyne shook his head angrily. "We're not inclined to ruin——"

"Stop sounding like one of King Arthur's Knights. Men of sense and good judgment don't request their enemies to meet them on a field of honor. Instead, a state of war is assumed and from that instant on, A is looking for a chance to stab B in the back because he knows that B will cut him off at the hips if he turns his back for a moment. Honor on the battlefield is accorded only to a defeated enemy; up to the time he is defeated, anything goes. And if both sides know that open warfare means total destruction, the process on either side is one of boring from within, or gnawing at the foundation. But this is a bad place to get involved in a discussion of ethics. Where do we go from here?"

"If I knew how to run that ka-dodie in the Lancaster we'd head for Sol—if I knew where Sol was from here."

"And how about Howard?"

"I don't know about Clevis," he told her. "The thing to do would be to hike home as fast as we could and spill our tale to the people who would know what to do about it. Let's face it, Norma. They can mingle with Terrans because they can speak our language. But I couldn't mingle with them to locate Howard. I'd be picked up in a minute."

"So how do we get back?"

"Why do you think they brought the Lancaster?"

"Probably to fit her out as a bona fide hellflower runner."

"Okay. We'll hide out in my cubby until they run her back."

"You go hide out," said Norma. "If they find me missing, they'll know something smells bad."

Farradyne chuckled. "From what I know of them, they're as arrogantly secure as the Gods of Olympus. Some part of their gang is still expecting me to turn up near Terra on an escape course, and the only smart thing I have done is to be where they didn't plan me to be. So we'll be where they don't expect us to be and maybe we'll get away with it. Come on, let's hide out."

The hitch in their plans came when Farradyne led Norma down the stairs to the last deck below and stopped, holding up a warning hand.

"What's the matter?" she whispered.

He pointed. The hatch he had used was lying to one side and a beam of diffuse light was coming up from below. There came also the triple-tongued voices of two men.

Farradyne led Norma one deck above where he could speak without attracting the attention of the men below. "They've installed the space drive in the inspection cubby," he said. "That's probably what all the work was about. It's been taken from the bottom deck and permanently installed down in the cubby where it wouldn't attract attention on a casual tour. Maybe a different unit, I wouldn't know; the temporary job might have been only a harness-job to be used until they could haul the Lanc' to base for a real tear-down and rebuild."

"I didn't see any work-wagon," said Norma.

"Maybe not, but the workman is here, and tuning up the drive. We can't get below now."

"So what do we do?"

"I've half a hunch that they won't leave this ship standing idle long. Let's hide in the cargo hold until they stop tinkering."

Norma nodded thoughtfully. "Let's wait it out," she said. "Then if we have trouble, I can slope and run out of here like a startled rabbit and draw the chase away from you."

"You make the escape," he suggested, "I'll do the hare and the hounds."

Norma shook her head. "Let's use logic, and not emotion," she said calmly. "I'm known to be here, you're not. So if I cut and run and they catch me, that's it. But if you're caught running loose on this joint, they'll also start looking for me. If I carry my point, you'll still be unexpected. Follow? And someone may get back—the other way, no?"

"I suppose you are right."

"You know I am. It's just false chivalry. You get caught and we're all licked."

He took a deep breath. "You're right, of course."

"Now, here we are and can we be safe here?"

"I think——" He held up a hand abruptly. His ears, attuned to life aboard a spacer, had caught the sound of someone coming up the landing ramp and into the salon a few decks above. Then faint as if it were a hundred yards away but audible in the silence of the ship, they could hear the triple-tongued piping of a man.

He was answered by Carolyn Niles. "Speak Terran!"

Farradyne nudged Norma. "That's the line I used and it worked," he chuckled.

Carolyn's companion said, "Why use this mono-voice junk?"

"You know the rules. It's not smart to relax, you idiot."

"All right. So what's the answer?"

"Ask me in Terran."

"All right, Your Highness. I was merely inquiring as to the imminence of your take-off."

"Don't be insolent! We're taking off as soon as we're all aboard. Now get along with your work!"

The next voice scared them both out of a year's growth; they had been straining to hear Carolyn and her companion high above them in the salon, and now, with every nerve tense, the sound of the ship's intercom roared at them with terrifying volume. "Carolyn Niles! Go aloft, will you, and put the——" there came a triple-voiced syllable "——into standby!"

Carolyn's voice replied, "Aye-firm. But look, boys, shouldn't we have some Terran term for the space drive?"

"We ought to," acknowledged one of the men in the inspection cubby. "But how do you translate it into Terran terms when they have no term for it themselves?"

The other man said, "We could always use 'space drive'."

"No good. Better we didn't mention it at all. Leave it as it is."

Farradyne whispered, "They're a canny bunch. Talk the language always, act the part always, live the life always; and cut your enemy short when he's looking for something alien."

Another pair of feet came up the landing ramp, and Carolyn said, almost at the same time. "It's on. How's she working?"

"Fine. We're finished. Coming up."

"I want to see."

"Okay, so you come down and see. We're coming up and getting started."

"Pincered!" said Farradyne to Norma.

He drew her to the cargo hold and handed her down the service ladder. He followed, closing the door behind him and then, before he snapped out the lights, he reached up and removed one of them, saying, "I don't think we'll have an inspection, but if we do, having one lamp missing will cast a shadow we can stand in. This is a dimly lit joint at best." He waved at the shadow caused by the empty socket and then snapped the lamp off.

They sat with their feet pulled up beneath them, not daring to say a word. Her breathing, and the faint pressure of her shoulder against his told him of her presence beside him.

They waited in the dark silence, listening, and

occasionally tensing instinctively when someone clumped past the wall outside or seemed to come near the cargo hatch above their heads. There were voices and calls and running feet from time to time, and then the humming sound of the conveyor-belt.

The hatch above was opened wide but the lights were not put on.

And then from the end of the loose-cargo conveyor came a tumbling shower of hellblossoms. They landed on the floor in a conical heap and kept coming until both Farradyne and Norma were shoulder deep in them. The air filled with the thick, syrupy perfume. Farradyne felt a slight spell of dizziness from the heady odor and then wondered with horrified interest just what effect this completely unpredictable overdose of dope would do to the woman.

The shower of hellflowers came on and on, and Farradyne was forced to stand because of their depth. Still they came and he found himself swimming off his depth in them; it reminded him of treading in a haymow.[3] The rain of blossoms ceased as the hold filled and the lights went on briefly for an inspection.

Farradyne was propped neck deep, his head barely below the ceiling and he felt quite safe from detection unless the inspectors put their heads down into the hatch to peer around the edges of the cylindrical hold. He looked at Norma. She had scrabbled up and a-top the pile and was lying on her back with her arms thrown over her head. Her eyes were closed, but as she drew in a deep breath, the lids went half-up and she looked over at Farradyne and smiled ecstatically.

The hatch slammed down, and she said huskily, "Such nice friends you have, Charles."

He wanted to ask her if she didn't find this friendship

---

[3] A stack of hay.

a bit overpowering, but instead he said, "They're certainly no friends of mine."

"Nor mine. But this is . . ." and her voice trailed away to a whisper that he could not catch.

Pressure came upsurging and Farradyne felt that he did not have to explain that the Lancaster was on its way to space and perhaps back toward home. In the midst of the take-off pressure she found his hand and drew it toward her, she snuggled her face against his palm. Her free hand came over and touched his cheek, then ran back around his head. She pulled him forward until she could rest her head against his shoulder with her forehead against his face.

Her fingers ran through his hair and pressed his face to hers. He tried to free himself, but he could not escape without being rough about it and he believed that any bold move to elude her would bring forth either pleas or bitter demands loud enough to bring the enemy on the run. He struggled a bit, his hands closed on either side of her waist but instead of moving away, her body came forward against his.

Then, abruptly, the pressure of the drive went off and they floated free.

Their weight upon the cushion of flowers was released and the springiness of the hellblossoms thrust them up, hard, hurling them against the ceiling.

Norma's hands were dragged free of his head and, in clutching at him frantically, her fingernails raked his cheek. The pressure he held against her waist thrust her away as soon as she lost her leverage. Her head hit the ceiling with a dull thunk, followed by the soft sound of her body hitting flat. A sigh came from her lips, but it was the sigh of an unconscious person.

The hold was filled with hellflowers floating free and spread apart by the tiny pressure of the ends of their leaves and petals; Farradyne fought them away frantically, but only succeeded in digging himself deeper in the room.

Eventually he found the service ladder and clung to it, waving himself a breathing space by pushing the floating blossoms back.

Norma's inert hand touched him limply. Farradyne toyed with the idea of reviving her but gave it up instantly; let her sleep it off, and preferably alone and elsewhere in this hold. He gave the hand a push and she floated from him in the dark, pushing through the free mass by her heavier inertia.

The exertion had called upon his reserves and he drank in lungfuls of air that was stickily laden with the heavy perfume. It made him dizzy again and he fought for air, only succeeding in drawing more of the thick scent into his system. He wondered haphazardly what the effect of an overdose of love lotus might have on a man; the experiment had been tried but not to this extent. So far all it did was to make him feel as though he were being doctored with a dose of nitrous oxide.

He scrabbled up the ladder and opened the hatch cautiously. It was as dark outside as it was inside and Farradyne pushed the hatch up further to put his face in the clean air and take a deep breath. Then, because he felt better, he climbed out of the hold and floated free in the air above the hatch. He latched onto a handrail and closed the hatch carefully with a breathed, "You like 'em, baby. You breathe 'em until I get back!"

Then he sat in mid-air with one hand hooked in the rail and, with deep breaths of the clean air, tried to think what to do next.

19

He prowled the cargo hold level, floating along the circular corridor. He knew it was not the safest thing to do but preferred anything to a return to the hold. He did not stop to decide whether it was the perfume of the lotus or the presence of the doped woman that kept him away from his cover.

An hour passed, then two, and Farradyne was growing bolder by the minute. He had covered the entire lower level of his Lancaster and had stopped above his former hiding place speculating whether to hide or not.

He decided not, and went floating upward through the ship until he came to the stateroom level. He floated around the corridor noticing that the little flags that indicated that the door was locked from the inside were all down except one. One of his "guests" did not trust his fellow travelers completely.

He floated on upstairs to the salon and almost ruined his silent flight by trying to put on the brakes. On the divan lay a man in his clothing, restrained by the hold-down safety strap. He was sound asleep.

Farradyne floated over, and then taking hold of the strap to keep himself from flying free with the motions, he deepened the man's slumber with a vicious cut of his revolver.

He floated on into the control room, where the silent and

distant stars watched. Some of them were moving down; these would be the nearby stars, while the rest stood as immobile as he had always known them. He would have preferred to stay and watch the effect of traveling faster than light, for the aspect of the sky directly above was very strange in color and in constellation. But he knew that he had started something and he could see this odd, stellar phenomenon at some more leisured time.

He took a roll of two-inch adhesive tape from the medicine supplies and taped the unconscious man's wrists and ankles and then slapped a length over the mouth that sealed up the gash along the side of the head at the same time. Then he went down to his own quarters and opened the door slowly.

A second man slept there, but Farradyne did not lash out with the pistol. He holstered the gun and clipped the enemy along the side of the jaw with a sharp chop of his hand. Tape was applied quickly and effectively.

That made two.

He considered the situation carefully. So long as his batting average stayed at one thousand he was in fine shape. All it had to meet was one error and he was out of the game. His chances were not too good, but they were helped by the fact that he was an unknown enemy among them.

This was some sort of undeclared war, but the Lancaster could hardly have been termed a warship, since there were no space battles to fight. The ship ran itself, there was nothing to watch, so they did what all spacemen do, sleep. If he could catch them one by one . . .

He opened Stateroom One. It was empty. That put a different light on things. Maybe this was not a fully loaded transport. Maybe it was just like the average cargo-haul with only a couple of passengers.

He opened Stateroom Two and found it empty. That sort of proved it. He opened Stateroom Three and found a man asleep in the bunk. The enemy was stirring as Farradyne scanned the room, and he moved just as Farradyne hastily launched himself across the cabin. Haste ruined his aim so that his down-slashing hand clipped the man on the skull instead of hitting him alongside the ear. The man grunted and swung out blindly, hitting Farradyne and moving him up and away. Farradyne caught the upright of the bunk, staying his free flight, levered himself around and swung again.

The enemy parried the blow and let out a roar that sounded like three angry locomotives tooting for the right of way. Farradyne pulled himself down and around, then kicked out with both feet, catching the man in the face and chest. The force drove his man deep into the mattress, from which he rebounded to fold up over the hold-down strap. He flopped up and down, limp, an inert mass caught between two springs. The same force drove Farradyne out toward the open door.

His aim was still bad, his outsweeping hand caught the leading edge of the door and he and it swung on the hinges until he came flat against the wall behind the door. He fought his body around and came out of the room feet first.

Catching at the handrail he stabilized his flight, then he took notice of his surroundings, expecting the whole enemy horde to come boiling out of their staterooms.

A door down the hall opened and a man came sailing out. He caught sight of Farradyne and launched himself at the spaceman. Farradyne met him with a slash of the pistol, which was parried by a block of the man's forearm against Farradyne's wrist. It stopped the enemy's flight but tore Farradyne's hold loose.

Farradyne recovered first, hauling himself erect just in time to let the other man peer down the barrel of the gun. "Hold it, friend," he snapped.

The enemy, about to kick himself forward, took a firm

hold on the handrail behind him and retracted his feet from against the wall.

"You can't get away with it, Farradyne."

"I can try, Brenner. So happy to meet you again."

Warily he listened. There were no other sounds along the corridor, only the one he expected, and soon the little flag on the lock went in and the door opened. Carolyn Niles came out in pajamas and coat, her eyes blinking slightly. "What's the——" Then she gasped. "Charles!"

"Howdedo. Any more hiding in the dark, Carolyn?"

"How did you get here?"

"I walked," he said flatly. He turned to Brenner. "You stay there, schoolmaster. I'm scared to death and a bit touchy."

Brenner shook his head. "I know you're scared. I'm scared, too. Scared to move."

"Relax—but do it slowly. Now turn around and make it hand over hand toward the salon. You follow the gentleman," he said to Carolyn.

Farradyne followed them both, calling to Brenner that if he tried any tricks, Carolyn might get in the way of the shot intended for him. They went up the stairway, one, two, three, and floated into the salon, Farradyne making a bit of a time of it because of his full gun-hand. He hooked his legs around the guardrail and eyed them coldly.

"Carolyn, let's see how good a job you can do on Brenner's wrists with a chunk of this tape." He tossed the roll at her and she clutched wildly and missed.

"Go get it!"

Carolyn performed some intricate free-flight maneuvers before she caught the roll. Then she went to Brenner, who held his hands out behind him while she ran tape around the wrists.

"I'd be willing to bet that's a slipshod job," said Farradyne. "But it will probably hold until I can relax. Carolyn, coast over here and force yourself to sit in the straight chair."

Farradyne taped her to the chair by the wrists and the ankles and took a slight hitch in the hold-down strap. Then he added some security to Brenner's bond and taped the man to the legs of the divan at the ankles. With his hands behind him and the strap tight across the man's hips, Farradyne felt that Brenner would be thoroughly immobilized. He propped the still unconscious one up near Brenner and taped him similarly.

Then he took time to go below and collect the third from his cabin and bring him up. The man was struggling against the wide tape and glaring at Farradyne over the plaster on his lips. Farradyne hurled him backside first at the divan and followed him, to catch the man on the rebound from the divan. He taped him as he had taped the others, then he took a small flight to the bar, where he perched on top of it by hooking his feet around one of the bar stools.

"Aren't we a good-looking bunch?" he chuckled. "Shall we sing?"

"Stop it, Farradyne," snapped Brenner.

Farradyne's twisted smile faded. "We'll play this game according to my rules for awhile."

"How long do you think you'll be able——"

"Long enough. I'm running this show."

"You can't get away with it."

"You said that before. Convince me, Brenner."

"Why bother with you? I'm the one that counts."

"Cut it out," Farradyne said contemptuously. "I should think your position would feel a bit awkward for a conqueror."

"The sooner you free us, the——"

Farradyne laughed in one loud humorless bark. "So I'm still your prisoner?"

"In a way. You wouldn't care to die without telling what you know about us. You'll do anything to stay alive."

"You damn well bet! And I'll do anything to learn a bit more."

"You can't make me talk."

"Want to bet? I don't think I could squeeze anything out of you by torture, but I have a hunch you'll sing loud and long after you watch me take Carolyn's fingernails off with long-nosed pliers and listen to her stifled sobbing. An old-fashioned torture, but still effective."

Carolyn looked at Farradyne coldly. "Come to think of it, Charles, I don't think you have enough sadism to perform the operation on me."

Farradyne looked at her. He held enough dislike of what she stood for to do almost anything with cold deliberation, for he thought any pain was small retribution. But she was still a woman.

Carolyn sniffed cynically, and Farradyne realized that he had mumbled the last few words of his thoughts. "Just retribution, Charles, but have you the guts to collect your revenge?"

He looked down at her. "No, I haven't. But I've someone with me who might."

He took aim and sailed down the stairs. He soared around the stateroom corridor and ran full-tilt into a flurry of floating skirt. He hurled Norma from him and recoiled. When he caught himself again, he had one hand braced against the handrail and the pistol aimed at the middle of her stomach. She righted herself as he let out his breath and relaxed his gun-hand.

"Don't ever do that!" he said sharply.

She looked at the gun and her face went white with the realization of how close it had been. She looked at him searchingly as if seeking company for her fright. She apparently found it, for her face relaxed and she took a deep breath, let it out slowly. Then she fought the hem of her skirt down again and blushed.

Farradyne chuckled, "Go into Number Four and swipe a

pair of Carolyn Niles' pajamas," he said. "They don't float. Then come up to the salon."

He turned and headed back slowly, stalling until he heard her return to the corridor.

He went first and helped her make the curve around the railing at the top. Solicitously,[1] he steered her to the divan and fastened the seat strap.

Then he faced Carolyn and the rest. "Speaking of retribution," he said slowly. "I'd like you to meet a woman I know. Miss Norma Hannon. She's a hellflower addict. Whatever she does is basically your responsibility." He said directly to Carolyn, "You have me fairly well pegged. I couldn't do it. But I think that Miss Hannon might enjoy a bit of an emotional binge with the people who fed her the first hellflower and caused the death of her brother." Farradyne turned and sailed across the room to Norma's side. He reached out quietly and removed the love lotus from Norma's hair, then recrossed the room to hurl it into the disposal chute.

"Just sit there quietly until the effects of that thing wear off," he told her. "I'm going to take a tour of inspection of the gewgaw they installed in my ship. I'll be back when they decide to answer questions."

Farradyne dived down the stairway again. He had no idea how long it might take, especially after Norma had been literally sleeping in a smothering roomful of the things for hours. Probably long enough for them all to get the whim-whams just thinking about it, he concluded.

He conned[2] every stateroom on his way down. He was reasonably certain that the ruckus would have awakened them all, but he wanted to make sure that no one in them was lying doggo[3] until he could make his bid. They were all empty, so Farradyne went on down in the Lancaster,

---

[1] In this context: eagerly.
[2] To study or examine carefully.
[3] Lying quietly and motionless to escape detection.

checking the supply rooms and the galley and workshop, the other cargo lock and the storage room. He looked into the inspection cubbies and the wiring hatches until he had covered every nook and cranny that was large enough to contain a human being.

The ship was clean.

He stopped once more to eye the four metal cases bolted to the floor and discovered that the gentleman who had occupied the place when he and Norma tried to hide had put nuts on the bolt ends and run the cables neatly below-deck so they no longer trailed. He went up, then, all the way.

"Any talk?" he asked brightly as he soared through the salon.

"Farradyne, you can't do this!" snapped Brenner.

"Who, me?" asked Farradyne, in mock surprise. "I'm not doing anything!"

Norma was still sitting in her seat on the divan. She had not changed position. But her face was losing its softness and her attention was no longer diverted easily. "I'm waiting," she told him as he passed upward to the control room.

Somehow, Farradyne believed, it would not be very long waiting.

20

Farradyne paid no attention to the oddness of the sky because it could tell him nothing and he had more interesting things to inspect. The little auxiliary panel was gone. The controls had been incorporated in the main panel, neatly and as if they had always been there; in such a way as to make any but a completely critical inspection pass them over. They blended with the other myriad controls, so that only the pilot of the ship would be able to find them.

There was a small meter, calibrated arbitrarily in three sectors of colors. The needle stood high in the middle of the blue region. Below the meter was a cross-bar toggle switch and on either side of the toggle were flat buttons set flush with the panel, blue to the right and red to the left. The wiring was concealed, Farradyne found by looking under the panel that it had been neatly inserted into the main bundle of cables and wires as though it had been installed with the Lancaster's construction.

He considered the installation carefully.

In the history of warfare, Farradyne had heard of no one installing a device that would blow up a whole equipment if the operator used the wrong combination. In fact, designers worked hard to make such equipment fool-proof because they knew how rattled a man can get in the heat of battle.

The worst he could do was probably the blowing of a fuse if he tampered with it. On the other hand . . .

So much for that, he thought, and went on to the next matter: destruction charges.

Big prime movers like battlecraft and stationary installations seldom fell into the hands of an enemy in any condition to be reused. Either the big stuff was shot to hell before the enemy captured it and was therefore unfunctional, or there was time for the crew to render the big stuff useless long before the installation was abandoned. There were booby-traps, of course, but these were usually improvised on the spot, or at least installed from a stock closet at the time of possible capture. No thinking nation would ever install a booby-trap permanently because of the possibility of the operator punching the wrong button.

Self-destruction devices were another item. These came shortly after the Military discovered the electron, and at a time when there were basic new designs of equipment the function of which it had been necessary to keep secret from the enemy. Countless pieces of apparatus had been equipped with self-destruction charges heavy enough to addle the insides of the gear, and possibly bulge the case a bit. But a man could sit on one of them while the charge went off and the most he would get would be a sharp kick in the pants.

But such destruction charges were controlled from a separate panel. There could be no mistake or error; no one could hit the wrong button. Destruction must be performed with deliberation.

And so Farradyne eyed the new installation calmly. It might hold a self-destruction charge, but the probabilities of having the control handy enough to be used in the heat of excitement were remote, especially since such a condition would leave a ship and crew marooned in the depths of interstellar space to die because someone's finger slipped.

Farradyne was even certain that not much could happen if he tinkered with the toggle, so long as they were in deep space by some light years distant from anything large and hard.

He took the toggle bar in his right hand and pulled. It did not pull so he pushed. It did not push. He turned the cross-bar slightly and exerted effort. The bar moved downward in a wide arc and as it moved, the seat of the chair slammed upward against the seat of his pants, and all of a sudden up was up and down was down, and the stars were all in their right places. The toggle came to a stop and the accelerometer read one gravity. The needle on the meter still read halfway into the blue.

Farradyne chuckled aloud. He had it now. If the traffic lights flared blue-green for "GO" and red-orange for "STOP" he had this combination as well. Start your spacecraft and punch the blue button for start. That was the beginning and the warm-up and nothing could happen until the meter read into the blue section of its scale. Then the toggle controlled the action of whatever generator of force was used, more or less as the toggle was advanced or depressed. The equipment stayed in readiness all the time. The red button was undoubtedly the cut-off button to close the gear down once the flight was completed.

It was as simple as that. Farradyne had spent many an hour in spacemen's bars up and down the solar system in spacemen's happy arguments regarding the complexities of exotic equipment, so he could theorize on both sides. The pro side was a matter of insisting that electromechanical principles were universal and therefore an alien bit of gear would function in a recognizable manner. The con side considered the fruitless arguments that something new might be discovered or that the evolution of instruments from the original principles would follow the normal dexterity of the alien life-form involved. But Farradyne knew that buttons

ch. ends p. 191

are buttons and therefore meant to be pushed, not pulled; and similarly, D'Arsonval[1] had invented the same kind of galvanometer[2] as Ugthrybb, on Vega, with a moving coil between the poles of a magnet, and just because one race was right-handed and the other left, the principle did not change.

Then, being of a practical frame of mind, Farradyne forgot the subject and began to wonder about his position and what he was going to do about it. He squinted into the point-of-drive telescope and caught sight of a tiny yellow star on the crosshairs. That must be Sol, distant, small, and far weaker than Sol as seen from Pluto. It was a true stellar point from here.

Then he looked through the point-of-departure periscope and automatically cut the drive so that the flare would not blind him.

Behind was the constellation of Lyra and on the crosshairs was another star of no particular consequence. No more important than Sol. He got out the Spaceman's Star Catalog and opened it to Lyra. Among the listings were a number of the F, G, and K classifications, and one of them, about twenty-seven light years from Sol was listed for the right position in the constellation. Farradyne grunted; it meant nothing to him. It was merely Lyra.

The sound of a whimper cut into his thought and he remembered the possibilities of the scene in the salon. He waited. He snapped on the intercom and listened, wondering whether he could sit there and let Norma go to work on Carolyn. Man's inhumanity to man was a pale and insignificant affair compared to the animal ferocity of a woman

---

[1] Jacques-Arsène d'Arsonval (1851–1940) was a French physician, physicist, and inventor of the moving-coil D'Arsonval galvanometer and the thermocouple ammeter.

[2] An instrument for detecting and measuring electric currents.

about to settle up a long-standing account with another woman.

"Charles, come down here and take this madwoman away!" cried Carolyn.

Farradyne sauntered down the stairs. Norma stood before the bound Carolyn. Her eyes were glassy, her face cold. In one hand she held a small bottle of acid from Farradyne's workshop, in the other a small, pointed brush. As he came down the stairs, Norma dipped the brush in the acid and approached Carolyn, holding the brush as she would a pencil.

Farradyne held her hand. "Wait!" he said.

Norma looked at him with a trace of anger in her eyes. "Don't stop me," she said. "I'm going to write 'Hellflower' across that alabaster forehead—among other words."

Farradyne shuddered. His imagination had stopped working at the point of removing fingernails and applying lighted cigarettes to the skin. Now it leaped forward again and he could see the outcome of this assault upon the woman's pride and beauty. A formerly flawless skin covered with scar-tissue lettering of accusals, viciousness, and probably lewdness.

"Take her away!" said Carolyn. "There is no point in this."

"Why not? Or are you ready to talk?"

"I'll talk. I'll talk because you will never get a chance to use it."

"You talk and I'll take my chances on that. Give me the works."

Norma struggled a bit. "Please, Farradyne?"

"Maybe later," he said soothingly. "Sit down now, and wait."

Angrily, Norma turned and headed for the divan.

He turned to Carolyn. "What the hell is going on and why?"

"This is war," she said.

ch. ends p. 191

"Like hell it's war. This is backstabbing. But it'll be war as soon as we can fight back."

"It is war," she repeated. "Let it go at that. The process should not be unfamiliar to you; you've done it yourselves time and again. First you weaken the enemy by undermining his resources, lowering his resistance, by turning his efforts toward advancement against some stumbling block. Then——"

"I presume that doping the women of a race is a right and honorable practice?" sneered Farradyne.

"It is better than dropping a mercurite bomb.[3] Face the fact, Charles. We got to interstellar space first and met another people as racially jealous as we are. We could have made a landing openly, but if we had, the warfare you are threatening would have been here and done with long ago and there would be nothing left of either of our people but smoldering planets to mark the meeting place of two stellar peoples."

"You can say this knowing that no Solan has the barest notion of how this doodad in the hold can permit us to travel faster than light?"

Carolyn looked at him with pity. "I'll tell you what would happen," she said. "You'd greet us with cheers and invite us in—long enough to steal our warp-generator. You'd trade us your medical science for our chemistry and your electronics for our gravities, and then you'd meet us face to face to prove to yourselves that even though you got a second-place start, you could move faster and hit harder than we could. You'd carry your war to us, and we'd carry our war to you, and there would be cause and effect and attack and retaliation with each blow a bit more vicious until your people would be planting mercurite at the same time we were. And then, as I say, the next interstellar race to visit this section of

---

[3] A fictional bomb created by Smith, but alludes to mercurate, which means to treat or combine with mercury or a mercury compound.

the sky would find the radioactive remains of two cultures. I know because our people come of the same stock."

He looked at her cynically. "Is that so? Where I come from it takes three people to sing a trio, Carolyn. How do you explain that?"

"That's a recessive mutation."

"All right," he snapped. "So you've justified your own actions to yourself."

"Of course. Everybody is self-justified."

"And you justify the doping of our race by calling it better than meeting us face to face."

"Remember your own history. Even before the First Atomic War everybody realized that warfare was a bankrupt measure to be undertaken after all else had failed. You conducted your conflicts undercover, by boring from within, by undermining the moral fiber and lowering resistance. So, when your people have lost the ability to fight back, we'll move in quietly and make an asset of you instead of a vicious enemy; ultimately a ruined structure that must be rebuilt completely before it is of any use to us."

"Got it all figured out, haven't you?" sneered Farradyne. "All except a few of us who happen to catch on. Then what—if we don't exactly cotton to the idea?"

There was a yelp from behind him and he turned just in time to intercept Norma. She was advancing on Brenner with her acid-brush poised. "Don't, Norma," he said gently, turning her aside.

"But you said——"

"Later." He gave her a gentle shove toward the side of the room and she went reluctantly. "Brenner," he said sharply, "I want information."

"Ask," replied Brenner. "What can we lose?"

"Navigational data," said Farradyne, ignoring the question. "Where are we and how fast does that gizmo run us?"

"I'd guess about six light years out from Sol. The warp

generator permits a top speed of about two light years per hour in Terran figures. So go ahead and drive this can somewhere so we can get this fool rigmarole over with. But take the dame aloft with you. I don't want my face lettered like a washroom wall."

"Somehow it seems appropriate," chuckled Farradyne, but he took Norma by the hand and led her up the stairs. She followed like an automaton[4] until they were out of sight, and then she came alive.

Visibly she relaxed. The granite set to her face faded and became soft. Her lips curved gently and her eyes were animated. She walked briskly across the control room, and turned down the outgoing gain before she turned to face Farradyne.

"Charles, that was the hardest acting job I've ever done."

She snapped her acid bottle into one of the spring-containers so that it wouldn't float all over the place under weightlessness and then she went to the co-pilot's seat and dropped into it casually. She relaxed with her head leaned back.

"How long after a sniff of hellflower does the effect last?" asked Farradyne.

"Depends. I could feel the euphoria fading shortly after you took mine out of my hair. The odd part of it was that it seemed different, somehow. I feel so odd. Dizzy and weak and somehow frightened. I'd like to be held, gently, and caressed like a kitten." She sat up and half turned to look over the back of the co-pilot's seat. "This is honest, Charles. I know, I can feel it; it's true and it's good, Charles. Oh, yes," she said in a matter-of-fact voice, "I remember everything. This isn't an act, Charles. This is the real thing. I've seemed to regain my feelings again. Actually, I can almost feel sorry for them, you know?" Her voice ended on an upward note.

---

[4] In this context: one who acts or responds in a mechanical way, much like a robot.

Farradyne looked at her. Bemused, he said, "Could it be the hair of the dog?"

"Hair of the dog?" she repeated automatically.

"The one that bit you," he said. "You were in an awful overload dose, Norma; maybe the overload burned the dross out, like fire cleansing a wound. Maybe——"

Norma blushed. "You were very gentle," she said.

He realized what she meant. He recalled the stories he had heard of sophisticates who took their hellflowers to heighten the emotional thrill of a symphony or a dinner; of men who had enough love for their women to let them plumb the depths of emotion without using the exhilarant as the cold means to a crude end. He had been with her through her emotional binge and he had seen her through it quietly. The fact that he had not wanted her, in fact repulsed her, had helped. She had not been burned by piling passion a-top a heightened emotional response.

He looked into her eyes critically. They were alive and soft. Could it be that an overdose of the same devilish stuff could cure the effects of its own?

"How do you feel?" he asked gently.

"Weak, washed out, but I can go on and on," she said confidently. She didn't look it, but maybe she could, he thought. Excitement would carry a person through a lot of trials. He looked at her again and understood that he was right. She would go on and on, until the strain was over and then she would probably come completely unglued for some time.

Farradyne put out a hand and stroked her cheek. She sighed against his hand and moved her head from side to side. She reached up and pulled his face down to kiss him on the lips. It was brief but warmly satisfying.

She laid back in the co-pilot's seat, relaxed. "It's all there again," she said dreamily. "That same fast pulse and the tingle—and the rather interesting feeling of danger. I'm a woman again, Charles; just a very little bit concerned about

ch. ends next p.

being marooned in a spacecraft with you. Let's get back home where I can enjoy my feelings. Please?"

Farradyne gave her hand a squeeze. "Done!" he glowed. Silently he wondered whether she were really cured. He looked at her, at the glow in her eyes and at the blush on her face, and he hoped so.

He slipped over the back of the pilot's seat and pushed down hard on the toggle bar. The weightlessness came, and the compressed springs of their seats tossed them up against the restraining straps. From below there came a moan, but beside him, Norma relaxed in full confidence and watched him work the controls with interest.

Two light years an hour . . . Farradyne ran the Lancaster for exactly three hours and then cut the super-drive. Together they inspected the heavens and found a brilliant yellow star on their quarter. Farradyne turned the ship to face it and pushed the toggle up and down. The star reappeared without change. He kept his eye to the point-of-flight telescope and raised the toggle slowly. Sol changed color, racing toward the blue and the violet first and then turning a dull red and rising through the spectrum again until it became violet once more. It went through another spectrum change and started to increase in size.

Whatever caused this phenomenon could not be explained by Farradyne; perhaps by no living Solan physicist until many years of research brought forth a theory.

But regardless of the theories-to-come, Sol grew in size like a toy balloon hitched to a high-pressure air line until its flare frightened the pilot. He shoved the toggle down and Sol winked back into the familiar disc of blinding sun, about the size as seen from Mars.

Farradyne oriented himself with his knowledge of common celestial navigation, consulted the spaceman's ephemeris and pointed at a large unwinking spot. "Home," he said.

Two light years an hour . . . Farradyne went to the computer and made some calculations. He returned, pointed the Lancaster at Terra and flicked the toggle up and down, counting off a few seconds for drive. Sol whiffled past, changing in color as its position changed in the astrodome, and when Farradyne drove the toggle down, Terra was a distant disc in the sky above them.

Farradyne turned the outgoing gain on the intercom. "Terra dead ahead," he called to the prisoners below. "Still want to bet?"

Brenner growled. "You've got your bet. It's our lives against yours."

"Done!"

"Don't try to collect too soon," snapped Brenner. "You're not leading your squadron of spacebombers yet."

Farradyne picked up his throat-whistle and put it in his mouth. He worked it back with his tongue and said, "The hell you say, Brenner." The result was a humming, whining, groaning travesty.

21

"We'll not repeat," said Farradyne. "Norma, hike below and see that our visitors stay taped to their chairs. I'm going to land this crate without interference."

Norma nodded and went down to the salon. "They're still secure," she reported over the intercom.

Farradyne replied, "Aye-firm," and then made his first ranging-radar contact with Terra. He set his deceleration drive accordingly and the integrator-needle crept over to the center-scale zero, informing Farradyne that zero separation from the surface of the spaceport would result in zero velocity of the Lancaster.

Then Farradyne fired up the radio and called: "Washington Tower. This is a Lancaster Eighty-One requesting landing instructions. Registry Six-Eight-Three. Farradyne piloting."

"Tower to Six-Eight-Three. Take Beacon Nine at one twenty thousand, Landing Area Five. Traffic is zero-zero, but eight repeat eight Spaceguard cutters are in formation at sixty thousand." The voice changed in tone slightly. "Spaceguard, Code Watchung. Calling Watchung."

"Watchung to Tower, go ahead."

"Tower. Watchung, we are away from Beacon Nine. Lancaster Eighty-One coming in. Give position and course."

"Watchung to Tower. Position azimuth[1] six seven zero, altitude sixty thousand, distance nine miles. Course twenty-seven North azimuth. Will miss Beacon Nine by thirty-three miles. Recheck?"

"Recheck and aye-firm, Watchung. Tower to Six-Eight-Three: Did you follow that?"

"Aye-firm!" called Farradyne.

"Watchung to Six-Eight-Three: Pilot identify yourself."

"Pilot Farradyne here, Watchung."

"Aye-firm. Watchung Five, assume command of Six, Seven, and Eight. Take alert pattern at two hundred thousand feet and stand by. Watchung Two, Three, and Four compute and take closing course on Six-Eight-Three and convey to Landing Area Five. Farradyne, prepare to accept convoy."

"Deny, Watchung. Request reasons."

"Prepare to accept inspection, Six-Eight-Three."

Farradyne growled angrily and dropped the radio formalities. "Why?" he snapped.

"You are suspected of hauling a cargo of hellflowers. Prepare to stand inspection upon landing."

From down in the salon came the sound of cynical laughter. Brenner said, "We'll let your own people punish you, Farradyne. Hellblossom running, resisting arrest, kidnapping, operating with a forged license, operating a ship with a questionable registry. I'll bet that life you offered."

Farradyne knew what Brenner meant. Taped tight in his ship were Carolyn Niles, daughter of one of Mercury's leading citizens, and a schoolteacher supposedly named Hughes. There would no doubt be a lot of other witnesses prepared to perjure him into three hundred years of hard labor on Titan. He wondered how they had managed this; certainly they had not been prepared for losing their captured spacecraft

---

[1] The horizontal angle measured clockwise between a celestial object and the northern point of the horizon as seen by the observer.

so quickly. Yet the counter-preparation looked as though such an eventuality had been expected.

"Six-Eight-Three, respond!"

Farradyne snapped his mike-switch and said, "I resent the accusation and demand an explanation!"

"There is no accusation. We have an anonymous tip-off. You are not accused of illegal operations, only suspect. Will you permit inspection?"

"No!" snapped Farradyne. "Deny!"

"Code Watchung: Intercept Six-Eight-Three. Prepare to fire."

"Fire and be damned," said Farradyne in a growl. His hand reached for the toggle and shoved it home for ten seconds. When he turned the ultradrive off, they were far a-space and the radio was silent.

"Give it up, Charles," said Carolyn from below.

"Go to hell!"

Brenner said, "You might as well, Farradyne. No matter how you figure it, you'll either be grabbed by your own people or get picked up by ours. We can't lose."

Farradyne went below and faced them. "And what happens if I dump you out of the spacelock and your cargo with you?"

"You could do that to Cahill," said Carolyn, "because Cahill was not registered as a paying passenger. I am, and when the authorities find me missing—as they will very soon if they haven't been so informed already—you'll be called to account for me."

"Just what sort of act do you suggest?" Farradyne asked cynically.

"Surrender and turn this ship over to us. You will be detained as a prisoner of war and imprisoned among your own kind."

"Doing what kind of prison labor? Growing hellflowers?"

"Not at all. We wouldn't consider that ethical."

"What a cockeyed code of ethics you have!"

"Let's not discuss ethics now. Surrender and you'll be placed on a Terra-conformed planet with every freedom among your own kind except the right to space flight."

"No, thanks," said Farradyne dryly. "I had four years of slogging in a fungus marsh because of your kind. I'm disinclined to give up after one miss. It——"

"Charles!" cried Norma through the squawk-box. "Come up here! Radar trace!"

Farradyne raced up the stairs just in time to see the long green line of the radar settling down to a solid signal pip at the extreme end. He flipped the switch that coupled the telescope to the radar and looked through the eyepiece. At the extreme range of the radar beam was a spacecraft, either the same starship that had chased him before or its sister ship. It was closing the range fast.

Farradyne dropped into his chair and snapped the belt. He turned the Lancaster by ninety degrees and grasped the toggle on the ultradrive. Ten seconds later he resumed normal flight for a few seconds and then, at another angle, he used the ultradrive some more.

He paused here long enough to take his space bearing, then plunged the ship down between the orbits of Jupiter and Saturn, far to the south of the ecliptic with a flick of the enemy switch.

"Norma," he asked quietly, after he had inspected the sky to be certain of their freedom, "who is Howard Clevis' boss?"

"Howard reports to Solon Forrester directly."

"Oh fine," groaned Farradyne. "Getting to the Solon is no picnic. How do we go about it?"

From the intercom came a suggestion: "Walk into his fourth under-assistant sub-secretary's office wearing a hellflower and ask for an audience."

A flick of color caught Farradyne's eye and he turned to look at the radar. The line had wiggled slightly and, as he watched, its extreme end formed into a signal pip. He looked through the telescope and saw the starship again. Whether they had one with supervelocity tracking methods or several hundred covering the solar system like an interception net, it made no difference. They were on his trail.

Farradyne played with the high-space drive again, cutting some more didoes back and forth across space, ending up this time not too far from Mercury.

"Having fun?" asked Brenner.

"Shut up!" snapped Farradyne.

From below there came a rapid conversation in multi-tones, like someone dusting off the keys on a pipe organ played in mute.

Farradyne swore as he sat there looking at the big chronometer on the wall, counting off the seconds. Seventy of them went under the sweep hand before the radar trace hiked up into the same, familiar extreme-range warning.

Deliberately, Farradyne turned his ship toward Terra and hit the ultradrive. "They called me a hot-pants pilot," he gritted. "Now I'll really be one!"

Yellow-green Terra raced up and up and up through the spectrum and burst in size from an unwinking pinpoint of light to a shockingly large disc that zoomed toward them frighteningly. They saw its roundness come out of the sky in myriad colors until it filled the dome above them. Norma screamed, but by the time her voice had stopped echoing through the control room, Terra was past them by a good many miles of clean miss and Farradyne had cut the ultradrive. He grunted unhappily because he was now as far from Terra on the other side as he had been before he took the chance. This mad use of the enemy ultradrive in ducking around the solar system was something similar to trying to make a fifty-ton clam-shell digger split a cigarette paper; at two light years per hour, their speed was enough to take them from Sol to Pluto in one second flat. He could not control it finely enough to do more than zoom off out of sight. Without a doubt the big starship could maneuver at ultra-velocity with their drive cut in at microsecond intervals mechanico-electrically, of course, which was a setup that Farradyne did not have.

He shrugged, and then he patted Norma on the shoulder. "I don't think that my aim is good enough to hit the thing," he said. He turned the Lancaster end for end abruptly and tried a quick flick of the toggle. Once more Terra leaped at them, a swirling kaleidoscope of color, looming into monster size, flicking past.

When they came out of it Terra was again behind them by a few million miles. Farradyne thought for a moment, started to say, "Maybe we——" when he reached out and pressed the red button on the auxiliary panel, "——are being traced by the generator doodad they put below."

"But what are we going to do now?"

"Hit for Terra!"

Farradyne set the drive for Terra and then sat there, tense and waiting. He had not long to wait. The radar wiggled its warning trace almost dead ahead.

They moved to intercept him, but Farradyne raised the drive to four gravities and plunged on. The starship grew and behind it Terra grew, but slower. The radio burst into sound and Farradyne grabbed the microphone and said, "Come and get me, fellows!"

"Stop," came the demand, "or we fire!"

"Start a shooting match here and you'll have all of Terra wondering why the fireworks," Farradyne said.

"Stop!"

"No!"

"One last warning. Stop!"

Farradyne touched a lever. "Maybe you'd like to polish a few rivets?"

The Lancaster turned ever so slightly until the starship

was directly on the point-of-drive. His other hand touched the drive and the acceleration increased a bit. Caustically, Farradyne said, "Go ahead and shoot! You'll find your own living room full of byproducts if you do!"

He was right. The Lancaster was on collision course with the starship and if the Lancaster was blasted at this moment shards and fragments of the spacecraft would spread like a shotgun charge, and if the starship escaped being hit with a rather uncomfortably large mass of jagged metal it would be because of sheer luck.

"Veer off!" came the strident cry.

"I'm going to ram you, damn you!" roared Farradyne.

The starship flared at its tail and at the same time a torpedo-port winked as a missile blasted off. Farradyne gauged the missile and the starship and kept his nose on the starship's lead. Gritting his teeth he watched the missile come at him as he held his course by sheer nerve. At the last moment the missile veered aside, obviously controlled by the enemy to keep from hitting him. It was a war of nerves.

The starship loomed big in the astrodome and Farradyne aimed the Lancaster amidship.[2] The interstellar monster grew rapidly until the individual plates could be seen. Then with a silent, dark flicker that was as shocking as a loud blast and a searing flare might have been, the starship quietly ceased to exist as an obstacle in front of them. They had resorted to the ultradrive at the last moment. The sky was clear ...

Except for the missile, seeking them and with no control to stop it.

It had curved in a vast circle behind them and was now closing in from behind. The radar pip leaked across the screen; the missile must be coming at them by several thousand gravities.

---

[2] At the middle of a ship.

"You'll have to take this," gritted Farradyne to Norma. "Hunker down in the seat."

His hands ran across the board and the Lancaster turned in space slightly while the drive went up to six gravities. The flare behind them lengthened with the increased power, and the Lancaster took a slight side-vector to its course as the flare was aimed at the seeking-missile that was homing on them.

Insensate,[3] unable to understand the maneuver, the missile followed its finding-gear and roared up into the long trail of reaction flare. The flare was a byproduct of water, stored in its tank as a reaction-mass. It was heated by the atomic pile to an energy that destroyed the molecular affinity of hydrogen for oxygen and then stripped the electrons from their orbits, and when that was done, the nucleus of the oxygen broke up into eight protons and eight neutrons and added their binding energy to the drive. The flare was sheer gamma and sheer bombardment and the word "heat" had no real meaning, until the reaction blast touched something that was massive enough to absorb the energy.

The missile absorbed this energy, was bombarded back from the Lancaster, and ultimately melted to join with the flare because its mechanism could not function to start the fission of the atomics in the warhead.

There was a sparkling burst from behind, like a monster signal flare. That was all.

Farradyne cut the drive back to a more comfortable level and relaxed a moment to let his body rest. Norma had blacked out briefly, but came to as soon as the drive had been cut.

Ahead of them Terra loomed moon-sized in the middle of the astrodome, and behind them the radar wiggled its tail

---

[3] Lacking sense or reason.

at extreme-range again. The range closed, and Farradyne with a grunt juggled his levers. The drive rose once more and the pressure increased. The range closed more slowly, but still the starship came on.

"You can't make it, Farradyne," the radio blared exultantly.

Farradyne laughed into the microphone and cut it dead with a flick of his hand. "We may not make it," he told Norma, "but we won't end up as live cowards!"

Terra loomed larger and larger as the range closed between the Lancaster and the ship behind it. Norma cried out, and Farradyne looked through the telescope to see the giveaway annular flare. The enemy had fired another torpedo.

He laughed and Norma touched his arm; he turned to smile at the deep concern and puzzlement on her face.

"They know we can louse it with our drive," he said. "And they know that while that thing is coming up from behind we cannot possibly make a turn-over and start decelerating for a landing. It's a thoughtful tactic on their part—they hope."

"But I don't see——"

"Well, they know I won't pile up on Terra. I'll steer to miss. No doubt they have another starship on the other side of the planet, waiting to intercept us out here after I elude the missile. Maybe they have a whole space net flung out. So hunker down, while I cut some didoes."

The radar showed the picture. The starship, now fearful of being detected by one of the long-range jobs on Terra, veered away on a tangent, while between them came the missile. Before them, the huge, solid-looking pip that indicated the bulking Terra, crept closer and closer. Farradyne cranked the rate-of-change dials and looked at the figures and nodded; the enemy had computed their missile's drive beautifully. It would meet the Lancaster at about the same time the Lancaster met Terra. Since everybody knew that

Farradyne was not going to plow into Terra head on, he would have to steer to one side, but in order to keep from being hit by the missile, he would have to keep on driving right past Terra and out into space again—into the arms of the net on the other side, waiting outside the radar range from Terra.

The alternative was to cut the drive and try to land, and if this were tried the missile would blast the Lancaster far above Terra, long before the ship could signal its home planet that there was danger in space.

The missile's range closed home and Farradyne hiked the drive until the reaction-trail was a sun-bright fury and consumed the missile in its fierceness.

He cut the drive dead just in time to hear the first screaming complaint of the superstratosphere. Farradyne hit the upper reaches of Terra's air blanket at a point so high that the air there was a fairly hard vacuum, but the speed of the ship was high enough to pile quite a bit of air in front of it. The accelerometer went crazy, reading peg-stop against the end of the scale to the left. Their seat belts cut their thighs and the blood rushed to their heads. Norma's arms were flung above her head, but Farradyne fought the pressure that tried to lift his arms; he kept his hands on the control panel and caressed his levers gently so that the Lancaster pinwheeled.

The screaming of the air grew louder as the ship turned broadside, then diminished as its tail came around to align itself with the course of flight. Then with the pressure coming from the right direction again, Farradyne waited until the scream of tortured upper stratosphere faded away and the braking pressure stopped. He hit the drive as the Lancaster soared on past Terra.

Though the enemy must have been awaiting him on the line of flight past Terra, the Lancaster came nowhere near them. Its course had changed from the usual straight line to a long ellipse and the first turn of the curve had wound their course so far from the anticipated point that the enemy could not move over in time to intercept him. Terra rotated madly below and to the side, then came moving up in the angle of vision until it was at forty-five degrees off the nose and still rising.

Once more Terra loomed close and once more came the scream of air, deeper and yet shriller as Farradyne cut the drive and let the air-brake take over. They went on around Terra in a close ellipse, the air-screech rising and falling as their altitude changed.

Three times around Terra they went, then Farradyne turned his tail straight down with a few hard blasts and started to drop like a plummet.

Far to one side came a light flare and the radio gabbled something that Farradyne was too busy to catch; in the distance a jet freighter trailed a line of vapor and far to the south ultra-brightness of a spacecraft take-off trail climbed into the sky. Farradyne, busy checking the controls, the autopilot and the computing radar altimeter, aimed the Lancaster for the southern edge of Lake Superior, and they came down in a screaming fall.

The flare parted the waters of the Lake and sent up a billow of steam for about a hundredth of a second. The autopilot cut the drive and the violence ceased as the Lancaster sank into the deep, cool waters, to stop, to come rising buoyantly toward the surface again.

Farradyne hit the switch that opened the scuttlebutt of the water tank and the lake waters rushed in, killing their buoyancy.

The astrodome porpoised[4] once, gently, and then the Lancaster sank very slowly. Farradyne waited until the ship was resting tail down on the bottom; he turned it slightly

---

[4] To move through the water like a porpoise, alternately rising above the surface of the water, then submerging.

to one side and opened the drive by a bare fraction. Water churned below them and the ship moved logily sideways, toward the shore. He wondered whether he had enough power coming from the motor to cut up a stream of bubbles and steam, hoping that the cooling water would kill the rising turbulence so as to conceal his operation.

He spent an hour testing and trying the depth along the shore until he found a place that was just deep enough to let the Lancaster stand upright with its dome a foot or two below the surface.

A small fish goggled at the shining metal hungrily.

Farradyne stretched. "We got this far anyway!"

Norma looked at him dizzily. "How?"

"My pappy used to tell me about this sort of come-in," he said. "Seems as how he once knew a gent that had piloted one of the old chemical rockets that used braking ellipses for landings. That was a heck of a long time ago, before we had power to burn. But anyway, it wasn't expected, I gather, because we succeeded."

"Now what?"

Farradyne grinned. "This is going to be a bit wet," he said. He took the retractable antenna from its stowage and wound it with insulating tape half way up its length. Then he pulled out the astrodome plug and ignoring the stream of water that splashed on the control-room floor, he shoved the antenna into the hole and made it fast. The water stopped. The upper half of the antenna projected above the surface of the lake.

Farradyne tuned the radio to a local broadcast station, and waited, relaxing in his seat, until the music stopped for a station break. "The latest news flashes on the system-wide hunt for Charles Farradyne. The search for the notorious hellflower operator still goes on. It has narrowed down to North America because of several reports, some official and some unofficial, of activity a-space in this region.

ch. ends next p.

"Farradyne is also charged with complicity in the disappearance of Howard Clevis, high undercover operative for the SAND Office. It is believed in some circles that Farradyne may be much higher in the love lotus ring than a mere handler or distributor. Some officials have indicated that Farradyne may be *Mr. Big himself*.

"An early interception and arrest is anticipated. Keep tuned to this station for the latest news."

The music returned.

22

"Very neat," said Brenner.

"I thought so," replied Farradyne coldly.

Brenner's smile was serene and it made Farradyne want to push his face in. "Glad you made it. I wouldn't want to die in space. Now that we've landed it's going to be easier to pick you up."

"Stop crowing, Brenner. I'm not licked yet."

"Why don't you give up? You can't begin to realize how isolated you are from the men who might listen to you—if you could get to them."

"Look, Brenner, I've no doubt that you have your henchmen neatly planted in many high offices. But you can't cover them all."

"How can you tell which is which?" laughed Brenner. "You can't get through, Farradyne."

Carolyn stirred and groaned. Farradyne looked at her as she opened her eyes. "Can't take it?" he sneered. "But how you can dish it out!"

"Where are we?" groaned Carolyn.

"Wouldn't tell you on a bet," he snapped. "You might be telepathic as well as multitonal. I——"

Farradyne's eye caught a flicker of motion and he whirled. The other two men were struggling against the tape that bound their wrists and ankles, and they glared at him over the white sheet of tape beneath their noses.

"Shut up!" roared Farradyne.

Brenner sneered. "Just how do you hope to do anything?"

"I have a few ideas."

"With every roadway plugged from top to bottom? And if you did succeed in getting to a SAND office without being shot to bits, how would you convince them of anything?"

"Sometimes it's better to start at the bottom and work your way up," said Farradyne. "The idea is to make enough noise so that a large cross-section of the population can hear you."

Brenner laughed. "You think you can convince the public?"

"You may be surprised."

Farradyne lit a cigarette and relaxed. "We'll wait until dusk to be sure," he said.

Hourly, the radio went on telling how Farradyne was being cornered. Radar nets and radio-contact squadrons were scouring the North American continent with special attention being given to the North Middlewest. A ship of the enemy must have arrived with some information that could be pieced together, for another report said, "Charles Farradyne, sought on many charges involving hellflower operations, has been implicated in the disappearance of Carolyn Niles, according to her family. Her father indicated that Miss Niles had not returned home after a date with the criminal. This is a familiar pattern with hellflower dopesters. Be careful. The man is cornered and desperate. He will not hesitate to shoot, he may even bomb a village or neighborhood if his freedom is threatened!"

Brenner and Carolyn did not even jeer at him. The situation was obvious; Farradyne and his white flag would be shot to pieces before he could tell his name, let alone make explanations.

But now it was dark outside. The stars were bright above the astrodome and they danced with the motion of the water. To one side a wavy trail passed across the sky and high above there was the flicker of a space patrol crossing the sky at fifty or sixty miles. The radio was alive with reports and the police bands were busy with their myriad reports and directions. Farradyne pricked off their calls on a map with a drawing pencil. Ground and air patrols were combing a vast area and space squadrons were holding a dragnet high in the sky above. For a very brief interval Farradyne could hear a distant network in operation which indicated that the same sort of complete search was underway in other districts across the face of the continent.

He inspected his map and hoped that he had them all. Then, very cautiously, he lifted the nose of the Lancaster above the water line and eyed his radar. Pips showed here and there, a couple within a few miles of him. He waited until they turned away, waited until they went beyond the radar horizon.

Using just enough power to waft the Lancaster into the air, Farradyne placed the ship in a gully a few hundred yards from a state highway. The trees covered it from direct observation at night and the flat hills and ravines would cover it from radar detection . . .

It was almost two o'clock in the morning when a lonely moving van came along the highway. The brakes screeched as the driver caught sight of a crumpled body lying alongside the road. Red sogginess contrasted with the length of white thigh, uncovered by a ripped skirt, and more redness dribbled wet from the corner of Norma's mouth. The driver piled out of one door and his helper from the other. They ran to kneel by the woman's side.

Then they smelled the ketchup and stood up, raising their hands immediately.

"That's not blood spilled," said the driver loudly. "Let's keep it that way."

The driver's helper added, "This is a bum job, friend. We're carting secondhand furniture, not gold."

"I don't want your load," said Farradyne, stepping into the glare of the headlights while Norma got up and dusted herself off. "I want your truck."

They looked at him and he saw recognition in their faces. Obviously every news agency had his picture presented in full color. He saw that they apparently understood why he wanted the truck, for there was also contempt on their frightened faces.

"What's the next move, Farradyne?" asked the driver in a surly tone. "Do we take the high jump?"

"No. I just want your truck."

"Getting a bit brash?"

"Maybe I have to. Driver, what's your name?"

"Morgan. This is Roberts."

"Morgan, you drive that truck into the ravine there and I'll see that Roberts plays hostage. Get it?"

"Behave, Al," pleaded Roberts.

"I will, but I think we'll get it anyway."

"Act like you believe that and you will," snapped Farradyne. "I have neither time nor patience."

Morgan climbed into the truck and drove it from the road through the trees until they came to the Lancaster. Both men goggled at the big ship parked there and Farradyne let them look at it for a moment. Then he waved his gun. "Unload it!" he said sharply.

It took them an hour to move the load from the truck to the ground, and Farradyne spent that hour in nervous watching. He could not trust them not to make a break, nor could he hope to explain. When the van was emptied, he faced Roberts against it and said, "Norma, tape Morgan's hands behind him."

She did, and while Farradyne stood over them, she taped Roberts. Each man knew that the other's life was dependent on him and, while either man might have made some break for safety, he would not so long as the other might suffer.

Their lips curled in contempt as the conveyor-belt came out of the cargo lock and the white blossoms tumbled along it to drop into the van. Both Morgan and Roberts were honest men, but they lacked the higher education that was necessary to be pilot of a spacecraft; therefore, they resented the fact that Farradyne had this training yet used it to such ends. They were rough-hewn and hard-boiled and, perhaps like other transcontinental truckers, they had a woman at either end of the line and a few strung along the way, but their love conquests were lustily honest and they scorned the idea of hellflowers as an aid to passion. Even in their fright they sneered at the spaceman.

Farradyne left them sitting there on the ground after the loading was finished. He and Norma went into the salon and he faced Brenner. "Better take this quietly," he said. "It's inevitable, Brenner."

The radio made him pause:

"Ladies and gentlemen, the late news: The system-wide search for Charles Farradyne is hurrying to a close. Indications are now that the infamous hellblossom king is hiding in the Lake Superior region and all forces are being hurried to that area to create the most leakproof dragnet in the history of man's manhunt. A special session of the planning committee of the Solar Anti-Narcotics Department has been called to deal with the problem, and any information pertaining to Charles Farradyne may be delivered by picking up your telephone and calling SAND, One-thousand.

"This information is being disseminated freely. We know that Farradyne is listening to this broadcast, and the Sandmen have instructed all radio stations and networks to deliver the following announcement:

"'To Charles Farradyne! A reward of fifty thousand dollars has been offered for your capture dead or alive. You cannot escape. The forces that are blanketing the Lake Superior area are being augmented hourly by additional men and materiel.[1] You will be arrested and brought to trial for your life. However, the reward of fifty thousand dollars will be turned over to you to be used in your own defense if you surrender at once.'"

Farradyne grunted. "Very tasty dish," he said sourly. "Very competent people you have, boys and girls. Someone really thought that one out most thoroughly. Can you picture me walking up to a patrol and saying 'Fellers, I've come to give myself up so I can have the reward' and then have the patrol take me in on that basis? I'd go in on a shutter, and the patrol would divide the loot. To hell with you, we'll play it my way. Norma, go ahead."

Norma slipped off one high-heeled shoe and advanced on Brenner. The enemy agent tried to shy away, but Farradyne went over and caught his head between the palms of his hands and held Brenner fixed. Norma swung the slipper and crashed the heel against Brenner's jaw.

Brenner slumped, and the heelprint on his jaw oozed a dribble of blood mixed with mud.

Farradyne slung Brenner over his shoulder and carried the inert man out. He propped Brenner in the helper's seat and handed Norma into the driver's seat. He stood on the runningboard and watched Norma strip the tape from Brenner's wrists and replace it with fresh tape from the truck's own first-aid kit.

---

[1] Military materials and equipment.

"The ankles, too," he warned her. "You have to cover up the tape-marks."

Norma taped Brenner's ankles. Then she looked up at Farradyne. "I'm shaky."

"I know," he said. "But you have to hold yourself together until this gambit is played out."

She smiled wanly. "That's what is holding me together. Charles, wish me luck!"

He leaned into the truck window and put his lips to hers. It was a very pleasant kiss, their first kiss of real affection and mutual confidence, though it lacked a compelling passion. Then he swung down from the truck with a wave of his hand and Norma put the big engine in gear with a grind that set Morgan's teeth on edge.

The truck turned onto the highway and roared off down the road.

Morgan asked, "What do we do now?"

"We wait in the spacer," Farradyne replied, "and go back under water."

Roberts shrugged. "Hope we like the trip," he said. "I've never been in a spacer before."

They went up the landing ramp and into the salon, to stop short as they saw Carolyn and the other pair.

"Quite a collection you have here," said Morgan. "Is this Carolyn Niles?"

"I am," replied Carolyn. "Aren't you going to do something about it?"

Morgan showed her his taped wrists. "Not in this garb," he said. "This man-about-space has too many things his own way."

Farradyne smiled and left them. He went aloft and returned the Lancaster to the lake. "Now," he said, "we'll wait it out."

ch. ends p. 223

Morgan shook his head. "With the net they've set up you'll never see your girl or the truck again, or the hellflowers."

"Maybe I want it that way."

"Oh? Putting the finger on the bird you carted out of here?"

"Precisely."

"And how about the dame?"

Farradyne laughed. "In this cockeyed society of ours, even a streetwalking slut can rip her dress open, point at a man, and holler 'Rape' and half the community will start yelling 'lynch the sonofabitch' without looking too hard at either of them. She'll get by, but it may go hard with him."

With some amusement he saw two different expressions looking at him silently. Morgan and Roberts were scornful, angry, and ready at any instant to do whatever they could to overcome him. Only the tape kept them from trying. But on Carolyn's face was an expression of mingled defeat and admiration. She knew as well as Farradyne that Brenner was in for a rough time.

Farradyne relaxed. He lit a cigarette and mixed himself a highball. Carolyn groaned and tried to flex the wrists that were secured to the arms of the chair. Morgan growled at the sight of her helplessness and asked if Farradyne had harmed her. Carolyn replied, "Not yet. I happen to be immune to hellflowers."

"Scorpions," said Farradyne, pointedly, "are immune to their own poison."

It made no difference. Morgan and Roberts still wanted to get free so they could take him on in a rough and tumble, and Farradyne knew that either one of them would be more than a match for him. Tooling a truck was not hard in this day of mechanical and electrical aids to human muscle, but manipulating furniture was something else again.

Either one of them was capable of bending him double and straightening him out again afterward.

He listened to them discuss him. It was amusing, in a way. The first remark was made with a sly glance in his direction to see how he reacted. As he merely smiled, their observations became bolder and more damning. They wondered how and why his degradation had been so complete. They considered his family for a number of generations of inbreeding and illegitimacy.

In all of this he had to admire Carolyn's ability to dissemble even while she was playing a losing battle. She was determined to carry on high until the bitter end, and she added to the slander with a fine regard for the well-turned phrase and amplified all the truckmen said. They were working on his chances for a painful Hereafter when the radio music faded again:

"And here is the latest news on Charles Farradyne. Within the past half hour the area of search has been narrowed to a ten-mile circle by the interception of a moving van laden with hellflowers. The arrest was made by a state highway patrol with the aid of a woman who gave her name as Norma Hannon.

"Miss Hannon was in a state of hysterical collapse after days of imprisonment at the hands of the lotus ring, a brutal physical assault, and threats of being forced into love lotus addiction. The driver of the truck was carrying a license made out to Walter Morgan, but information from the Bureau of Identification indicates that Morgan is also known as Lewis Hughes, a prominent teacher of Ancient History in a Des Moines school. During the struggle Miss Hannon succeeded in rendering the alleged criminal unconscious by hitting him on the jaw with her slipper, after which she taped——"

Farradyne chuckled. "You see?" he glowed.

ch. ends p. 223

Morgan grunted, "My license!"

Roberts cried, "Our truck!"

Carolyn said, "And what's it got you, Charles?"

"——the first-aid kit," went on the announcer. "Morgan or Hughes is being held on a John Doe warrant pending the true identification of the man, charged with hellflower possession, abduction, illegal restraint, assault and battery, rape, and driving an interstate truck with an improper license.

"Miss Hannon collapsed after driving the truck to within sight of the dragnet set out for Farradyne. Her statement will be taken by the Sand Office as soon as she is recovered. The point of hospitalization has been kept secret by the Sandmen, who are now confident of an early arrest. Indications are that Hughes or Morgan has turned state's evidence and is willing to inform on his racket-boss."

"Hah!" glowed Carolyn.

"Did you a lot of good, didn't it, Farradyne?" snarled Morgan.

Farradyne ignored Morgan and spoke to Carolyn. "Unless Norma is being tended by someone of your gang, this is the end, baby."

She eyed him superciliously.[2] "How long will they believe her after they discover she's an addict herself?"

"Maybe she isn't."

Carolyn laughed, "Everybody knows there is no cure."

"And how about our pal, Brenner-Hughes-Morgan?"

"You leave me out of this!" snapped Morgan.

"Sorry," said Farradyne with a smile. "I didn't mean to include you, Walter."

Carolyn said, in a self-confident voice, "Brenner is one of us. He is just as willing to die for our cause as——" She suddenly remembered the truckmen present, who were

---

[2] Arrogantly.

probably as puzzled as men can be over the trend of conversation. But she didn't have to finish. Farradyne realized with a start that the enemy culture and training must include a high degree of blind patriotism which demanded that the agent in danger of discovery must be ready to eliminate his discoverer even though it cause the death of both of them. The Semiramide——

A searchlight swept across the lake and its light, refracted downward from the waves, caught Farradyne's eye. He left them in the salon and raced up the stairs to the control room. Through the astrodome, distorted by the water, Farradyne could see the headlamps of a big truck. The searchbeam crossed the water again and flashed ever so briefly on the slender rod of the antenna. The truck paused in its course, the beam swept the woody shore and stopped; the truck turned toward something in the woods and rumbled off through the trees.

The radio music died again. "Ladies and gentlemen, we are about to bring you a very startling program. John Bundy, our special events newscaster, has joined the forces scouring the Lake Superior region for Charles Farradyne. Inasmuch as an early arrest is expected, and possibly a running gun battle, John Bundy will take the air with an on-the-spot account. Come in, John Bundy!"

"Hello, this is John Bundy! Our convoy of trucks, men, guns, radar, and radio control resembles a war convoy. We have everything from trench knives to one-fifty-five rifles aboard as we scour the northwoods for the criminal who has been so successful up to this time. We arrived at a point along Lake Superior which must be close to Farradyne's operations, according to the description given to us by the arrested truck driver. Sand and mud from Miss Hannon's shoes correspond to that district.

"Flying above us now are eight squadron bombers

carrying heavy depth charges because Farradyne is believed to be hiding his spacecraft in the waters of the Lake. A submarine from the Great Lakes Geodetic Survey has been hastily equipped with some ranging sonar from the War Museum at Chicago and is seeking the submerged spacecraft. It——"

There came a distant crash in the radio and seconds afterward the Lancaster resounded with the thunder of an underwater explosion.

"One of the depth charge patterns has been dropped," explained Bundy excitedly. "Perhaps this is—no, it's not. Sorry. Just a hope, but the submarine has just covered the explosion area and reported only an underwater mountain peak instead of a hidden spacecraft. No place will be left unsearched——"

A thin, pure ping of a pitch so high it was on the upper limit of Farradyne's ability to hear came and lasted for less than a tenth of a second. It came again in about twenty seconds, repeating at like intervals again and again. The interval dropped; the volume of the ping increased noticeably until the singing tinkle, something like tapping a silver table knife on Haviland china, was coming fast.

Ping! Ping! Ping!

Farradyne looked above. Circling there were skytrails of jet bombers making loops in the sky. There came another flash of the searchbeam against the antenna.

Ping! Abruptly the pinging changed in tone. It became frequency modulated so that it rose in a chirp, and Farradyne knew that the submarine was coming closer.

Norma! Get through, wherever you are!

Along the shoreline something blossomed with an orange flash. Seconds later there was an eruption fifty yards from the Lancaster that shook the ship hard enough to make the plates groan. A trickle of lake water oozed through the ceiling of the astrodome.

The pinging came louder.

Underwater bursts ricocheted and flashed and hurled their gusts of force against the spacer, buffeting the Lancaster.

Farradyne's hands hung above his controls. He could escape this holocaust; all he had to do was to blast free from the water, make a brief run for it, and then come down hard on the enemy ultradrive toggle-bar and his Lancaster would virtually disappear right under the guns of the squadrons that sought him. He could hide in space for a day or a week and return after Norma explained.

But this was wrong. To be sure he had the enemy equipment in his hold and enemy agents in his salon who could explain the science behind the device. Eventually it could be reproduced—but only if there were time.

For Farradyne realized that his act had been the first overt move that could start the First Interstellar War—but the enemy would not permit Sol to take the second move. Once their secret was out the starships would hover over Sol's planets with their loads of mercurite and it would be slavery or death. He would land to find a ruined Sol and a few remnants of humankind reduced to savagery. The only result would be the locating of a mercurite stockpile and a blow of retaliation.

And then someday, another sentience would come to visit the stars and find only the smoldering ruins of two systems that could neither live with each other nor permit each other to have supremacy.

Another bouncing crash shook the Lancaster.

The radio was rambling on and on as John Bundy gave the world a blow by blow description of the first action made toward its ultimate death.

ch. ends p. 223

"——and to those people who have stood out against the expenditure of monies for arms and training, I say they should witness this attack upon an enemy of society. Yes, warfare is dead, but the conflict goes on against evil and ruthlessness, and only by preparedness of strength and preparedness of mind—to be as ruthless as the fiends that bore from within—can mankind combat his own weaknesses.

"They are evacuating the area now. Farradyne is trapped and unless he surrenders within the next half hour, atomic weapons will be used. We may never learn the thoughts of the mind that has directed the decay of the moral fiber of our people. We may never know why a man, given the opportunities that many finer men have been denied, chose as his life's work——"

Carolyn laughed hysterically and Farradyne went below for a look.

Morgan and Roberts fell upon him and hauled him down the stairs. They pinned him to the deck and held him there. Carolyn stood above him.

"We don't mind dying," she said, "in order to take you with us! You and your money and your paid agents and your bribed officials! Permit you to surrender? To stand mock trial and be acquitted? Never!"

The Lancaster shook with the throb of depth charges.

Farradyne struggled against his captors. He'd been as blind a fool as he had ever been, to let them sit there without taping them separately.

"Let me up!" he stormed. "Let me up so we can escape this bombing——"

"Shut the hell up!"

Farradyne struggled.

There was a blasting roar that stunned them all; it shook the Lancaster viciously. The trickle of water through the astrodome was covered by the ear-splitting thunder, but less shockingly loud as the Lancaster hiked into the open air and braved the fire of the squadrons.

Farradyne fought himself awake. "Let him escape and we——"

Carolyn's shrill laugh drowned out his weak voice.

The radio went on as accursedly unanswerable as always. "Farradyne's spacecraft has been trapped and fired upon and now the pilot himself has been flushed from cover. He is making the criminal's last-stand. The rascal is hoping to flee through the most thorough skycover that has ever been assembled. He cannot hope to win though, ladies and gentlemen. I wish we had video here in the early morning light, so that you could see this vivid spectacle of the eternal battle between the forces of good and evil!

"But we'll all be there when Farradyne goes down to the death of flame he so richly deserves. Above him now are the jet bombers and above them lie the Interplanetary Space Guard to fire the final coup de grâce—if Farradyne can run this gauntlet of righteous wrath that far.

"His flare trail is dimmed by the pinpoints of flashing death that seek him out. On every side of me are ships vomiting torpedoes, guided missiles with target-seeking radar in their sleek noses that will end this reign of terror and dissolution once they find their mark."

Farradyne looked up at Carolyn and saw a glow of excitement in her eyes. She looked down at him and said, "Charles, you almost succeeded——"

The radio clicked audibly and a forceful voice came on: "Attention! Attention! All listeners hear this. This is the office of the Secretary of Solar Defense, Under Secretary Marshall White speaking. All persons, whether official or unofficial, whether citizen or military, are hereby charged with the safety of Charles Farradyne and the Lancaster model Eighty-One in his possession. This is a 'Cease Fire' order. All citizens and military personnel, officials and non-officials are hereby ordered to offer Charles Farradyne whatever he may request in the nature of manpower, machinery, supplies, protection, material, and safe conduct so that he may deliver his spacecraft to the Terran Arsenal at Terre Haute, Indiana."

Morgan looked at Farradyne with a scowl.

Carolyn cried, "Friends in high places!"

Roberts spat on Farradyne's face.

The Under Secretary's voice went on, "Within the hour, Miss Norma Hannon, one-time associate of Howard Clevis, undercover agent attached to this office on free duty, has presented irrevocable evidence to show that the hellflower operations have been a part and parcel of an unsuspected plot against humanity by denizens of an extra-solar culture. Since Farradyne's spacecraft contains the only known device enabling matter to exceed the velocity of light, its delivery to the Arsenal is deemed top priority. All persons are charged——"

Farradyne shrugged himself out of the grip of the truckmen. "Go the hell aloft and grab that bastard running the ship!" he snarled at them.

The other enemy rushed forward and Roberts caught a hard fist on the jaw and reeled back. Farradyne wheeled with a wide swing and chopped the edge of his hand hard against the side of the alien face. The blow hurled the other back against the little bar, against which he crumpled and slipped to the floor in a flaccid heap.

"Watch her!" Farradyne yelled to Roberts, who was recovering from his blow. Morgan dashed up the stairs and Farradyne was at his heels.

The truckman raced across the control room and caught the enemy pilot by his right wrist, whipped it out, around, down, back and up in a hammerlock. He jerked once and then lifted the screaming pilot out of the chair; hammerlock in one hand, his other arm clenched around the pilot's throat.

Farradyne slipped into the pilot's chair and reversed the controls. He oriented himself, and then boldly turned the Lancaster on its side and sent the ship screaming through the upper air toward Indiana.

In the control room there were some flashes high in the sky. Terran forces had made contact with the enemy.

●

He turned in his pilot's chair as he heard them struggling up the stairs. Carolyn was fighting her way up with tooth and nail and crying, "I've got to see him!" Roberts was still stunned from the blow, a bit groggy and also a bit reluctant to lash out and crush a few bones.

Farradyne jeered, "So I couldn't get through?"

Carolyn faced him, "You poor simpleton," she said, "you've just sealed your own doom."

Farradyne shrugged. "Sometimes it's better to kill the dog than let the fleas multiply. It saves the rest of the dogs."

"Do you realize what you're doing? You're giving up! You're admitting——"

"Oh, shut up, Carolyn. What's your alternative? To surrender quietly and let your rapacious gang walk in? Of course we can't win. But you can't win either because we're going to deprive you of victory. When the next galactic race comes this way they'll find a couple of glowing monuments to a culture that preferred death to slavery."

"But you couldn't possibly——"

"Oh yes, I can. That's why we're heading for the arsenal now. I'll get my load of mercurite there, and deliver it to your system while you and your gang are ruining ours. I call it retribution."

"You don't offer any alternative, either," she whispered.

"Complete surrender," he suggested.

"And you know what that would mean."

Farradyne looked at her. It was an impasse and he knew it as well as she did. The law of an eye for an eye and a tooth for a tooth is only good when there is a higher authority to see that it goes no further. When there is no just authority to pass judgment, the loss of an eye is revenged with interest, and the anger and resentment and desire for counter-revenge grow and pyramid until nations and planets and solar systems are involved in punitive wars that leave both sides weak and broken. Primitive and ruinous it was. But then, so was all revenge.

It need not be ruinous. There could be a better way to pride, to personal or national integrity. It had been done before in the middle of the Twentieth Century and it had been the start of a consolidated Terra. For there is personal pride in knowing that you have let your defeated enemy live; in letting your defeated enemy know that you feel strong and secure enough to hold his efforts in contempt.

Farradyne looked at Carolyn. "Surrender," he suggested to her. "Then we'll move in quietly and count off your people. We've lost many of ours, so we'll just tally off so many men to be murdered in cold blood. So many virgins to be ravished. So many wives to be left without husbands and so many husbands left without wives. Children left homeless to such and such a number." His voice rose. "So much hunger; so much pestilence; so much famine; so much death. What in the hell do you think we are, Carolyn, a race of God damned vultures?"

"What do you want me to do?" she whimpered. "You're in the driver's seat."

"No, I'm not!" yelled Farradyne. "And I'm not going to be held responsible for anything that wasn't my idea in the first place. Your outfit started this and now if your outfit does not care for the end-game, it's for you to say. Now—do we drop mercurite?"

She searched his face and saw nothing but hard determination. She shook her arm from Roberts' clutch and walked to the radio. Into the microphone she began to singsong. She went on for some time; staccato, musical now and discordant then, her triple-tongued voice rising and falling as she spoke rapidly.

Then she turned from the radio. "You win," she said. "Somehow you always win. And maybe—maybe I'm glad it's all over!"

Tears welled in her eyes and she turned away from them to stumble down the stairway blindly.

23

Farradyne looked down at the white face, almost as pale as the hospital sheets. Norma looked up at him, her face wan and her smile weak but genuine. He reached down and pressed her hand gently. "Relax, Norma, it's all over and done with."

"You're sure?"

"Of course I'm sure. Dr. Fawcett told me this morning that you were obviously on your way to a cure."

"I'm feeling fine," she said. "I'm weak, but I do feel better. This is just from the strain. I held my nerves together too long and it's left me sort of washed out. But I'll be all right."

"You've got to be," he said seriously. "This is all too good to miss."

"What's happened? Charles, you talk. I'm——"

"Sure. Well, you never saw so much gold-braid and striped-trousers a-space before in your life. After I set the Lancaster down at Terre Haute, they came aboard and sat on two of the guys for hostages against my return, and a bunch of us went to Lyra Three-Fifty-Seven with Carolyn as interpreter. We made 'em cough up Clevis and about a hundred other bright guys who'd been too smart for 'em. They—the gold-braid and striped-trouser set—moved in and they've been conferring ever since. Seems as how I guessed right; both sides seem to think that there's been enough strife, and that more can be gained by pooling our efforts. Anyway, it's out of my hands now and I'm just a spaceman again."

Farradyne took a deep breath and chuckled. "I've my license back, clear and honest. There's nothing too good for Farradyne, former bona fide louse. I've also got enough interstellar shipping contracts to set me up in rare style. Within a year I'll own a whole fleet and then I can retire and pay someone else to go a-spacing. Does that sound good, honey?"

Norma looked up at him out of soft eyes. "Is this a proposal of marriage?"

"In the first degree," he said.

Norma pulled him down and gave him her lips. They were soft and warm and pleasantly affectionate, as they had been on the road in Wisconsin. Then she let him go and he stood up. He saw her eyes fill with tears.

"Norma?" he said.

"Charles, it wouldn't work."

"But——"

She smiled gently. "It's not that, Charles," she said slowly. "I'm not thinking about Frank and the years of hate. Since then I've come to know you and admire you, but you see, I don't really love you, Charles. I——"

He saw something in her eyes and understood; he hoped she would not get involved in any long discussion and, to forestall it, he asked, "It's Howard?"

She nodded. "I loved him before Frank——" Her eyes glowed a bit and were dry again. "Howard is a strong man, Charles. He used Frank, and then he used me, and then he used you. And the hellflowers took Frank, and then they took me from Howard and finally they took Howard, too. But you've brought them all back but Frank. To me, Charles, and I've got——"

He bent down and stopped the flow of words with his

lips. "Be happy, baby," he said against her cheek. "I'll finish it all up in fine style."

Farradyne left the room quickly. In the corridor he paused long enough to shake the growing vacuum away, and then he went down to the waiting room . . .

"Howard? She's awake and feeling fine, although she's still weak as a kitten. A bit of the sight and touch of you would work wonders, Howard. She wants you."

Clevis got up and gripped Farradyne's hand hard. "You're quite a guy, Charles," he said.

"I want to be second-best man, Howard."

"Any damned day in the week," replied Clevis. He left and Farradyne was alone.

Farradyne sat down and lit a cigarette. He blew smoke at his toes and wondered at himself. He should have been feeling despondent. Instead, he felt a peculiarly satisfying glow of contentment. He couldn't win everything; somehow this single loss was meant to be and it was right that he should not have Norma.

And then the plume of smoke curled around a pair of slender ankles and Farradyne realized that his loss of Norma was not a loss at all; the slight vacuum filled full as Farradyne knew where his last piece of unfinished business was.

The waiting room resounded with a gentle musical chord. It was operatic in quality; angel, hoyden and devil singing bacchanal. He smiled and looked up at her.

"Any damned day in the week," he promised, getting to his feet.

Against his face, Carolyn laughed softly. "But you can't even pronounce my name."

"I'll get along," he said. "We'll figure out something."

Arm in arm they went out into the bright sunshine.

George O Smith
HONORARY HEATHEN

*HE BEGAN TO UNDERSTAND
THAT THE MATTER OF BEING
LOST IS ONLY A DISLOCATION
OF YOUR OWN FRAME OF
REFERENCE.*

www.ingramcontent.com/pod-product-compliance
Lightning Source LLC
Chambersburg PA
CBHW061552210726
48287CB00006B/2154